For Jem —
Thank you,
my friend and ...
me so patiently how to write.

COLLISION COURSE

Love,

Susan

11/03

Susan Nichols Ferrara

PublishAmerica
Baltimore

First printing

ISBN: 1-59286-764-2
PUBLISHED BY PUBLISHAMERICA, LLLP
www.publishamerica.com
Baltimore

Printed in the United States of America

To my beloved father – Lt. Gen. Robert Lee Nichols, Jr., USMC Retired, whose joy in life was an inspiration and who showed me the glory of the stars. He enlisted at the age of 17 and proudly served his country for 40 years through three wars with decorations too numerous to mention. He died on the Fourth of July, 2001.

My father gave me three valuable pieces of advice: "Never pick up hitchhikers, always check the oil in your car, and forever beware the military/industrial complex."

ACKNOWLEDGEMENTS

I am grateful for the help and encouragement of a number of individuals. First and foremost I want to thank Professor Catherine Houser of the English Department at the University of Massachusetts, Dartmouth. At various times while I revised this novel, she was my English professor, my mentor, my editor, my sidekick, and more than anything else, my dear friend. Her encouragement and support helped make it possible for me to fulfill my dream.

I am also grateful for the tireless tutoring I received from Jim Huston, who helped me when I first began to write. The mark of his red pen cleaned up my act and taught me some discipline as a writer. I want to thank my original writers' group in Newport, Rhode Island. Besides Jim, the group included Bob Bent, a man of fabulous style and substance; Skip Burns, a true artist who blew our minds each week; and Arliss Ryan, a woman whose precision and purity inspired us all. And I will never forget gentle Celeste and her tales of horror. These friends taught me through their fine example and with their gentle prodding. We had a lot of fun.

Many thanks to Eric Ryan, Arliss' husband, who volunteered to sift my words through his scientific mind. I want to thank my writing professors at Vermont College – Tom Absher and Charlotte Hastings who were both encouraging and instructive during the early stages of this project, as well as Charlotte's brother Dr. Roger Hastings who educated me in physics concepts. And many thanks to the astrologer Anne Lathrop for her encouragement after reading the manuscript. Also, I gratefully acknowledge the assistance given me by various faculty members of the Physics Department at Brown University. I am grateful for the publishing advice I received from Professor

Peter Owens at the University of Massachusetts, Dartmouth. And I want to thank Jimmy Ferrara for his computer acumen and for his creativity with the cover design.

My daughter Erin has always inspired me with her spirit and spunk, with her beauty and laughter. She believed in me all along the way. Last but never, ever least, I am so thankful to my husband, Arthur, who feeds my soul with his big-hearted love. He came along just in time — and made me believe in miracles.

PROLOGUE

Years ago in the small town of Waxahachie, Texas, the U.S. government attempted to build an underground Superconducting Super Collider.

As the largest scientific instrument in the world, the SSC would have reproduced conditions 15 billion years ago, just after the Big Bang. It would have been the greatest experiment in the history of the world. But after spending $2 billion, Congress eliminated funding for the SSC. All that remains is 14.7 miles of tunnel under the Texas prairie.

Today, in a desert in northern Chile, one determined man has succeeded where the U.S. failed. He built the LIFT Accelerator, capable of accomplishing everything the SSC would have done – and much, much more.

CHAPTER 1

The silver "L" engraved in the steel handle of Pierre Lorillard's ice axe glinted in the sharp mountain light. Lorillard dug the metal spikes of his Foot Fangs deeper in the crusted snow and, like a king surveying his domain, he regarded the earth's noble monuments laid before him.

To the south the shimmering white cone of Mont Blanc ruled over the foothills of France, dwarfing its valleys and lakes. To the northeast he could see the spire of the Matterhorn, and beyond, breaking through settled layers of gray clouds, the craggy presence of Mischabel.

From his commanding realm, Pierre Lorillard gazed down the mountain at Dr. Nikolai Potapov and shook his head, grinning. Even though Nik was tall, athletically lean, and only in his forties -- young enough to be Pierre's son -- the man clung to the last icy ridge like a snail sucking a wet rock. An hour earlier Nik had informed Lorillard he couldn't make it any farther, it was time to turn back.

"A sarpé!" Lorillard yelled down at him, laughing. "You climb like a sarpé!"

"We've gone far enough." Nikolai's dark beard and eyebrows were stiff with ice.

Pierre laughed. He knew a good climb would disclose a man's true character. Through years of experience with Americans, both on the mountain and in business, he had come to understand that they were afraid of death. His Canadian countrymen could be fools, but not cowards. This Russian was new to the mountains. But if he was to be of use, Pierre must know what Nik was made of.

When Lorillard turned sixty-nine his doctors told him to give up climbing. Today, standing in the protected pass between two peaks, he flexed the taut muscles of his short legs, felt their strength beneath his solid frame. He was built like a buffalo, his neck and shoulders thick from early years of wrestling and later, weight lifting.

"Not like a sarpé," Pierre hollered down the pass.

Dr. Nikolai Potapov understood sarpé meant serpent. It was the mountain patois of the Chamoniard natives, their term for weak clients who clung to the rocks like lizards. An accomplished athlete himself, Nik's inability to keep up with this older man infuriated him. But Nikolai had heard the tales, that Lorillard confronted a challenge the way a ravenous animal attacks fresh kill. Lorillard himself had credited his relentless passion as the reason for his success: he was one of the three wealthiest men in the world.

Squinting into the reflected light of the French Alps, Nik saw Lorillard grinning down at him. You bastard, Nik thought. You're enjoying this. You're going to bully and prod until we reach the top of that ridge. But Nik didn't trust Pierre's judgment. The man's sense of danger seemed distorted; he didn't understand fear.

In their ascent they had traversed the upper snowfield and then climbed the rock step above the dangerous gully that ran from the summit of the west ridge. To reach the highpoint they would have to climb around the snow-covered boulder just ahead and tunnel through the icy crevasse that led to the summit.

"Come on now!" Lorillard's deep voice betrayed impatience. Vehemently he waved his arm through the air. "Use my anchor. We're almost there." Pierre wiped his gloved hand across his frosted, brittle moustache, and his cracked lips bled. His tongue found the taste warm and sweet.

Forcing himself to try once more, Nik took a deep breath. At this altitude the oxygen was thin. He struggled to haul himself up, but the muscles in his forearms cramped in knots and burned with the exertion. Despite the gloves he wore, the skin of his aching hands stung. It was no good; he could not go on. He knew they should rappel down to the ledge mid-way, rest, then continue back to the lodge.

"That's far enough," Nik hollered. Hanging loose in his harness, his arms fell free at his sides. He felt like a puppet, and he knew Lorillard had been pulling his strings all day. "It's dangerous to go on," he yelled. "We should head back."

Pierre could hear the anger rising in Potapov's voice. So the Russian's hitting the wall, Lorillard thought. Evidently the young man doesn't like how it feels.

"Nonsense! You can do this. Put your mind to it. You must see the frozen arch." Pierre watched as Nikolai made one last, feeble attempt, then fell back and hung against the icy ledge of rock. Lorillard could see it was no use. "If you can't make it," he yelled with disgust, "stay there. I'm going myself. I'll be back."

Stunned, Nikolai watched Pierre remove the safety lines from around his waist. He dropped the nylon rope to the ground, leaving Nik safely secured to a series of pitons, but himself utterly unprotected. He was breaking the first rule of climbing.

"You can't go up there alone!" Nikolai called. "What are you doing? Don't be a fool!"

Nik watched helplessly as the old man used a lieback technique, pulling both hands to one side of a raggedly thin crack and pushing with his feet in the opposite direction. His motions were economical, graceful. Nik was astounded at the power of Pierre's body.

"Lorillard! Stop!" Nik called. "It isn't safe!"

But Pierre never looked back. In a matter of minutes he was around the boulder. Nik watched him disappear into the narrow face of the crevasse.

* * * * *

Dr. Selena Hartmann sat alone at a long table facing the ten-member, all-male panel. In her lap she twisted a paperclip into furious contortions while silently she cursed the good senator from North Carolina. This was the fourth time he'd interrupted her testimony before the congressional hearing of the Science and Space Committee.

"Gentlemen, I think we're all familiar with the impressive qualifications of our lady astronomer Ms. Hartmann, here." Senator Whiting nodded to Selena. "But in the interest of saving time..."

"Excuse me, Senator Whiting." Selena leaned closer to the microphone. "That's *Doctor* Hartmann, sir." You gray-haired old lummox, she thought. She squeezed her hand into a fist until the sharp end of the paper clip pierced the soft flesh of her palm. Startled by the barb of pain, her dark eyes grew wide, her tone more forceful.

"If you'd allow me to continue uninterrupted, Senator, *that* would be in the best interest of saving time."

Several panel members looked disparagingly in Ralph Whiting's direction, and, reluctantly, he took his seat. He was one of the chief supporters of a proposed Star Wars nuclear defense program. Selena had been sparring with him for the last forty-five minutes and she was on the verge of showing him just how much of a lady she wasn't. Instead, she crossed her legs, cleared her throat, and continued.

"An asteroid's capacity for destruction is greater than all our weapons combined. It's greater than we can conceive. The impact of Comet Shoemaker-Levy 9 with Jupiter in 1994 proved that. There are over 300,000 near-Earth asteroids, gentlemen. This is problem number one. It is not of our making."

"Which is precisely my point," Senator Whiting said, rising from his seat. He was a large man who wore his belt under the swell of his belly. His tie was too short. Selena thought he behaved like a bumbler, but she knew he was the Chairman of the Armed Services Committee and a close advisor to the president.

Realizing he was too far from the mike to be heard, Senator Whiting sat down before continuing. "Since Dr. Hartmann has graciously enlightened us as to the potential dangers involved here, surely it would not behoove us to twiddle our thumbs. This nuclear defense program will provide both future protection and sorely needed jobs. I urge your full support, gentlemen."

Right, Selena thought. And you have the full support of Dawes Orbital Corp. that plans to procure a hefty contract in this deal.

Senator Whiting continued his monologue while in the rear of the chamber, a small man in a generic dark suit and black-framed glasses entered quietly. He remained standing, his attention on the floorshow. Representative Pete Chapman from California was now speaking.

"Excuse me, Senator Whiting, but we've already spent $65 billion on ballistic missile defenses and we haven't a single working system to show for it. Now could we please let Dr. Hartmann finish her testimony before we waste any more money?"

Whiting spread his arms as if to say, 'Please, be my guest.'

"Thank you," Selena said. "Our second problem, gentlemen, if it comes to pass, would be of our own creation. The program suggested by the good senator would enable the use of nuclear explosions in space to deflect incoming asteroids that threaten our planet. But what if that same technology were used to literally shove an asteroid onto a collision course with Earth? The Russians used to call this strategy "Ivan's Hammer." Unfortunately, their dream is now a very real possibility."

"Dr. Hartmann?" Representative Chapman said. A short man, he leaned close to the mike and adjusted his bowtie, taking the pressure off his large

Adam's apple. "What about the asteroid you're studying? Isn't Hartmann 2009 on its way to Earth right now? And don't you expect it to arrive sometime in 2009? Shouldn't we begin now to protect ourselves by putting a deflection system in place?"

As if on cue, three sharp sneezes from the back of the room seemed to underscore Chapman's questions. The man in the black-framed glasses appeared uncomfortable when several people turned to look. He rubbed his red, watery eyes.

Through the years Pete Chapman had been a major supporter of Selena's work. He was one of her few allies on this panel, and she knew his questions were designed to allow explanation, not to antagonize.

"Hartmann 2009 is expected to pass by Earth in the year 2009, but it's not a certainty that it's on a collision course with our planet," Selena said. "I hope to present evidence to the contrary at the annual asteroid symposium in Chile in less than two weeks. Nuclear warheads in space, however, are an absolute prescription for the most devastating pool game in the history of mankind."

"What do you suggest?" Chapman said.

"The potential of outer space is beyond our comprehension. The natural resources available could prove to be a literal lifesaver for our planet in the future. We can't afford to destroy those opportunities. We're simply not ready for the responsibility of nuclear weapons in space."

"Shall we just wait until it's too late?" Senator Whiting demanded. "Compared to the loss of one city, I think our investment is more than reasonable."

"Senator," Selena said," when raising my daughter I encouraged her to take responsibility for herself as soon as I thought she could handle it safely. I wanted her to explore, to try new things, and to grow. But if I felt the activity was beyond her ability or if the consequences were too dangerous, I made the decision that she should hold off, that she should wait until she was older and able to protect herself better. As I'm sure you understand, with freedom comes responsibility. And just because we *can* do something doesn't mean we *should*. Not until we're ready."

"Let me just interrupt for a moment," Senator Whiting said. "I'm certain you were a very good mother, Doctor, but surely we're not children here. At least I hope not." He snickered and looked down the panel of grinning men. The audience laughed, too.

"In the history of the universe," Selena said, "our civilization isn't even an infant. We're embryonic. And we're not ready for this responsibility. We don't begin to grasp the danger involved or the consequences to be paid. We're still thinking in terms of individual countries, but if we move our war games to space, we must be able to think on a planetary level. And as a planet, we aren't socially and politically mature enough to protect ourselves from the potential devastation. If this is the pool game from hell, gentlemen, once somebody down here yells, "Set 'em up!" it will be impossible to lower the stakes. It's not a bet I'm prepared to lose. Are you?"

The audience broke out in enthusiastic applause. Even the panel members concurred, some more reluctantly than others. As Pete Chapman thanked her for her testimony, the small man in the back of the room slipped quickly out the door.

Selena Hartmann brushed back a wave of her short, auburn hair and, holding her tall frame erect, she walked gracefully from the room, leaving behind the mutilated paperclip.

* * * * *

Dr. Nikolai Potapov unhooked the carabinier, pulled the jumar upwards, and then leaned back into the harness. With the weight of his body, the jumar tightly gripped the rope. Settling back in the snow-reflected light of the mountain, Nik felt a great relief from the pressure of having to keep up. Pierre was a fool to go on alone, but for the moment, Nikolai was in no hurry for his return.

Nik had run into Lorillard at CERN, the European laboratory for particle physics in Geneva, Switzerland. CERN was celebrating its fiftieth anniversary, and Pierre Lorillard was their guest of honor. Eight years earlier in Chile he had begun what others called an impossible project: the building and operation of the LIFT. The Lorillard Industries Future Technology or LIFT accelerator would be a superconducting proton collider. Because the U.S. Congress had cancelled the SSC in Texas, Pierre Lorillard, a businessman, became a hero to the worldwide community of physicists.

Nikolai Potapov had left Russia nine months earlier, and Lorillard immediately pursued him to run the LIFT's Superconductor Laboratory. Nik refused, insisting he was committed to Stanford University and a research project there, but Pierre remained relentless. Nik was beginning to feel like he was Lorillard's challenge of the moment.

Safely hanging in his harness, Nikolai removed his thick gloves, rubbed his cold fingers together and massaged the sore muscles of his forearms. You're supposed to be on your way to Hawaii, he told himself, to lie on the beach with Selena in your arms. You should know better than to tell a man like Lorillard he's too old.

At a CERN cocktail party just 48 hours earlier, the two men had been admiring the distant view of Mont Blanc, dreamlike in the fading light of early evening.

"I understand you did some remarkable climbing in your day," Nikolai said. "I've climbed a few times, but nothing like you used to do."

Lorillard smiled, his pale little eyes squinting. Nikolai imagined he was remembering some high adventure of years past. Then Pierre offered to take him on his first climb in the Aiguilles de Chamonix.

"You mean you still climb?"

"I do my best," Pierre answered, chuckling. Lorillard told the Russian he'd have his private helicopter drop them at a lodge halfway up the west passage.

"Some of the most extraordinary climbing in the world," he'd said. "I'm going to show you the frozen arch at the top of the east ridge."

Remembering the look in Pierre's eyes, Nik realized he should have known better. He knew he wouldn't see the arch today and that was too bad, but his exhausted body was relaxed for the first time in hours. He closed his eyes to enjoy the warmth of the sun on his face and within minutes was on the verge of dozing.

"Aaaghhhhh! Aaaghhhh!"

Nik jolted at the distant sound of frantic screams. There was no doubt it was Lorillard's voice, except now his bullying tone was desperate.

Nik hollered up the mountain. "Pierre! What's wrong?" There was no response, only Nik's echo in the icy canyons.

"Hello! Lorillard! Pierre?" He waited; with each second his fear intensified. Something had gone terribly wrong. An injured, still body would be defenseless against this cold.

Nik began his ascent, following the exact course Lorillard had used. After a mighty effort to pull himself up to the next ledge, he managed his way to the boulder with little trouble. He felt stronger now, refreshed, and was able to marshal surprising stamina. When he reached the impasse he again followed Pierre's example, executing the same lieback technique.

Once beyond the boulder Nikolai crawled on his knees. The pack weighed heavily on his back. He thrust his ice axe deep in the crusted snow, pulling himself up inches at a time. When he reached the narrow opening of the crevasse, what he saw alarmed him.

An oval tunnel shot almost straight to the sky, directly through the snow. Steely crystals hung frigid and blue along the pass. At the far end, silvery ice gleamed like liquid mercury in the harsh sunlight. I don't think I can make it through, Nik thought. Except for the low whistle of the wind as it blew against the frozen lip of the tunnel, he was alone in the silence of the mountain.

"Lorillard!" he called again. Only his echo responded. Nik knew he had no choice. "I'm coming to get you, Pierre. Hold on!"

Adrenalin rushing through his limbs, Nik began the climb through the open shaft. He braced himself against his pack, pushed his crampons sharply into the icy crust, then pressed with all his might. Within ten minutes he reached the top, amazed at his strength and agility.

Breathing hard, Nik scanned the immediate area. A trail of broken snow led to the north. He ran quickly in the direction of the footprints.

"Pierre!" he called out and turned sharply under an immense overhang. "Where are you?" Suddenly his feet sank beneath him in the deep snow. He fell forward gasping, his bearded face hitting the crusted ice. When he raised his head, blood dripped from a gash over his eye. But Nik didn't even notice, because right before him sat Pierre Lorillard, cross-legged beside his pack, drinking a hot cup of coffee.

"Hello, my friend," Pierre said, smiling. "Would you care to join me?"

Nikolai wiped the snow and blood from his face and struggled to his feet.

"What the hell?" The words spewed out wet and angry as Nik gasped for air. "Damn you! I thought you were hurt!" Nik looked down the mountain and saw the treacherous climb he'd just made. He choked on his anger until he could hardly speak. "I could have killed myself trying to save you," he said, as if realizing the danger for the first time.

Pierre chuckled. "But you didn't. I must commend you. You made that climb in excellent time, especially for someone who was so tired." Lorillard nodded approvingly as he studied the younger man. "I knew you could do it, Nik."

Nik remembered the terrifying crevasse he'd just climbed and his rage grew. "Who the hell are you to make those decisions for me? Who do you think you are?"

Pierre spoke quietly, unmoved by the anger. "It takes most men many years to achieve that level of climbing. Isn't it remarkable what you can do when you set your mind to it?"

Nik hated the bastard, but he reminded himself he still had to get down the damned mountain. This was no time for a brawl. He turned away, walked a few steps, refused to look at the old man.

"Of course, being young helps," Lorillard continued. "But nothing, absolutely nothing, compares with determination. My congratulations," he said and offered Nikolai a steaming cup of coffee.

As Nik's anger began to subside, his exhaustion quickly took over. He sat down on the snow and reluctantly took the proffered cup. "You had no right to do that," he said, somewhat calmer.

Pierre ignored his words. Instead, he looked out at the majestic expanse. In the distance, dazzling in the afternoon light stood the graceful arch of ice.

Nik's eyes smarted in the magnified light of the crystal formation as he marveled at the fiery sculpture. It looked like the gateway to heaven. The rising heat of the coffee warmed his face, and he recalled his determined effort to scale the crevasse, how efficiently his body had worked. He'd never attempted anything like that before, hadn't known he was capable of it. After a while, Pierre spoke.

"When I was a boy, I used to climb with my brother in the Laurentians. Bertrand was a natural, tall like you, and agile. There was such grace to his movements. I tried harder when I climbed with him, did things I never thought I could do. I trusted him." Pierre smiled affectionately at the Russian. "You remind me of Bertrand."

Nikolai didn't know what to say. Eventually he turned and stared out at the frigid blue-white landscape. He was still angry. Lorillard was crazy. But Nik knew Pierre was also right. Nik had climbed with the boldness and conviction of an expert.

"Climbing is like a siege on life. And this is the reward," Pierre said, raising his arms to the mountains beyond. Moments later he added, "Of course there's something far more ancient than the mountains." He seemed lost in some personal reverie, no longer talking to Nik. "It's the only real challenge left. Up there." Pierre pointed to the sky. "Far beyond that pale slice of new moon."

Nik could see Lorillard's deeply lined face brighten with the allure and mystery of what he saw. The intense sunlight made his blue eyes eerily pale.

"That's my goal. That's the only challenge. There's nothing left for me to do here."

"What about the LIFT accelerator? Your work in Chile?"

"Anyone could do that. Except those fools who run the U.S. government,"

Pierre said. "The real adventure is out there."

"Not in our lifetime," Nikolai said. His scoffing tone was not lost on Pierre. "Someday, but we won't be around to see it."

Pierre Lorillard ignored Nik, letting his gaze linger on the distant skies. When he turned to face the Russian, it was with a look of disappointment.

"You've forgotten already," he said, shaking his head. "I told you, my friend. Determination is the most powerful weapon." Rising swiftly to his feet, Pierre gathered his pack and ice axe, then charged ahead, his words trailing behind. "Come now. Enough resting."

Nik struggled to get up, his sore muscles already cramped from the cold. Hurrying after Lorillard, he thought he heard the old man say, "I've got a surprise for you in Hawaii."

Nik had no idea what Lorillard was talking about. And he wasn't sure he wanted to find out.

CHAPTER 2

If a ten-watt light bulb was burning on the surface of the moon, Dr. Selena Hartmann could have seen it with the 200-inch Hale telescope on California's Mt. Palomar. It's just that powerful.

Zipping her orange insulated bodysuit, Selena said, "Let's open it up, Charlie," and she walked out of the heated control room. Charlene Muller, the woman at the computer, brushed back her long mass of gray-streaked brown hair and punched in the data.

To prevent distortion of the telescope optics, the temperature inside the observatory must be the same as the mountaintop outside. Tonight the frigid air in the cavernous dome was numbingly cold, but Selena was elated to be back at work and finished with the frustration of the congressional hearings.

Inside the dome Selena stood perfectly still, her breath billowing up into the air, her face raised expectantly to the ceiling. It wasn't the "light" of the month, when the moon was up, so viewing would be exceptional. Within moments she heard the rumble fill the hollow dome with a deep echo and she felt a sharp, hungry slice of excitement. The mammoth steel shutters slowly parting the ceiling revealed to her an unobstructed view of her universe, the cosmos.

In near darkness she stepped onto the metal grating of the open-air elevator, her thin body dwarfed by the massive tube of the telescope. It was at night Selena felt most vital, most alive, and as the lift followed the interior curve of the dome to the prime focus capsule, her excitement expanded like a helium bubble, making her chest hollow and tight.

She saw the stars as a crystal birthmark on the universe. All she had to do was look at them on a night like this and a certain knowledge spread inside her like energy, reminding her of the rightness of life and her part in it. She could feel a physical connection, an unspoken closeness, like looking across a room awkward with strangers into the warm eyes of a dear friend, then seeing those eyes blink in recognition.

As a child her father told her God had taken her mother away to be with Him. And God lived in the heavens, didn't he? In Selena's young heart her mother had become a celestial body orbiting the earth, fragile yet fiery, and beautiful beyond words. Selena had longed to capture the spirit of her mother, catch it in a net and bring home that little piece of heaven that was meant to grace her life.

Coming to a smooth stop, the hum of the elevator ceased. Selena took a deep breath and stepped inside the cramped space of the capsule. It was here, in the eyepiece of the telescope, that the light rays gathered by the two-hundred-inch mirror of the Hale telescope converged. Straddling the viewing equipment, she checked the star image centered on the crosswire. During the course of the night the telescope would slew from east to west, gliding on gears so frictionless it was possible for Selena to move the 530-ton telescope with the steady pressure of just one finger.

"Okay, Charlie," Selena said into the intercom. "Let's black it out."

"Amen to that," Charlie said. "Here we go."

Suddenly every trace of artificial light vanished. Looking up at the astonishing night sky, Selena felt like someone trapped in a cold apartment yearning for the glittering excitement promised in the distant lights of downtown. She tried to envision the cosmos before the Big Bang, when it consisted of matter and energy so dense the entire universe was smaller than the head of a pin, yet trillions of degrees hotter than the center of the sun. She wanted to comprehend a universe so expansive as to have more stars visible than there are grains of sand on all the beaches of planet Earth. If the earth was just one, tiny grain of sand among so many, Selena couldn't help but wonder, might there be another civilization out there?

She knew each and every one of us is composed of stardust. It's in our bones in the form of calcium. It's in our blood in the form of iron. Still, she found it was impossible to grasp. Our galaxy, the Milky Way, is so big it has 200 billion suns. But there were billions of other galaxies, each containing hundreds of thousands of millions of stars. Tonight, as she looked through the lens of the telescope, Selena reminded herself the light she viewed had traveled through space for billions of years before it reached the green iris of her eye.

As the telescope slewed to the correct position, focusing on the coordinates of an exact spot in the cosmos, Selena brought her concentration to the work at hand. Asteroids, like Mars or Venus or Earth, orbit the sun in approximately the same plane, like balls circling a roulette table. Because of the media's recent focus on her research, it felt as though the world were placing bets, waiting to see where her asteroid, NEA Hartmann 2009, would land.

Based on the results so far, Selena could not predict or disprove the possibility of a collision. When interviewed by the press, she steadfastly refused to speculate, but the pressure was building, and there wasn't much time. Even a fragment of Shoemaker-Levy 9 would have taken out the entirety of Los Angeles. What if she couldn't be certain? There wasn't a moment to waste.

* * * * *

After registering in the lobby of the Koamala Hilton for the Makapuu Point Hang Gliding Competition, Dr. Nikolai Potapov decided to return to his room. It was still early in the evening, but he could not shake the feeling of disappointment that Selena hadn't joined him in Hawaii. Her message had said she was held up in Washington because of the congressional hearings. She had not returned his calls to her hotel.

Alone in the elevator, Nik was scratching his beard and thinking about the postcard he'd just mailed to her, wondering whether it had been a mistake. He had planned to tell her this weekend about the new developments in his research on superconductors. It was a risky thing to do, but the breakthrough would be the greatest achievement of his scientific career. He had grown so close to Selena; he wanted to share it with her. Nik was thinking perhaps he shouldn't have sent the postcard after all, when a man slipped his hand between the closing elevator doors and forced them open.

"I saw you checking your gear in the parking lot," the stranger said as the doors closed. He pushed number seven. The elevator began to rise, but the man remained with his back to the doors, directly in front of Nik. "I'm writing a book on gliding," he said. "Why you nuts do it. What the attraction is. How about an interview? Maybe tomorrow?"

Nik nodded in agreement. There was something in the stranger's tone, in his expression, that made the question sound anything but a request. Nik appraised the man. He was lean in build but looked powerful. In the closed space of the elevator his energy felt overwhelming, as shocking as the single streak of white hair that bolted back from his right temple. It served to distract, if only for a while, from the scar tissue that disfigured the right side of his face. Nik thought he must have been burned. The man's nose appeared to have been broken several times, and his right ear, while partially concealed by hair, was clearly mutilated. Yet his dark, keen eyes asked for no pity, Nik thought. They seemed to be laughing.

"The book's dedicated to people who died in gliding accidents," the man said. He was grinning, as if he found this humorous. "I'm afraid of heights myself."

The words struck Nik as incongruous; the stranger didn't appear to be frightened of anything. When the elevator reached the seventh floor, Nik felt relieved, but instead of getting off, the man stood in the pathway of the automatic doors and continued to talk. Nik found it difficult to listen, however, because the doors were jamming against the man's body, butting against his broad shoulders. With each jarring impact, Nik felt his own body brace, but the stranger seemed impervious to the repeated blows.

Just before he left, the man added, "Do zavtra," then swiftly backed up, allowing the elevator doors to shut. It was a Russian greeting, a friendly "I'll see you tomorrow," and Nik was stunned by the familiar dialect of his parents' native province. Reflexively, he stepped forward, reached out to the man, but it was too late. The doors shut tight. The stranger was gone.

* * * * *

Three hours into the second shift at Palomar, Selena was immersed in the cosmos and talking to herself in the dark, cramped capsule.

"That's what I call romantic," she said, peering into the viewfinder. "You've been burning for five-hundred-thousand years. Nik can't keep it alive for a week. Definitely not in the same league."

Nikolai Potapov had left a message for Selena at her hotel in Washington. Two messages, actually. First, he wanted to postpone their trip to Hawaii by a day so he could go mountain climbing. Then he cancelled it altogether. Couldn't break away. She'd been hurt beyond disappointment, but now she told herself it was just as well she hadn't gone. I might have told him about Katya, she thought. Selena thought of her sixteen-year-old daughter and worry tightened her eyes. It was good she hadn't told Nik, she thought. It would have been a mistake.

Charlie's voice on the intercom was prefaced by the irritating scratch of static. "I'm back from the lab."

22

"How's the clarity?" Selena asked. "Have we got it?"

"You can say that again. Especially the second batch." Selena took a deep breath, then let it all out before asking, "Time for one more set?"

"It's almost five, kiddo. Show's over for tonight."

She flipped off the intercom, but before packing up the equipment, took one last look at the object of her attention: the near-Earth asteroid (NEA) Hartmann 2009. She wouldn't be face to face with it again, up close like this, for almost a week. Of course, she'd be with the King then -- Keck -- on the Big Island of Hawaii. Keck was the largest, most powerful telescope in the world. Selena knew she would need every bit of that documentation to stop Senator Whiting. She also knew the potentially apocalyptic consequences if she failed. Nuclear arms in space would almost certainly generate disaster, but a collision such as that of Comet Shoemaker-Levy 9 would destroy our planet a dozen times over.

At the thought, Selena bit the raw cuticle of her thumb until it began to bleed. Scientific objectivity had nothing to do with the compulsion she felt to prove tragedy wasn't imminent. The desperation was more than a vigil. It was an immense "if only," and she knew it was dangerous to the work. Did she really believe she could will this tragedy away, unlike another one, by force of her commitment and determination? But this loss she must prevent. She had to try.

For five years Selena had meticulously tracked the orbit of Hartmann 2009. The asteroid's swing by planet Earth in 1993 had been uncomfortably close by astronomical terms: it missed us by only 89,000 miles. Considering our moon is 250,000 miles away, the next pass could very possibly be a direct hit. That wouldn't happen until the year 2009, but if Selena's research demonstrated a collision was inevitable, defense programs must be implemented. She would present her findings at a major symposium on asteroids in Chile in less than two weeks. Her documentation must be precise.

* * * * *

In Hawaii, Nikolai Potapov left the Koamala Hilton for the gliding competition at Waimanalo Bay. Classical music flowed out the open window as he drove the red Taurus, a yellow hangglider on the roof rack, along Highway 72. The road skirted the ledge above the ocean and followed the coastline of pristine beaches.

Nik saw storm clouds crowding the peaks of the Koolau mountain range, moving south in the direction of the sea. He knew the rains would be forceful but pass quickly, not interfering with his day of gliding.

At Koko Head the road turned inland and snaked through the stratified cliffs of hardened volcanic ash and mud. By the time he reached Hanauma Bay, winds were lashing the palm trees against a charcoal sky. The waters of the Pacific darkened like squid ink. Within minutes, the downpour hit. Rain drummed emphatically on the roof and slashed against the windows. Nik slowed his car.

Leaning forward to peer through the frenzy of the windshield wipers, Nik was surprised when he saw a man dressed in a yellow rain slicker. He was standing on the road beside a Jeep, waving his arms above his head. Nik slowed to a stop and lowered the passenger window before he saw it was the man from the elevator, his bold streak of white hair clearly visible above his forehead. The man leaned in, water dripping off the tip of his disjointed, pale nose.

"I tried to get some shots of the storm clouds," he hollered over the noise of the wind. "Can't get the car started."

"There's a pay phone at the park," Nik said. "Get in."

As the man slid into the passenger seat, Nik noticed his snakeskin cowboy boots were soaked, but the crease in his dark pants held with the persistence of polyester. It occurred to Nik the stranger wasn't terribly concerned about comfort, wearing an outfit like that in the Hawaiian heat. When the man turned to face him, the only dry thing Nik saw was the metallic grey revolver pointed directly at his face.

"Nice gun, isn't it, Dr. Potapov? It's a Glock Semiautomatic. Austrian. Used against terrorists."

Nik's first thought was of the movies, gangsters, and guns. It all seemed so American he wondered for just an instant if it wasn't some kind of a joke. He wanted to look at the man, to understand the cold laughter on his face, but Nik's eyes were magnetized to the dull grey metal of the gun barrel. His stomach tightened in fear then clenched in anger. He felt an intense urge to lash out. He gripped the steering wheel tighter, his heart beating with the frantic pulse of the wipers.

"They're very accurate," the man said casually, tilting the gun from side to side. "For a long time they wouldn't let the cops near these babies. The trigger's touchy. Just the slightest bit of pressure," the man said. He raised the barrel higher, pointed it directly between Nik's eyes. "The least bit of tension, and boom! Accidental death!"

24

* * * * *

When the elevator came to a halt on the observatory floor, Charlie was there to greet Selena with a cup of coffee.

"Thanks, I'm beat," Selena said, rubbing her neck. "I never feel it when I'm up there." As they walked back to the control room, she pulled off her wool cap and shook her head. At five foot ten, Selena stood almost a head taller than her assistant.

"Good stuff, Doc," Charlie said, closing the door behind her. Above her gold granny glasses a black baseball cap bore the faded, but unmistakable symbol of the seven-pointed marijuana leaf. "I think we've almost got it," she said.

"God, I hope so." The elation of the night's work was fading and the deepening exhaustion made the responsibility feel overwhelming. Selena looked at the raw cuticles of her right hand, then made a fist. She had no idea why, but she never bit the left hand. Charlie began to massage the tight muscles in her neck, and Selena, closing her eyes, let her head drop.

"Any word from Katya?" Charlie asked.

"Not yet, but the tour company said postcards would be hard to come by in the jungle." Selena's shoulders began to warm and loosen. "God, that feels good."

"Don't get too relaxed." Charlie patted her on the head. "Owens wants to talk to you. Pronto."

"At this hour?"

"He's in New York."

Selena grimaced. "What's his problem?" She found the new head of the CalTech Astronomy Department, P.D. Owens, more of an astute politician than a scientist.

Charlie shrugged. "Maybe he's on your case about the SCB." She picked up the receiver. "Ready?"

"Put it on speaker," Selena said. The SCB was a superconducting bolometer being produced in Chile at the Lorillard Superconducting Laboratory. Working like night-vision goggles, it sensed and recorded infrared waves in space. When completed, the SCB would effectively detect the fainter, less reflective asteroids such as Hartmann 2009, and Selena would no longer be considering probabilities, she would know for certain. Since Selena had specifically requisitioned the SCB and been instrumental in its design, she was responsible for overseeing its development.

"Yes, Dr. Owens," she said. "I spoke with Dr. Sadler in Chile yesterday. Things are progressing well at the lab."

"That's fine," Owens said. "But I just received a personal call from Representative Chapman. He commended you on your testimony before the congressional hearing. Said you did a stunning job."

"So what's the problem?" Selena asked. She and Charlie looked at each other with raised eyebrows.

"Not a problem, really. Chapman wants to speak at the asteroid symposium in Chile. Maybe a closing address. I told him we'd be honored."

"It's a science conference," Selena said. "Not a media event. Why would he want to be there?" Co-sponsored by CalTech and Lorillard Superconductor Laboratories, the conference had been organized by Selena. She liked Pete Chapman but had purposely kept a low profile on the event, wanting to avoid public alarm, not heighten it.

"Between you and me," Owens said, "I think one of his biggest financial supporters is exerting some pressure."

"Who's that?"

"I don't know. It doesn't matter. Evidently he's as strongly opposed to the nukes in space program as we are."

"Are you sure this financial supporter isn't more interested in the marketability of the SCB?" Selena asked. "Does Lorillard have anything to do with this?"

"Hardly," Owens said. "He's about as pro-Star Wars as they get. Stands to make a fortune in government contracts. Chapman asked as a personal favor, Dr. I promised him you'd take care of it."

Selena stopped biting the cuticle of her thumb.

"You shouldn't speak for me, Dr. Owens. I'll have to get back to you on this." She gave Charlie the signal to cut him off. The dull buzz of a dead phone line filled the control room.

* * * * *

Within half an hour the sunshine repossessed the island of Oahu as if the earlier storm had never occurred. The red Taurus rental car registered in the name of Dr. Nikolai Potapov pulled out of the Koko Crater Road onto the Coast Drive. Its roof rack held a yellow hang glider. The radio blasted rock 'n roll through the open windows as the driver made his way to Waimanalo Bay.

There were over one hundred hang gliders participating in the Makapuu Point Competition that Sunday. Colorful wings highlighted the air. They flirted with the wind like gracefully choreographed butterflies, then circled to the east, landing on the sandy beaches of Maunaloa Bay.

The bearded young man driving Dr. Potapov's rental car arrived at the event later than planned. He quickly unloaded the gear from the roof rack, assembled the bright yellow, state-of-the-art glider, and carried it to the launch for check-in, his goggles already in place.

"Hey, Tom," he said to a guy with a nametag and clipboard. "Looks like another tough day in paradise."

"Sure beats the hell outa Nebraska," Tom agreed, noticing the man's nervous excitement. Between the goggles and the beard it was difficult to make out his expression. "Nice glider you got there. One of those rocket-powered parachutes, isn't it?"

"Yeah, thanks," the young man said, sounding terribly pleased. "My name's Potapov. Nikolai. I registered last night at the hotel for the 'Best Glide' contest."

"You bet, Doc. Gotcha right here on the list. Number 93." Tom helped slip the numbered vest over the man's head, securing it under his arms. As No. 93 continued his pre-flight check of the wires and sails, Tom noticed his awkwardness with the equipment and decided the glider must be brand new.

"Have a good one," he said and moved on to the next contestant.

Thirty minutes later, the yellow glider was soaring on the powerful wind currents that rushed against the 1100-foot cliffs. Seeing the waves beneath him turn to foam as they hurled themselves against the unfeeling boulders, he anxiously secured his gaze on the steadfast horizon where the smooth edge of blue sky sealed itself to the ocean below.

After ten minutes, the man carefully maneuvered the sensitive glider back towards the land, letting the body of upward-moving air push with exhilarating force against the yellow sails, lifting him higher and higher. He reached a thousand feet, then swooped off the rising ridge of air and turned back towards the ocean to lose altitude.

When the Dacron wings of his glider began to tear, No. 93 could feel the power of their resistance fail. It was a hollow moment, the loss of support jolting his stomach like an unexpectedly deep step. In disbelief he looked over his shoulders, first right then left. The clean rips in the brilliant yellow wings silhouetted the exceptional blue of the Hawaiian sky. His face contorted in confusion when he saw the wings were torn in what looked like the shape of a hammer and sickle, the symbol for the USSR.

Terrified to near-paralysis, the man diving to the sea below struggled to open his parachute. Over and over again his thumb struggled with the release button on the control frame of the glider. The rocket would not fire. The parachute would not deploy. He grappled in vain with the harness that kept him tied to the plummeting glider. Through the lens of his goggles, his eyes looked as if they were screaming, but his voice could produce no sound to echo his final moments of flight.

CHAPTER 3

Selena slipped a CD of Brahms Double Concerto into the dash of her '64 Porsche and started the long wind down Mt. Palomar on County Road S6, the black speedster gleaming in the sharp rays of early morning light. She had rebuilt or replaced every belt, bolt, and bumper on the car, but whenever she threatened to buy something practical like a Toyota, Charlie protested.

"It's the one lovely, irrational thing you've ever done," she'd say. "It's healthy for a control freak like you."

Once she reached the lower elevations Selena opened the car window, enjoying the flow of soft, warmer air on her still-cold face. Turning north onto Highway 76, she thought about the discussion she'd had with Charlie just before leaving the observatory. She regretted it.

"Anytime she wants to know," Selena had said, "she just needs to ask. I've made that clear."

"It's your responsibility," Charlie insisted. "Not your daughter's." Charlie wanted Selena to tell Katya about Nikolai. She believed Katya's troubled behavior of late was directly related to the father issue.

"It's been fifteen years," Selena said, her hands clenched at her sides. "You think because Nik suddenly shows up he's going to solve all our problems?"

Charlie had looked surprised and hurt, then backed off without saying another word. Selena hadn't meant to say Charlie had no right to interfere. That wasn't the case. Charlie had loved Katya from the beginning, starting as surrogate father in the labor room.

On that day fifteen years ago, Selena had refused to take any pain medication. Still, she couldn't remember very much. Charlie loved to tell Katya how towards the end of labor Selena rose up in bed and announced with absolute sincerity that she'd had enough for today. She was going home. She'd come back tomorrow and finish the job. Selena laughed, picturing Charlie's reenactment of the scene for Katya.

Pulling onto the freeway, she moved quickly to the passing lane and settled in for the long ride north to Pasadena. I'm just tired, she told herself, thinking once again of Charlie. It's the pressure to finish everything in time for Chile. It all seemed to be happening just when Katya needed attention.

Selena knew sending her daughter off to Costa Rica on a rainforest eco-tour with her school friend, Naomi, was only a stopgap measure. It got Katya away from the freaks at Venice Beach for a while, but she would be home before Selena returned from Chile. Naomi's parents had agreed to let Katya stay with them, but Selena was still concerned. What if Charlie were right? What if Katya was piercing her nipple and dying her hair black because she wanted to know her father? What would she do next? And would Selena even be there to stop it?

* * * * *

The brass paperweight on Mr. Clive Bingham's desk was given to him by his wife, Eunice. Engraved beneath a wide-eyed, pipe-smoking fisherman holding his arms as far apart as they could reach were the words, "The One That Got Away...." At CIA headquarters in Langley, Virginia, they frowned on personal objects cluttering employees' desks, but Bingham wasn't worried. He was retiring in the fall from the clandestine service of the CIA, the Directorate of Operations, or as the insiders call it, DO.

A tall, balding, but chipper man of sixty-two, Clive Bingham held the position of Deputy Director of the Latin American Division. He reported directly to Mac Mulroney, a true member of the old guard. Most of them had already gone, and Bingham didn't blame them. He couldn't wait to retire to his future cabin on Lake Chauncey and catch another fish like the iridescent, stuffed trout that hung on the wall behind his desk. Clive was deeply absorbed by these thoughts and the inspection of two newly made flies when his assistant entered the room.

"Good morning, sir." Norman Hambly was only five feet four inches tall but he stood stiff and upright before his boss. His red, allergic eyes stared out from beneath dark-framed glasses.

"Where is Lorillard now?" Bingham demanded.

"On his way back to Chile, sir." Norman felt a bout of sneezing coming on and reached for his handkerchief.

"Listen, Hambly. Mulroney was just in here. He got a call from the seventh floor. The Oval Office is monitoring Operation Blue Whale, and I haven't gotten any information worth shit from our agent down there. I can't afford any surprises."

Hambly understood why the President would take such an interest in Operation Blue Whale. As a senator from Texas, he had championed the Superconducting Super Collider. When the project was cancelled, it was a personal defeat and a humiliation he never forgot. From the moment he learned that Pierre Lorillard had made difficult-to-trace but massive contributions to PACs and lobbyists fighting the SSC, the President considered him an enemy. Now the son of a bitch was building his own supercollider. Operation Blue Whale was payback time.

Bingham continued. "Mulroney's making a move for upstairs. Personally, I think he's nuts, but if that's what he wants. At any rate, he needs Blue Whale in his pocket. We've got to get somebody else in Chile, somebody with access to Lorillard and that lab."

"I understand, sir."

"I looked over the imagery from the reconnaissance satellites again. They've worked it every which way, computer enhancement, digital reconstruction. Nothing. It's simply not in the picture. But something's going on down there."

"Yes sir." Hambly knew the smooth success of this operation was vital not only to Mac Mulroney but to Clive Bingham as well. As his boss put it, "Then I can get the hell out of here before any more liberal shit hits the fan."

Bingham looked at his assistant with an expression of exasperation. Hambly was smart, no doubt about it, but he was such a wimp.

"Hambly," Bingham said, "when this is over the Missus and I want to have you out for dinner. With your lady friend. The one who's so keen on you."

Norman Hambly looked anxious, but Bingham warmed to his subject.

"You know, there's nothing like having a woman at home for support, somebody taking care of things. It might help you loosen up a bit. Have some fun. Eunice and I are celebrating our fortieth anniversary in a couple weeks." Bingham beamed a self-satisfied smile. "You should see the surprise I have in mind."

"Yes sir." Hambly could feel another sneezing attack coming on.

"You'll have to come up and visit us at the lake. The fresh air'll toughen you up a bit. I'll teach you how to fish. How about it?"

Hambly's eyes began to water and he quickly reached for his handkerchief, covering his face as a series of three sharp blasts hit. Bingham winced with each outburst.

"I'm not sure my hay fever would like that, Mr. Bingham. But thank you anyway, sir."

"Hmmm. I see what you mean." Bingham cleared his throat and reached for the phone. They just didn't make men the way they used to, Bingham thought, punching numbers into the phone.

"Time to break the bad news to the little lady in California," he said.

* * * * *

By the time Selena took the exit for Avenida de Flores she was beat. Rounding the corner she saw her California-style bungalow up the road, the last house on a dead end street. The gardener had cut the grass and put extra mulch around the shrubs. Selena found the order of the freshly manicured yard reassuring. She realized she was starving.

Maybe there's one more can of soup in the refrigerator, she thought, even though it was breakfast time. She kept the soup cold to make the excess fat rise to the surface. These days it was too hard to burn it off once it settled on her thighs.

Dropping her briefcase in the front hall, she gathered the scattered envelopes beneath the mail slot. Amidst the junk mail she focused on a postcard of a glorious orange sunset. It framed the ample body of an American tourist dressed in a pink and blue muumuu, her arms overflowing with shopping bags.

Turning the card over, Selena noticed the collection of two and three cent Hawaiian stamps completely covering the upper right-hand corner. She read the message eagerly. "Sorry you couldn't make it. I miss you. Love, Nik."

Couldn't make it? What was he talking about? His message at her hotel had said he was postponing the trip. Had he called again, left another message rescheduling? Maybe she'd already checked out. Damn, I don't believe it. The frustration she felt was only slightly softened by the thought that perhaps Nik had not cancelled after all.

Just as quickly, Selena felt a fool. What kind of an emotional roller coaster ride was she allowing herself to take with this man? It seemed she was always reacting. Had she lost all control of her life? Tossing the rest of the mail on the hall table, her eyes rested on the framed photograph beside the phone. In the picture Charlie was teaching a three-year-old Katya how to bat a ball.

That day had been happy, but bittersweet. Sitting on the back stairs watching Charlie's patient clowning and Katya's wild swings, Selena had missed her child's father. She told herself a man wasn't needed. Still, she wanted Nik to share the joy of their daughter.

Selena suddenly realized there had been more involved in her defensive response to Charlie's suggestion that morning. Over the years she had gotten used to the lack of a father, had grown comfortable with their family unit as it was. She had forgotten the loneliness of raising a child alone, not just the scary runs to the hospital for stitches or the fevers in the night, but the worst part of all, the solitude of unshared joy.

She still harbored the hope Nik would renew their relationship, but now she wanted him to do it of his own accord, because of his feelings for her, not because Katya was his biological daughter. Once she told him about Katya, everything would change. That's why she hadn't wanted to hear the advice from Charlie. Selena knew she was still holding out for herself, for what she wanted.

For a moment she wondered if missing the trip to Hawaii was some sort of punishment for her selfishness, but she quickly told herself to drop it. That was nonsense. She didn't need to set her own booby-traps.

Flipping on the answering machine, Selena headed for the kitchen. With the postcard pressed between her lips, she searched the refrigerator shelves and listened. For the third time a woman named Edith from Sears wanted to sell Dr. Hartmann another year's service contract on the washer and dryer. Would he please call back?

Selena opened the last can of minestrone and placed a paper towel on the surface of the cold liquid, soaking up the congealed fat. She had turned the gas burner on high and was stirring the pan of soup when her attention perked at the sound of Charlie's voice.

"A Mr. Bingham from the CIA called. 703-833-2699. Said it was *mucho importante*. You got a job on the side I don't know about?"

Selena's first thought was relief that Charlie didn't sound upset about their quarrel. Quickly pinning the postcard to her collection on the kitchen bulletin board, Selena walked to the phone, an edgy concern growing in her stomach. The CIA? What's going on? Maybe it has to do with the new secretary's security clearance. But I thought that came through already. I'm sure it did. The CIA? Why would they call at this early hour? It made no sense. Before she dialed, she scribbled the phone number on a blue pad sitting beside the photograph of Charlie and Katya. Then it hit her.

What if it's Katya? What if something's wrong? Oh my God! She quickly punched in the number, hitting the wrong button for the last digit. She started again. Three rings before anyone answered.

"Thanks for calling, Ms. Hartmann," Mr. Bingham said. "I'm afraid I have some bad news for you. There's been an accident." A vacuum sucked the breath from Selena's chest. Her thoughts raced as the skin on her neck prickled, then went cold.

"Dr. Nikolai Potapov, ma'am. He was involved in a hang gliding accident. In Hawaii. I'm sorry, but it was fatal."

Selena's body and mind scrambled. "Nik! Oh my God!" The word "fatal" flashed like neon.

"Ms. Hartmann? Are you all right?"

"Where's Nik? What happened!" She was frantic for information, for facts to replace the fear.

"Evidently his glider failed."

"What about the parachute?" Selena demanded.

"That's just it. It appears to have been a suicide, Ms. Hartmann. Dr. Potapov left a note."

"What?" Selena simply could not believe what this man was telling her. "Nik would never do that!" she insisted. Her eyes darted from light switch to ceiling plaster to mirror frame, anywhere to avoid what had been placed before her.

"I know this must be a shock," Mr. Bingham said. She found his tone artificial and patronizing. "We're in the process of investigating. There are obvious security issues involved."

"Nik was an expert glider," Selena said.

"According to witnesses he fell into the sea from about two thousand feet. If it's any comfort, he must have been killed instantly."

"I want to see him," she said, half pleading, half demanding. "Where is he? When did this happen?"

"The accident took place yesterday. No body was found. We believe the sharks got to it before the Coast Guard made it to the scene.

Selena closed her eyes tightly and made a sound like a whimper.

"I'm sorry, Ms. Hartmann, but do you know any reason why Nikolai Potapov would want to take his own life? Did he seem upset to you, or depressed? Did he say anything?"

"No! No! He was the same. Nik would never do this!" Silently she kept repeating the words, as if each declaration were a rock in the barricade. He wouldn't do this. He couldn't.

"Well, if you should come upon anything that might help us in the investigation, any information or notes of Dr. Potapov's? Anything like that. Please let me know, as soon as possible. Anything at all."

Selena either could not or would not recognize this man's words. Some furious refusal had shut her down, blocked her ability to respond.

"Thank you for your help, Ms. Hartmann," Mr. Bingham said. "It's my understanding Dr. Potapov is the father of your child."

How in hell does he know that? she wondered, then realized Nik's name was on Katya's birth certificate. If the CIA wanted to find out, they could.

"You should know that in the suicide note, Dr. Potapov gave the name of an attorney in California. He'll be the executor of the will. I'm sure he'll be in touch with you soon."

Selena hung up the phone. She felt dazed. Walking slowly back towards the kitchen, she told herself it couldn't be, it simply couldn't be. The smell of soup burning on the bottom of the pan didn't register until she saw the black smoke rolling up the wall. She rushed to the stove and impulsively grabbed the silver handle of the pot, burning her right palm. Crying out in pain, she clutched a dishtowel and pushed the pan off the burner, then lifted the pot to the sink, letting the rush of cold water sizzle on the hot enameled steel. Her hand still burned as clouds of smoke puffed and rose to her face, stinging her wide, frightened eyes. She turned away, her teary, blurred gaze resting on the bulletin board, on Nik's postcard, hanging crooked from the corner.

Selena bent over the kitchen counter and lay her head down in her arms. The water gushed from the faucet, drowning out the sound of her sobs.

CHAPTER 4

Deep in the Monteverde rainforests of Costa Rica, Katya Hartmann scratched at the chigger bites around her ankles until they started to bleed.

"Shit," she said and leaned over to nudge the nighttime mosquito netting tight under the tent door. "This place is brutal." Spikes of Katya's dyed-black hair hung in her eyes and she brushed them back, then twirled one of the six gold rings that pierced her earlobe.

Naomi took another bite of a Mars bar she'd smuggled from home. "Yeah, it's brutal. But Federico is cool."

Katya smiled to herself. "No kidding," she said, twisting the cap tighter on a tube of oil paint. For the trip Charlie had given her the travel set of art supplies with a small, fold-up easel. Small compensation, Katya thought, for two weeks in hell. The eco-tour had been her mother's idea. Another part of the campaign for a "normal" childhood, Katya thought. More "Little House on the Prairie" crap. I wish she'd give it up.

"I can't believe how much Federico knows about the plants and wildlife around here," Naomi said.

Katya made a nasty face and stared at her friend. Typical, she thought. Their tour guide is gorgeous, and all Naomi can think of is flora and fauna. Holding up her latest painting, a purple and black wild orchid, Katya seemed pleased.

Naomi took the last bite of her candy bar. "I saw you flirting with him at dinner tonight," she said, leafing through the pages of *Mademoiselle* magazine.

"What's it to you?" Katya scratched her ankles again.

"Don't you think he's a little too old for you?"

"He's only twenty-eight. It's in the brochure." She picked at the black paint under her fingernails.

"That's twelve years older," Naomi insisted. She rubbed a freshly scabbed pimple on her chin. "You better be careful. Mom says sometimes with guys you get what you ask for."

"Give me a break," Katya said and frowned. Naomi was really beginning to irritate her. Looking in the mirror that hung from the center tent pole, Katya saw a smudge of black paint marking her cheek. Pleased by her eerie reflection in the shadowy lantern light, she brushed her bangs to cover her wide forehead and dark, straight eyebrows that were so much like her mother's. Katya liked her green eyes best. Her mom's were brown.

"We better go to sleep," Naomi said, poking her head out of the tent for one last look around. "Everybody else is."

"Ask me if I care," Katya said.

"I don't know what's wrong with you these days," Naomi said, then turned off the lantern and lay back on her air mattress.

Katya just sat there in the dark. She wasn't tired; she was bored. Brushing her finger across her nipple ring, she decided she would never forgive her mother for making her take this trip. She felt like she'd been sent to a babysitter's. She just wanted to dump me, Katya thought. So she could go to Chile, to her precious symposium. Well, there's no way in hell she can make me like this shit.

* * * * *

On the corner of 12th Street and Coney Island Avenue, Jean Levesque walked out of a Brighton Beach butcher shop holding a quart of plump, red strawberries in the palm of his hand. Despite the warm July evening, he wore a dark gray jacket. Looking over his shoulder at the plucked chickens hanging from their scrawny necks in the shop window, Jean's gaze lingered on their withered and yellowing flesh. Amusement slinked across his lips as the El passed noisily overhead.

Pausing on the curb, he adjusted a bulky package under his jacket, holding it in place with the pressure of his arm. The streetlamp highlighted a bold streak of white hair above his right temple.

The smell of freshly cut grass spiced the night air as Jean Levesque walked casually down 12th Street to No. 948. He stood for a moment in front of the old, brick row house and read the small, hand painted sign above the buzzer: "Marfa Ivanovna - Herbalist." Jean pushed the buzzer. While waiting, he carefully chose a ripe, unbruised strawberry, bit into it and smiled as the juice ran down his lips.

Responding in Russian to the woman's heavily accented voice on the intercom, he said, "Ya drug Nikolaya Potapova." I am a friend of Nikolai Potapov.

He entered the dim hallway and was greeted by the mingled scent of herbs. His cowboy boots scraped against grit as he mounted the stairs. The shop door was open.

Marfa Ivanovna's shop was dark and quiet, with candles illuminating the cluttered corners, dust particles dancing in the pale light. The room was lined with shelves. Jars and pots crowded every surface, each container labeled with the name of a medicinal herb, root, powder, or leaf. Through a beaded curtain Jean could see a back room that appeared to serve as both kitchen and laboratory. He rang the brass bell on the counter.

This is a waste of time, he thought. Just give me a free hand with the bastard. But when it came to that damned Russian, Lorillard was soft. And surprisingly foolish.

* * * * *

Katya Hartmann followed the footpath beside the winding backwater river. A khaki-colored canvas hat framed her olive skin and her clear, white, doe eyes. It was still morning, but underneath her pack she was already soaked with perspiration.

"I'm gonna catch up with the others," Naomi said and hurried past. Katya couldn't help but notice the immense wedgie in her friend's too-tight shorts. When Naomi's backpack whacked the arm of Federico, she apologized three times even though he told her it wasn't a problem.

Ever since breakfast, Katya could tell that Naomi was angry. It was probably because Federico had noticed Katya wasn't eating.

"At least a pancake," he'd said, standing over the fire. He flipped one onto her tin plate. "You've got to fill up those long legs with something."

Naomi had rolled her eyes and made a face. When Federico had gone she tried to mimic him, but nobody laughed. She's just jealous, Katya thought, then noticed Federico was calling her from up ahead, motioning her to hurry.

"Look!" he said and pointed high into the lush green forest. "Up there."

She moved forward, brushing her sun-browned, youthful body close to his. Searching the thick vegetation, she raised her binoculars and focused on a brilliantly colored Toucan regally perched in a tree not far ahead. The bird seemed to be defiantly staring at them, proud of its handsome beak of yellow, green and blue.

"I see it," Katya whispered. She was intensely conscious of the closeness of Federico's body. Letting the binoculars drop around her neck, she reached for her new Nikon. Thankfully, the telephoto lens was in place. She focused quickly, shot several frames, then quietly changed positions for another angle.

The path was narrow, forcing her to lean in front of Federico for the shot. Her balance shaky, he held her shoulders for stability. She felt heat from his hands penetrate the thin cotton of her T-shirt. Despite the majesty of the bird framed in her viewfinder, all her attention was focused on his touch.

Katya suddenly lost her balance and started to fall. Federico caught her, and the Toucan, disturbed by their noise, languidly flapped its wings and was gone.

"I guess he got away," Federico said, his arms still around her.

"But I didn't," Katya said, smiling up at him. Her eyes lingered on the gold streaks in his beard.

"I can see that," Federico said. He stepped closer and repositioned the binoculars on her chest. She could feel the hard muscles of his thighs pressed against her own bare legs.

"Federico!" Naomi called. A moment later she came running around the bend. Seeing them practically in each other's arms, she stopped abruptly a few yards away. "God," she said, her eyes big, her mouth hanging open. Naomi said nothing else, but quickly turned and ran back to the others.

Katya was blushing as Federico stepped back. "Thanks," she said, fidgeting with the assorted rings in her ear. "I think I got the shot."

"Good," he said, grinning. "I think we better catch up with the others."

* * * * *

Inside the small kitchen of Marfa Ivanovna's shop the kettle on the old gas stove hummed just below a boil. A yellowing window shade blocked out the night sky and the neighboring buildings. Straddling a chair by the lace-covered window, Jean Levesque ate his strawberries and tossed the leafy green tops at a large jar on the floor. The contents of the jar appeared to move, yet its clear glass looked solidly black.

Marfa Ivanovna, an old, frail-looking woman, was seated in the center of the kitchen and wearing, despite the heat of the third floor walk-up, a black dress and a heavy shawl. Her legs and arms were secured to the chair with silver tape, her mouth gagged. A pad of paper lay in her lap, a free hand clutching a pencil.

"I'm running out of patience, Marfa," Jean told the woman. He looked at the box on the kitchen table filled with teas and chocolates from Switzerland. A brightly colored silk scarf hung from the back of a chair. Old family photographs were spread across the table.

"We know Dr. Potapov stopped here on his way to Hawaii," Jean said. "You were his nanny. He loved you like his own mother." The thought of the Russian's affection for this woman made Jean's eyes sparkle. "You were the only family left for him. That's why he gave the photos to you. Tell me what else he left, Marfa."

The old woman stared at him, her confusion and fear puckering the wrinkled skin of her eyes.

"Ya ne khochu obidet tebya," Jean said in the same perfect Russian dialect he had used in Hawaii with Nikolai. "I don't want to hurt you." The woman's eyes widened with shock that he knew her language, as though he now had access to her thoughts, to her Russian soul. She gripped the pencil, raised it, and scribbled with her shaking hand the same word again. "NOTHING."

Watching her write, Jean noticed the liver spots that covered her bony fingers. Earlier he had considered undressing her, but was glad he'd decided against it. Placing the quart of strawberries on the spotless linoleum floor, he walked to the large black jar and carefully unscrewed the top.

"These little buggers are called Triatoma infestans, Marfa." Jean let some of the groggy black insects crawl onto the gold lid. About half an inch long, their prominent eyes and antennae protruded from elongated heads. Orange patches fringed their sunken abdomens. He held the lid of the jar close to the woman's face, and her eyes bulged in fear and disgust at the hideous creatures. Jean wished Nikolai Potapov were around to see the look on his nanny's face now.

"They suck blood. And they carry Trypanosoma cruzi," he said, carefully pronouncing each syllable. "South American sleeping sickness." Clumps of the bugs were crawling out of the jar onto the lid. He held it over the woman's head, letting the insects fall through her white, thinning hair onto her soft, pink scalp. As they began to creep, a visible shudder coursed through Marfa's body. She struggled harder against her restraints.

Placing the lid on her lap, Jean used his free hand to pull back the woman's shawl and undo the top two buttons of her dress. Watching her eyes, he shook dozens more loose, saw them fall against her pale, fleshy chest, crawl under her white slip. He stepped back a few feet and looked the old woman in the eye.

"They like to feed on mucous membranes," he said and watched the bugs crawl towards the old woman's mouth and eyes and nose. "Anyplace moist. They've been starved for months so their abdomens can swell like ripe berries filled with your blood." Marfa's body jerked and yanked desperately.

"Just write it down," he said, straddling the kitchen chair. "Tell me where it is and I'll let you go."

But Jean Levesque knew she wouldn't tell him. Lorillard was just a fool when it came to the Russian. Besides, there were other ways to get the information they needed. This old woman knew nothing. But if this were really what Pierre wanted him to do, Jean would oblige. It had been that way for years. As far as Jean was concerned, it always would be.

He took another bite of a strawberry. Wiping the juice from his mouth, he felt the strip of scar tissue that connected his reassembled right ear to his face. The rubbery, dead feel of the flesh made him remember that last operation, the anesthetist's familiar, "Sayonara, old buddy. See you at the other end." By then the words had become a ritual for Jean, a superstitious rite of passage. He'd been in the San Diego Naval Hospital for two years.

Jean had to admit that even as a boy in the small town of Red Deer just north of Calgary his older brother was always rescuing him from some mess. Those first years in the rodeo were the best he could recall, but then he wandered down to San Diego and, for lack of anything better to do, enlisted in the Army.

Once they discovered his unusual aptitude for languages he was shipped off to the Defense Language School in Monterey, California. Among other things, he learned to speak Iranian Farsi and was trained in explosives and clandestine surveillance for the Special Intelligence Unit.

When they sent him to Iran on a hostage mission, his instructions were to make contact with the extremists for delivery of funds in exchange for prisoners. But the U.S. aborted the mission, pulled out at the last minute. *Left me behind*, Jean thought, *exposed and expendable*. The fanatic religious sect he'd been working with tortured him for forty-six days.

Thankfully, he couldn't recall everything they did to him. He did remember them painting parts of his naked body with raw meat juice, then allowing the leash of a vicious and near-starved dog to slacken just far enough. He remembered the injections of amphetamines that kept him alive and awake while they brutalized his body.

Jean finished the last strawberry and threw the green top at Marfa Ivanovna's feet. Her struggling was beginning to subside, her eyes and nose covered by the black creatures. They were biting their way into her gagged mouth, working through her ears to the soft tissue of her brain. Jean rose from his chair and stretched, thinking, "No one's gonna help you now, old lady."

Luckily for Jean, help had come to his rescue – his big brother Louis. Levesque shook his head remembering. You sure as hell took your time about it, he thought.

Louis Levesque was a vice president for Lorillard, Inc., and his boss, Pierre Lorillard, even more than other Canadians, harbored a deep resentment of the United States. Also, Lorillard had lost a dearly loved brother. Jean learned later that Pierre had felt responsible for that death. Those sentiments made him doubly sympathetic to Louis' plea for help.

The company's oil rights holdings overseas provided the necessary connections. It took four million dollars cash placed in the right hands, but Jean Levesque was eventually released and dumped on the steps of the Canadian embassy, barely alive.

Jean ran his hand through the white shock of hair bolting back from his forehead. The white patch had appeared the morning after that final operation, together with a consummate devotion to Pierre Lorillard. Since then, that allegiance had been the sole objective of Jean's existence. Until, he thought, Nikolai Potapov showed up and things started to change.

Turning out the lights, Jean walked to the lace-curtained window. It would be hours before the insects had eaten their fill. For a moment he tried to imagine the woman's body afterwards. Instead he yanked on the window shade and let it fly up, spinning round and round, flapping against the sill. After he left, the light of the planet Venus shone through the warped panes of old glass and fell on Marfa Ivanovna's bug-covered head.

CHAPTER 5

The small, twin-engine commuter plane continued to circle the airport on the big island of Oahu. In the window seat next to Charlie, Selena attempted without success to concentrate on paperwork. Ever since her arrival in Hawaii she'd been keenly aware of one thing. It was here, in this so-called paradise, just four days earlier, she had lost Nik.

For most of the flight Charlie had kept to herself, deeply immersed in one of Carlos Castaneda's mystical lessons of Yaqui Indian wisdom. Selena knew Charlie was upset.

"Look out the window," Selena said, poking her friend's arm. They both squinted into the bright sun reflected off the plane's wing and took in the rich, green island buoyed all around by shimmering waters.

"It's glorious," Selena sighed. "Every time I see it, I'm amazed as if it were the first time. I've got to bring Katya someday." A look of concern crossed her face. Charlie noticed.

"Are you going to tell her about Nik?" Katya had now lost her only chance to know her father. Charlie had advised strongly against waiting to tell the child the truth.

"Maybe when she comes home," Selena said. She now deeply regretted her decision to hold off.

Charlie nodded, then said, "But what good would it do to tell her now?"

Selena did a double take. Were Charlie's words meant to sting with accusation? Selena's guilt and sadness hardly needed prompting. But Charlie had already returned to the mystical never-never land of her book, and her face held no malice.

What good would it do to tell Katya now? Exactly, Selena thought. It's too late. And what good will it do to finally spend time with her when she's all grown up? It seemed to Selena she was always running late, hurrying to get there in time. She felt like it was the story of her life.

The pilot's monotone voice came over the loudspeaker and announced they would circle the busy airport a few more minutes before landing. Selena nervously twisted the turquoise and silver ring she wore. It felt unfamiliar and rubbed against the tender skin between her fingers. Nik had given it to her sixteen years earlier in Aspen. With time, the cratered surface of the large, perfectly round stone had turned a rich shade of dark green, her favorite color. Made of heavy silver, the setting radiated like moonbeams from the center stone. She had worn the ring for years after Katya was born, then finally put it away, eventually forgetting all about it.

Selena wondered if she shouldn't have left the ring where she found it, lost in the bottom of an old jewelry box. She wondered, too, if it wouldn't have been better if Nik had never left Russia. He'd come to the States a year earlier, supposedly in search of work, but academic gossip held that Dr. Nikolai Potapov would never return to his homeland. An outspoken critic of the government long before the fall of the USSR, Nik persisted, it was said, in his disapproval.

When Selena first learned he had taken a position at Stanford, possibility crept into her heart, disturbing the comfortable certainty of her life with dreamy hope. But Nik didn't call. She told herself he was, after all, unaware of the connection that remained between them because of Katya. Then unexpectedly one Sunday he telephoned, asked to see her. Selena remembered how romantically foolish, how adolescent she'd felt after she hung up. That was less than a month ago.

The plane tilted sharply over the blue Pacific, and she looked down at a pearly, half-moon beach. Remembering how she and Nik had walked the California coastline a few weeks earlier, Selena's eyes stung. She swallowed hard against the longing.

They'd walked the water's edge just north of Los Angeles as the warm belly of the sun slipped beneath the line of the horizon.

"I still can't believe I'm here," he'd said. "In this wonderful country."

Selena found it difficult not to stare at him. The resemblance between Nik and his daughter was striking, particularly in his green eyes and the straight, stubborn line of his lips. Even some of his expressions reminded her of Katya, but of course that was impossible. They hadn't even met each other yet.

They walked in the dusk towards the lights of a pier; Selena's face was hot, her mind confused. How would he respond if she told him of his daughter? Would he be happy or disturbed? Could he love a child he'd never known? Would he leave again, return to Russia? Charlie said Katya had asked about her father recently. Maybe it was time. But maybe Katya didn't know what was good for her, Selena thought. Should she speak with Nik first, or her daughter?

She watched as Nik climbed out on some boulders that sheltered quiet tide pools. Hot colors of the sunset reflected off the still water.

"Come and look," Nik called.

He's as excited as a child, Selena thought.

"Quick. Here's a crab." He held out his hand to her and she climbed up the slippery rocks.

The questions continued to haunt her, but Selena told herself she couldn't think of all this now. Later she would understand what to do. Right now it felt so right just being there, close to Nik, feeling the warm skin of his hand wrapped around hers. She wanted to hold him. She wanted to give in to those same strong feelings of desire she'd known before. She wanted to believe everything would work out in time. She wanted to believe that this time it wasn't too late.

They walked on, farther down the beach until the last lavender spray of sunset was fading in the sky. Huge sea rocks by the water's edge were silhouetted in the lights of Port Hueneme, just ahead. On the cliffs an old Victorian house, red geraniums pouring from its window boxes, looked warm and inviting in the dusky light. A breath of music trailed down, muted by the sound of waves. "Montalvo Inn -- Bed and Breakfast -- Dinner Served," the sign read.

"Shall we?" Nik asked. Selena smiled, and they climbed the crumbling cement stairs.

The inn's dining room had an old world charm. Against the far wall a small fire burned in an ornately mantled fireplace while lace curtains, looking as ancient as the house, softened the dark paneling. The hostess led them across the empty dance floor to a booth by a window overlooking the ocean.

"Hi there," the waitress said. "How ya doin this evening?" Half her head was shaved and an assortment of earrings dangled from her left ear. She wore combat boots and a drab green T-shirt. Selena saw an exaggerated version of Katya and watched to see Nik's reaction. He was glancing at the waitress, pulling on the lobe of his ear, and scratching his beard.

"Something to drink tonight?" the waitress asked and handed them both large, faded blue menus with worn, white felt lettering.

"How about a bottle of this Bordeaux," Nik said.

"Good choice," the waitress said. "I recommend it." When she walked away, Nik's eyes followed her.

"American kids," he said smiling, then turned to Selena. "Your daughter doesn't look like that, does she?"

"Not exactly," Selena said, amusement spreading across her face. She hid her grin behind the menu, but found the entrees as alien to her as the waitress was to Nik. Stuffed pork chops with sour cream? Beef balls with sauerkraut?

"This is fantastic," Nik declared. "They've got knockwurst. Look, they even have Zupa Watrobiana. Wonderful."

Selena scanned her menu to find the source of his pleasure: "Polish Liver Soup." It was an enthusiasm she couldn't share. They agreed to share a knockwurst dish and a peasant stew with apples and sausage. The waitress returned and opened the bottle of wine, pouring a little for Nik to taste.

"Doskonaly!" he announced in Polish. The waitress looked at him as if he were beyond weird. Nik seemed to notice her disapproval and hastened to translate.

"Excellent! Very good!" The waitress walked away, rolling her eyes, and Nik grinned, shaking his head in mock disbelief. Selena imagined a future meeting of father and daughter and laughed. She felt suddenly grateful, as if the universe were on her side these days, as if things were going her way. She immediately felt she should knock on wood, but wouldn't let herself indulge in the superstition.

Instead, she noticed the tan skin around Nik's eyes, how it creased when he laughed, and she felt a wash of melancholy. It had taken years to make those wrinkles, much laughter, surely some tears, and many sunny days. Yet the time was over and gone. So were some of the people who'd brought the smiles to his face. She could feel the old familiar tightness in her chest, the wish to do this right before it was too late, not to lose what mattered.

Nik raised his glass to Selena. He looked serious.

"To the best of our memories."

Long ago memories, Selena thought, slowly sipping her wine. That's really all they shared. They had each lived full, separate lives over the last fifteen years. They didn't know each other, not as the people they were now, the people they had become.

"Tell me about your life in Russia," she said. "What was it like?"

He didn't look eager to discuss it. "Like here, in a lot of ways," he said. "Mostly work."

Years ago Selena had heard about Nik's opposition to Russia's military presence in Afghanistan. There had even been rumors of his persecution by the KGB, stories of house arrest.

"Have things changed?" she asked, not anxious to open old wounds. "Are they any better now?"

"Some people think so." He was nervously tugging on his ear now, his forehead creased. "Work conditions are abominable. My last week in St. Petersburg, my computer broke down six times. It could take days to get a simple photocopy." He was shaking his head, exasperated, when he suddenly laughed. "Do you know the average wait for phone service is thirty-two years?"

Selena had heard of his bitterness towards Russia. Still, she was surprised by Nik's intensity. She knew the American press ate these comments up, but it didn't please her to hear him ridicule his own country.

"And your family?" she asked. Might as well get all the touchy subjects over right away, she thought.

Nikolai seemed even more reluctant. "My wife is an engineer. We both worked a great deal. My parents died years ago, but Sofya has many relatives and we saw them often." He smiled. "Too often. She didn't want to leave Russia." He was serious now. "I couldn't stay any longer."

Nik looked away, out the window. A spotlight shone on the soft white line of surf. The beach was deserted.

"And what about you?" he asked. "Tell me about your life. Did you marry? What have you been doing all these years? Besides becoming one of the 'Ten Women Superstars of Science'?"

Selena laughed. Nik must have seen the article in *Scientific American.*

"I'll appreciate that compliment more when they drop the 'Women,'" she said. "Mostly I've been working. And raising my daughter. I lived with a man for five years, but it wasn't what I wanted." There was too much to tell, she thought, or was it too little? Instead she shrugged and said, "It seems like there's never enough time." Where could she begin? The years had flown so quickly, and there was something disconcerting about looking back. Too much life had passed without notice.

"I've heard about your asteroid symposium in Chile," he said. "With Lorillard Industries, right?"

"Yes," Selena said. "They're promoting their Superconductor Lab."

"And generating a lot of excitement."

"Too much," Selena said. "It's supposed to be a scientific gathering, not a media event. I just want to finish my research at Keck in time to present the findings. Only a few weeks left."

"A lot of scientists would love the hype. Pierre Lorillard must be encouraging it."

"The conference was his idea," Selena said. "Full sponsorship by his lab. But he agreed to let me run it. Without interference."

"So you've met him?" Nik asked.

"No. We discussed it on the phone. His office has been very cooperative, though."

"An unusual man," Nik said. "Remarkably stubborn. He keeps offering me more and more money to work down there at the LIFT Accelerator."

"Why don't you take it?"

"I'm too close to something at Stanford. It's very exciting. I'd like to tell you about it sometime. Anyway I can't leave now. And there's something about Lorillard. The man strikes me as ruthless. He's so certain he's right. I've seen that delusion coupled with too much power before, in Russia."

"But his partner in the LIFT is doing some good things with the technology. He's opened a proton therapy clinic for cancer patients."

"You mean Roosevelt Coons? He was in Geneva with us. We flew back to New York together."

"They say he flies patients in from all over the world free of charge. I hope to meet him in Chile."

"Quite the character," Nik said warmly. "But a wonderful man."

"Hello everyone!" A heavily accented voice interrupted from across the dance floor, and applause filled the dining room. Selena and Nik turned to see a short, heavy-set woman with obviously dyed red hair walk up to the microphone. Wearing a white satin vest with long fringe and sequins, she carried an accordion across her ample chest.

"That's Elsa," the waitress said proudly, placing huge platters of steaming food before them. "She owns this place."

Nik's face lit up. "Wonderful!" He finished his glass of wine and proudly told the waitress, "My grandfather played the accordion."

"Cool," the waitress said, looking impressed.

Nik turned to Selena. "He learned in Paris. It was all the rage."

Selena couldn't help but smile even though her mouth was full of knockwurst. She realized she was enjoying his pleasure, just as she did when

Katya or Charlie were happy.

"Now I play the Polka Holiday," Elsa announced. "This is by the King himself, Frankie Yankovich." As couples moved to the dance floor leaving their full plates waiting, Elsa pulled open the bellows of her accordion and began tapping her foot and bouncing her head up and down to the beat.

Conversation was no longer possible, and Selena was glad to just take in the scene. They ate, watching the spirited dancers and their big, jostling movements. Nik ordered another bottle of wine.

"Now I play the 'I Want Some Lovin' Polka," Elsa said when the first song was over. Taking a lace handkerchief from the sleeve of her blouse, she wiped perspiration from her forehead, then again began to tap her foot and nod her head to the beat.

The music was too lively to sit still, so Nik stood and beckoned Selena to join him. He placed his large hand firmly in the small of her back and began the one, two, three, hop of the dance, spinning her around and around to the quick, lively steps of the polka.

As they twirled past Elsa, Nik called out, "Mam wszystko co mi potrzeba!"

"Dobry!" Elsa answered gayly, her eyes following the tall couple as they flew around the dance floor.

Selena had no idea what Nik had said and she didn't really care. The room was spinning, and she felt swept up in the energy of the music. She told herself not to think about anything, just feel the secure pressure of his arm around her waist, just enjoy the closeness of him, the warm smell of his skin, his smiling eyes.

"Elsa's glad I'm so happy," Nik explained, his gaze holding Selena's, his arm pulling her closer. She returned his look for as long as she could, but her feelings were too strong. She had to break the connection, to look away, back into the safety of the people and their laughter. Nik continued to hold her in his eyes as they circled the room, their bodies moving easily together.

Elsa went right into the next song and then played two more while everyone stayed to dance. Selena's forehead and upper lip were shining with perspiration by the time they took a break.

"Come on," Nik said, still holding her close after the music stopped, still breathing hard from the dance. "Let's go outside and cool down." She could feel his warm breath against her neck, the rise and fall of his chest against her breasts.

On the patio she leaned against the wooden railing and looked out to sea, avoiding his eyes. Before her lay the black, endless water, and she could sense the danger out there in the darkness, waiting for her. It could come in with the mist, unannounced, find her unprepared as it had with her mother. She must be careful this time. There was too much at stake, both for her and for Katya.

Brushing her hair off her flushed face, she tried to hold the moment just a little longer, the lightness of it, the exhilaration and happiness. She wanted to calm her breathing and her heart but she could feel Nik's presence behind her, the heat from his body so close to hers.

"I thought of you," he said, his voice soft with loneliness, urgent with need. "So many times." He put his arms around her. She turned to him.

Gently, he pulled her close, holding her tight against his chest. She could feel the strong rhythm of his breathing, the warm, sweet smell of him. It was just as before. She raised her head, unable to resist any longer. They kissed, tenderly, then with growing need.

Like shards of light within her body, the energy enlivened her, charged her. But her mind threw shadows of caution this way and that, distracting her. Part of her struggled not to listen, to let herself go, but her thoughts pulled her back, told her to go slowly, to be careful this time. There was too much at stake. Finally, with all her will, she broke the bond, pushed herself away from him. Looking up, she saw longing and nearly desperate, haunting eyes.

"It's been a long time, Nik," Selena said, backing away.

"I know. I understand."

She turned to face the water again. The sea mist felt cool and she could smell the salt and seaweed, but the muffled roll of the breakers didn't calm her. Nik walked to the railing beside her and gazed down at the white surf frothing gently along the sand below. He was silent for a while, the moisture settling on his lined, rugged face.

"Beautiful California," he said, his tone light, distracted. "Easy. Warm. Not at all like Russia." Then, after a moment, "I must bring Marfa Ivanovna here from New York. She'd probably wear her heavy black coat at midday, but I know she'd be thrilled."

"Marfa?" Selena asked.

"She was my nanny in St. Petersburg. Came with us to Lomonosov each summer, to my grandfather's country estate. Her husband managed the stables. Mushkin was a crotchety old fellow, but Marfa was like a grandmother to me. She still is."

Nik turned to look at Selena, the lines of his face eased with affection and memory.

"At Christmas old Mushkin would take us for sleigh rides and Marfa would bake Christmas morning bread. Those are my best memories of Russia, the times on the farm. He loved the animals more than the people, I think, but Marfa is the kindest woman I've ever known. She was a healer, too, worked with herbs and nursed the peasants."

It pleased Selena to hear Nik speak fondly of his country. Still, she thought she could see a trace of the bittersweet shade the joy on his face.

"Do you still go there?" she asked. Sixteen years ago when she and Nik met at the Physics Convention in Aspen, he'd tried to put her off, told her he was married and had a five-year-old son. But Nik was her first love, her great love, and she didn't care about the price she'd pay later, the broken heart, the loneliness when he returned to Russia. She'd been so young, so determined. That's why she insisted upon keeping the baby, raising the child by herself despite her father's protests. Now Nik's son would be twenty-one. Selena took a deep breath and forced herself to ask the question. After all, she had made up her mind. His family must not be an unspoken thing between them.

"Do you still bring your son there at Christmas?"

Nikolai looked out to the dark water, then raised his head to watch a sheer cloud trail across the sliver of moon. When he didn't answer, Selena wondered if her question had been too abrupt, too personal.

Nik cleared his throat. "The house was sold long ago and my son........ My son was conscripted in to the Russian Army. He died in battle in Afghanistan."

Selena felt her skin prickle in waves of hot and cold. The sensation of loss ached behind her eyes, carved a hollow in her chest. It was the unbearable for Nik -- he had lost his child. She shuddered. Wrapping her arms around herself, she fought the urge to go to him, to hold him, to tell him all was not lost. Instead she turned away, dug her fingers into the flesh of her arms.

Nik had lost his son. How could she possibly continue to conceal the fact that he had another child, a daughter? Like a shadow under water, she let the emotions slide deep inside her. She wrapped her arms tighter.

"I'm so sorry, Nik," she said, knowing it was not enough. Part of her wanted to tell him, "You have another child! You have a beautiful daughter!" But she knew it wasn't the time. She would wait.

Nik continued. "The farm was sold many years ago. When the old man died, Marfa left Russia. I wanted her to move to St. Petersburg, to be near us. But her sister's family was in New York. She went there." Nik took a deep breath, then forced a tight smile and turned to her.

"I visit her, though. She has an herb shop on Long Island." Noticing that Selena was cold, he pulled off his sweater. "Here," he said, wrapping it around her.

Selena didn't speak, just held his eyes, trying desperately to let him know how sorry she was. A short scar across his right eyebrow reminded her of the first time she'd touched him, in Aspen so many years ago. Reaching out, she placed her thumb against his brow and gently followed the line of the wound. He took her hand, held it tight in his own.

She was feeling the warmth of his skin when Charlie's persistent tapping at her arm jolted her into the present. Someone's impatient voice was tugging at her consciousness.

"Excuse me, maam," the flight attendant said. "Excuse me. We'll be landing in Oahu momentarily. Please put your seat in the upright position."

CHAPTER 6

Clive Bingham stood at his CIA office window that overlooked the deep Virginia woods. He was snickering. That damned squirrel is still trying to raid the bird feeder, he thought. Two days earlier Bingham had hung not one but two aluminum domes over the top of the feeder, coating each with black engine oil.

The persistent squirrel had eventually succeeded in sliding from the tree limb down the fishing line to the top dome where he managed to precariously hold on. Then, like a kamikaze pilot, he kept trying to dive past the bottom dome onto the feeder itself. Each time he would crash against the edge of the dome, hit the feeder hard, and then plummet to the ground, badly shaken and increasingly covered with black oil.

Bingham held his breath as the squirrel deliberated once again. How much more of this could the creature take? The squirrel was rubbing his forefeet together. He shook his tail. Then, after a last, longing gaze at the birdseed, he gave up and backed off the limb.

"Aha!" Bingham cried out. "I got you, you bastard!" Delighted by his triumph, Clive Bingham rubbed his hands together in a gesture not unlike that of the squirrel. A knock on the door intruded upon his victory.

"Good morning, sir," Norman Hambly said, handing him a large manila envelope. "This just came in from our field operative in New York." As Bingham spread the series of photographs across his desk, Norman noticed with distaste his boss' blue tie. It sported a jumbled pattern of yellow and red fishing poles.

"My God," Bingham said, twisting the gray ends of his moustache. "Looks like the life's been sucked right out of her."

Hambly answered without emotion. "You could say that, sir. She was killed by hundreds of blood sucking insects. Her name is Marfa Ivanovna. Dr. Potapov's childhood nanny."

The photographs showed an elderly woman tied to a chair, her head hung limp on her deflated, bony chest. The woman's facial skin was a sickly shade of grayish blue and clung to her skull like wet cheesecloth.

"Blood sucking insects?" Bingham's eyes were riveted to the gruesome photos. "God, Hambly. I've seen my share of gore, but these pictures are repulsive. Where on earth did they get the little beasts?" Hambly took a timid step closer and laid some papers on Mr. Bingham's desk.

"South America, sir. Here's the autopsy report." Stepping back, he suddenly stopped short and pulled a white handkerchief from his jacket pocket. In a desperate gesture, he held his breath and placed his index finger tightly under his nose to stifle one of his monumental sneezes, but to no avail. Bingham grimaced at the sight. At least allergies aren't contagious, he thought. Regaining his composure, Hambly explained.

"The coroner had a hard time at first. There were no apparent wounds, but the corpse was drained of almost all its blood. On closer inspection thousands of puncture wounds were found all over the body. Even her eyelids, sir. Bitten. Hundreds of microscopic larvae were imbedded in her skin. The bugs had laid eggs."

Gooseflesh showed under the short sleeves of Bingham's white shirt. He rubbed his bare arms. "I see." Bingham visibly shivered as he looked at an enlarged photograph of Marfa Ivanovna's pock marked skin. Shuffling the photographs into a pile he said, "Rather extreme, I'd say. I wonder if he got the information he was after?"

"Dr. Potapov visited the woman on his way to Hawaii, left some personal belongings, photographs, some gifts for her. According to our surveillance, however, it's doubtful she had the recipe." Hambly was staring at the dull, liquid eye of the stuffed fish on Bingham's wall. The bass appeared to be looking directly at him.

"Hmmm. I'm sure that didn't stop our friend from enjoying his little torture scene. Tell me," Bingham said, pointing to the top photograph, "what are those things scattered around on the floor?"

"Those are the green tops from strawberries, sir. It appears the person administering the torture was eating fresh strawberries at the time."

"Jesus Christ," Bingham said, and looked up from his desk. "They're not going to stop until they get what they want, Hambly. Why is it so important

54

to Lorillard?"

Hambly didn't know what to say. He nodded.

"Do what you can to keep this quiet. No point in rattling cages, making nasty connections with Dr. Potapov."

"Also, sir, you should be aware that Dr. Selena Hartmann telephoned Marfa Ivanovna's apartment. An agent took the call and told her the woman had been quite ill. The official cause of death is anemia."

"I hope that satisfies her," Bingham said. "She called me about a postcard Potapov sent from Hawaii. She keeps insisting he couldn't possibly have committed suicide."

"She's a persistent woman, sir. She told the agent it wasn't possible the woman was seriously ill. She knew from Dr. Potapov that Marfa Ivanovna was fine."

"So be it," Bingham said, shaking his head. "If she doesn't let it go, we may have to put her persistence to use."

* * * * *

Charlie closed her book and reached for a *Vogue* magazine wedged in the plane's front seat pocket. Selena remained preoccupied with the idea of telling Katya about Nik's death. The vision of his glider in midair as he started to fall was like a presence, always on the periphery of her thoughts.

"Hey, check this out," Charlie said, holding up the page of astrological forecasts. "There's a full moon in Aquarius on the twenty-second."

When Selena first met Charlie years ago, she'd been surprised a scientist could believe in such nonsense. Charlie insisted it wasn't a matter of superstition, just another way of observing phenomena. She told Selena about all the great minds that had given astrology credence, from Hippocrates, to Kepler, to Carl Jung and Adler. Even Sir Isaac Newton, when challenged by Halley about his belief in astrology, had said, "Sir, I have studied the subject, you have not."

Charlie continued reading Selena's forecast, but the tone of her predictions turned dour. "A total lunar eclipse in Leo directly opposite your sun. You better watch out. That's a sinister aspect."

"Yeah, right, Charlie." Selena raised her eyebrows. "I'll be sure to keep that date in mind."

"I wouldn't be so quick to dismiss it."

"Oh, God, Charlie. Don't get all fuzzy on me now. You've got to maintain a healthy skepticism in life."

"Are you saying I'm gullible?"

"Yes. I think you need protection — from yourself. Remember what you told me about the signs in the New York taxis? The ones that read 'Communicate with TLC if you have complaints'? For years you thought the 'TLC' stood for Tender Loving Care instead of Taxi and Limousine Commission. Remember that?"

"Yeah, well," Charlie said, looking away. "A little TLC doesn't hurt, even with the Taxi and Limousine Commission."

"Okay. I see this is hopeless."

The plane's brakes screeched, reigning in its momentum. Selena felt her adrenalin rise and she was glad. To stay focused on her research she would need all the energy she could muster. The results were too important to allow anything, even Nik's death, to interfere. Not until the conference in Chile was over. Just another week, only then would she let her heart linger over the loss of him, the loss of her dream. At least Katya will be taken good care of while I'm down there, Selena thought, and pictured her daughter at the dinner table with Naomi and her parents.

Quickly packing her work papers into the briefcase nestled between her feet, Selena noticed something colorful and glossy in the side pocket. She pulled out the postcard from Nik. For the last two days she had carried the card with her, moving it from pocket to purse to jacket to briefcase.

"That's looking a little worse for the wear," Charlie said. Selena was smiling at the determined face of the shopping tourist on the front of the card. And, not for the first time, Selena was confounded.

"I just can't understand why," she said, striking her clenched fist against her thigh in frustration. "Why would he send such a happy postcard just before....?" She wouldn't finish the sentence.

"Did you tell that guy from the CIA about the card?" Charlie asked.

Selena nodded. "He isn't listening. And what about the Russian woman, Marfa? Can you please tell me how any of this makes sense?" She shook her head and massaged the tense muscles of her neck.

"Maybe we just don't understand," Charlie said.

"But Nik told me exciting things were happening with his research," Selena said. "He was close to finding a formula. Why would he give up now?" She bit the cuticle of her ring finger, then stopped herself and repeatedly rubbed the crown of turquoise on her ring. These damned planes are claustrophobic, she thought.

Nikolai had spoken enthusiastically about his work on high-temperature superconductors. Once when talking about the loss of his son, Nik had likened the character of superconductors to Eastern philosophy, to its precept that attachment to something -- a person, a thing, an idea -- only causes pain.

"They believe if you try to hold onto something," Nik had told her, "if you resist, it will hurt you. In a way it's like my superconductors. They carry electricity perfectly, with absolutely no loss of energy. Because they haven't any resistance, they're extraordinarily powerful." Then, looking away, he ran his hand through his thick, graying hair. "I have to let go of my son. I have to give up my mourning."

Selena could understand the physics involved in superconductors. She felt no resistance to the facts of science. Why was she resisting the fact of Nik's death? She told herself she was foolish, but her head and heart continued to revolt. It had been two days since the call from the CIA, three days since Nik's death. Still, she could not accept the loss of a dream she had come so close to living. It had been the same when her mother died.

Selena remembered returning to the house after the funeral. Strange people milled through the rooms, talking and eating, stopping to pat the top of her head and smile kindly down at her. The long mahogany table in the dining room was covered with food in unfamiliar serving dishes. Selena reached for a sterling silver fork, held it in both hands close to her chest, then walked through the kitchen and out the back door.

At the far end of the lawn she sat on the grass in her new dress. Methodically, she began digging up the flowerbed. She didn't cry; she couldn't. There was nothing to cry about and there wouldn't be, so long as she remained distracted and just kept digging and digging and digging. It was almost dark when her father found her there.

She had refused to believe it was true. It had taken years to understand, to realize she had blamed herself for not saving her mother. This time, however, she must accept the truth. She must let Nik go.

As if reading her thoughts Charlie said, "I know it's hard to believe." Looking at Selena she added forcefully, "But the evidence, it's all there."

Selena knew Charlie wasn't trying to hurt her. Her best friend had little patience with self-deception, her own or anyone else's. And she was right; the evidence was undeniable. A Japanese tourist had been videotaping the hang gliding event and recorded most of Nik's fall. He sold the tape to a local television station. CNN picked it up. Across the country the vision of Nik's yellow glider careening into the blue Pacific was aired over and over again, on all the major networks.

Newspapers mourned the loss of Dr. Nikolai Potapaov, one of the world's most talented physicists in the prime of his productive years. The Honolulu Homicide Squad said Dr. Potapov's wallet and a suicide note were found at the bottom of a canvas bag in the trunk of his rental car. The content of the note was being withheld.

The *San Francisco Chronicle* had run a photograph of the glider in mid-descent, showing the Russian hammer and sickle outlined on its shredded wings. In the photo, Nik's face was turned away. All she could see was part of his beard.

Every time Selena thought of Nik dying that way, it made her feel sick. The fear and terror he must have known in the moments before he hit the water. And the sharks. Oh God. The Coast Guard recovered sections of the Dacron wings still attached to the crushed frame of the glider. Police laboratories discovered the fabric had been treated with a chemical compound, consisting in part of hydrochloric acid. According to the Coroner's Office, someone, presumably Nik, used the invisible acid to paint the Russian symbols onto the yellow wings, probably the night before. By morning, the smell wouldn't be noticeable and the vaporization would have dissipated, leaving the fibers sufficiently weakened to disintegrate with pressure from the wind. To accurately time the effects, to find the precise mixture of acid and buffering compounds, would require someone knowledgeable in chemistry. Someone like Dr. Potapov.

The loss of Nik's only child was rumored to be the cause. Others hinted the underground KGB might be involved. But no one questioned it was a farewell. Nikolai had chosen his own way to die.

Still, Selena could not believe it was true. Turning the postcard over, she read Nik's message once again. "Sorry you couldn't make it. I miss you. Love, Nik." Again, she puzzled. He had cancelled the trip, not her. Had there been an awful mistake, she wondered, some fatal misunderstanding? She felt a hollow anxiety expand in her chest from that familiar fear, that need to hurry, to find answers. But, she told herself, it's already too late.

Moving her fingertips tenderly over his handwriting, she noticed the peeling stamps covering the right corner. Selena tried to smooth the brittle edges, but they immediately curled again. Figures written in ink were visible just beneath the stamps. With her fingernail she pulled up the stamps, just enough to see a series of numbers and letters.

During the last month Selena had watched Nik jot down work notes on matchbook covers, parking tickets, napkins, whatever was handy. Like an absentminded professor, he invariably left them in her car or on the kitchen counter. Curious, Selena considered peeling the stamps completely off, but she doubted the numbers would make any discernible sense.

"Earth to Selena," Charlie said. She was standing in the aisle, loaded down with both their carry-on bags. The plane was almost empty. Selena decided to keep the postcard intact and slid it back into her briefcase for safekeeping. After all, it was her last link with Nik.

* * * * *

Hambly's eyes followed Bingham as he paced, flipping through the list of LIFT accelerator personnel. "There must be someone else we can recruit as an agent down there," Hambly said, trying to be helpful.

Bingham looked disgusted. "I've got a dozen on the books now. I'm not even sure they all exist."

Hambly nodded. This was a touchy subject. The issue of agents had caused the scandal that lead to the resignation of Bingham's old boss, James Irving, and was primarily responsible for Bingham's early retirement. In the past the Agency had always pushed for more agents in the field. Bagging more field operatives meant promotion, more money. The pressure was so intense, some case officers had been known to recruit nonexistent people.

With the discovery of the Aldrich Ames debacle the press had begun its brutal frontal attack on the CIA, accusing the clandestine service of bungling its management, of being plagued by corruption and incompetence. At the time, Bingham was working in Cuban affairs under Irving. When a Cuban defector named Gabriel Malaga revealed to the press (with substantiated evidence) that every Havana agent recruited over the last ten years was actually working for the Cuban government and passing disinformation to the Americans, Bingham's boss, Irving, became the sacrificial lamb slaughtered to appease Congress.

Bingham was forced to testify against Irving before a Senate Intelligence Committee. Irving resigned. Bingham was transferred. That's when he decided it was time to get out—the sooner, the better. But he didn't want to make any mistakes, not now when he was so close.

"Hell," Bingham said. His head felt like it was in a vise. "If this operation fails they'll need somebody to hang. Guess who's gonna be prime beef?"

* * * * *

Charlie was washing her hands in the women's room of the Hilo Airport when she heard someone crying. Through the mirror she saw a young woman staring forlornly at a photograph. Charlie recognized her from the plane. Tall and attractive, she was hard not to notice, but the navy blue business suit and spectator heels made her look stiff and proper. Even her auburn hair was pulled tight and knotted into a neat bun.

The woman caught Charlie's eye and, through her tears, she ventured a pathetic smile. Charlie looked quickly away and concentrated on drying her hands, but in a moment the woman was standing at the next sink, her beautiful face reflected in the mirror as she tried to salvage her mascara. She laid the photo face-up on the aluminum counter.

"I'm sorry," she told Charlie, struggling to regain her composure. "I've just got to get hold of myself."

"No skin off my nose," Charlie said, stealing a look at the photo. It was a Keeshond, just like Charlie's dog, Sam, except this was just a puppy.

"They've lost Bear," the woman said, and suddenly began to sob all over again. "The baggage people. They can't find my puppy."

"That's awful." Charlie felt bad, but what could she do? She'd heard about the airlines losing people's pets. That's why she never traveled by plane with Sam. Charlie started to tell the woman a story about a dog that froze to death in the luggage compartment, but caught herself just in time.

"I bet they find her," Charlie said, though she wasn't at all sure. "They're great dogs. I have one, too. Samantha. She's eight."

"Oh you do?" the woman cried. "Then you must understand how I feel." That was all it took for her to start bawling again, only this time she threw her arms around Charlie. She must have been a foot taller, but managed to bend her long, porcelain neck enough to lay her head on Charlie's shoulder. She smelled like something creamy and apricot.

"It'll be okay," Charlie said, patting the woman on the back. "You should go and check. I bet they've found her already." Charlie pulled herself away, then checked her watch and frowned. "I better get going," she said and hefted her brown bag over her shoulder. "Good luck." She was out the door in a flash.

Selena was waiting at the curb with one of the yellow observatory jeeps, ready for the long drive up the mountain. Throwing their luggage in the back seat, Charlie saw her evaluate the cloudy skies.

"Wait until we get some elevation," Charlie said. "It'll clear up." Selena looked worried.

On the outskirts of Hilo they entered the Hamakuu rain forest. Winding through the dense jungle of ferns, Selena couldn't help feeling enchanted by the seductive tropical air, the luscious green, and the graceful pace. Even though Hawaii had taken Nik, its allure still tugged at her, energized her, and triumphed over the lethargy of her sadness.

"This place is like the ultimate carrot," Selena said.

"You gotta be kidding me," Charlie said. She shook her head and smiled. "Hawaii is paradise, pure and simple."

"My point exactly," Selena said. "The place is a big tease." It was an argument they had enjoyed over the years.

Selena believed the ability to appreciate beauty was a trick of genetics, another way to insure the survival of the species. To be captivated by loveliness was to be exhilarated by life. To feel attraction was to feel motivation. After all, humans were the descendants of the ultimate evolutionary survivors. Admiring beauty was one way they fed the voracious will to live.

"What's your point?" Charlie said.

"I'm agreeing with you," Selena said. "Hawaii seems like heaven on Earth. And part of the human condition is the eternal search for paradise. It's an illusion, of course, but you have to stay alive to pursue it. The long-awaited Hawaiian vacation keeps people slogging through the snow all winter. It's just a trick of the genes."

"If it's true, I don't want to hear about it."

"Dream on then."

"Whatever works," Charlie said.

Winding their way up the mountain to the Keck observatory, they broke through the cloud deck encircling the peak at seven thousand feet and found exuberant sunshine. Selena still worried the clouds might rise during the night, causing fog to drop moisture on the telescope, making it necessary to close the dome for protection. She must complete her research and present it in Chile. It was a serious survival issue, a danger she and Charlie were in complete agreement on.

The reign of dinosaurs had ended with a colossal cosmic collision. That asteroid hit earth like a mountain blasted out of the sky. On impact, it released a hundred trillion tons of TNT -- nearly a million times the total explosive force of all the nuclear weapons in the world.

The collision was a calamity for life on Earth, wiping out fifty percent of all species. One hundred billion tons of stinking sulfur blasted into the air, creating a murky haze covering the entire planet for almost thirty years. Shockwaves ignited forest fires for thousands of kilometers. Acid rain killed the plants while seismic reverberations kindled volcanic eruptions on the other side of the planet. It was an apocalypse.

When the sun finally came out, there were no more big, predatory animals. What remained was a perfect breeding ground for our genetic forbears: the burrowers, the sea bottom feeders, and the rodent-like animals. They had survived, and that relentless will to live was passed down as part of our genetic heritage.

Beauty might be mere illusion, but here in the paradise of Hawaii, Selena and Charlie agreed. Destruction of planet Earth was at stake -- whether by asteroid collision or by nuclear weapons in space.

CHAPTER 7

The Virgin Mary had given this day her blessing. Mariel Rosales could feel it in the warm, dappled sun that graced her assembled guests. She could hear it in the gentle patter and splash of the fountain at Casa Banderas, the Santiago estate that belonged to her father and his father before him. Yes, after more than a year of planning, no expense spared, the day of the wedding had finally arrived. July was the rainy season in Santiago, but Mariel Rosales' daughter had insisted the ceremony and reception take place in the formal gardens. Thanks to the Blessed Virgin Mary, the social event of the year was promising to be a day made in heaven.

To the melodic background of the Santiago Philharmonic the general's wife made her way down the grassy aisle welcoming her future son-in-law's family and friends on the left, and the best of Santiago society on the right.

"Everything looks lovely, my dear," Señora Montt said. "And the flowers, they're magnificent."

"Thank you, Gloria," Mariel said modestly, remembering the florist bill alone had been 3,264,000 new pesos. She figured that was about $8,000. Señora Rosales did most of her shopping in the United States and was used to thinking in American currency. That displeased her husband — as did the florist bill.

"I'm so glad you could join us," Mariel told Gloria. She held the woman's jeweled hand in her own. "I was afraid you'd be in Paris this month."

Señora Montt was the matron of Chilean society and a direct descendant of Jorge Montt, the officer responsible for winning the civil war of 1890 against the Chilean working class.

"Miss this for another shopping trip?" Gloria said. "Lucia will be the most beautiful bride."

Mariel Rosales kissed Gloria on both cheeks, then continued down the aisle, waving hello to the groom's parents, Smiffy and Les Rogers. Despite Enrique's insufferable behavior towards those charming people, they had remained most gracious. Thank God, Mariel thought. At least someone knows the meaning of refinement, even if my husband doesn't.

Señora Rosales understood why her husband would harbor such animosity for the Rogers, an old Boston Brahmin family. It was due in large part to his feelings of inferiority. It never failed to amaze her that so many people considered Enrique powerful, practically immune to intimidation. Of course the same people believed those horrible stories about him as a young man. But when she had fallen in love with him twenty-four years earlier, he was no more than a corporal with big ambitions, the son of a poor man who had worked in the copper mines. Remember, Mariel told herself as she reached the end of the aisle, those were U.S.-owned copper mines. This wedding could not be easy for Enrique.

All was proceeding smoothly. Still, the general's wife felt her head and neck pulled as tight as a violin string. Under the tents in the rose garden she noticed the servants preparing the banquet tables for the reception. Mariel's eyes rested on the ice sculptures she'd ordered, a pair of five-foot high angels with their wings spread wide, one playing the flute, the other the violin. A streak of late morning sun was glancing under the tent, melting the angels with each passing moment. Mariel impatiently signaled one of the maids to her side and instructed her to move the sculptures into the shade.

If she could just make it through the next six hours, she thought. She forced a smile of serenity on her unlined face, smoothed the loose strands of her rich auburn hair into place, and walked towards the arched double doorway of her husband's study. Again, she thanked the Blessed Virgin for her favor and beseeched the Mother of God for just one more blessing. If only Enrique would be good today, if only he would not create a scene, Mariel promised to make four novenas for the poor and downtrodden. "And I'll donate a hundred dollars to the needy," she added. "No, make it two hundred."

* * * * *

When Pierre Lorillard barged into the security room at the LIFT accelerator in Chile, he was already irate. He found Jean Levesque leaning back in his chair, his black snakeskin cowboy boots propped on an open drawer. The smiling face of Saddam Hussein looked up from the cover of *Soldier of Fortune* magazine.

"Turn that damned noise off," Pierre said referring to Johnny Cash wailing "Folsom Prison Blues" in the background. Jean hopped to it. When Levesque turned around, his tall frame towered over Pierre's, but it was Jean who felt put in his place.

"What is this?" Pierre demanded, shoving a series of photographs into Jean's gut. They were blowups of Marfa Ivanovna. Her sunken flesh looked like the withering, yellowed skin of a plucked chicken. "Why was this necessary? And still you have nothing!"

Lorillard reminded himself to remain calm. Levesque was becoming more than a nuisance, but Pierre considered it character weakness, as well as a strategic disadvantage, to put his emotions on display.

"That old Russian bag was useless," Jean said, unable to resist a smirk. "I'd have what you want tomorrow, if you'd let me handle it my way."

"Enough of that," Pierre said. Stiffening his back, he paced to the other side of the room, then turned abruptly. "What about security for the conference? Representative Chapman has agreed to attend. There'll be more press."

"I've got charter flights from Santiago for the science nerds. My people will check them at the airstrip. I'll send your jet for Chapman." Not looking at Lorillard he added, "I still think this was a bad idea. Too many people nosing around."

"I told you before, that's precisely what we want."

"I thought we're supposed to look like business pigs," Jean said. "Be pro-Star Wars."

"The press assumes we're promoting business, putting our superconductor technology on display."

"But what's your excuse for footing the bill for these goofs?" Jean looked down at the fingers of his left hand, crooked and arthritic from being crushed by the Iranians. He cracked the knuckles repeatedly, producing a popping, gristly sound.

"Stop that!" Pierre demanded. "Why can't you understand? The media think we're holding the conference because Lorillard Industries will be telecast all over the world." Striding to the window, Pierre turned his back on Jean. The man's crudeness was becoming increasingly difficult to tolerate. "What about General Rosales?" Pierre asked, still looking out the window. "Did you transfer his funds?"

"Done," Jean said. He noticed Lorillard's fisted hands in the pockets of his pants. Something's wrong, Jean thought. He never used to give me this shit. Not until he met that Russian. "I'd watch my back with Rosales," Jean added. "He's tough. I give him credit for that. But he'd sell his own ..."

"Nobody's going to pay a better price than I," Pierre said. "The general's nobody's fool. Just make sure he's received the payment. I don't want him forgetting his manners, the few he has. Particularly not at my dinner party with the representative and Dr. Hartmann."

Nothing I say is any good, Jean thought, then added, "That Hartmann bitch is gonna mouth off the whole time she's here."

"Which is exactly what I want. She and Chapman together present a powerful message against nuclear weapons in space."

"I don't like some bitch thinking she's running the show."

"That bitch, as you call her, is essential to my plan," Lorillard said. "Her research is our only insurance against the Star Wars bill, damnit."

"Why don't you just buy the votes," Levesque said.

"That would only stop the program for a year. We need more time. Have you checked her latest results?"

"We've already got her research," Jean insisted. "Who needs her?"

"We need her, you fool." Pierre felt heat spread up his forehead. His eyes tightened. "You hate women, don't you, my friend?"

It was true, Jean thought, but why in hell should he be blamed for that? His American fiancée had deserted him when he was in the hospital, mutilated and not sure he'd recover.

"Hartmann was involved with the Russian," Jean insisted. "She could make trouble."

Pierre shook his head, and then looked away. The man is mulish and impossible, he thought. He walked quickly to the door and left the room.

* * * * *

In the oak-paneled study of Casa Banderas, General Enrique Rosales pushed aside the heavy maroon drapes and scrutinized the crowd of people wrecking his lawn and gardens. A herd of peacocks, he thought, strutting about in fancy duds. He noticed his wife walking across the lawn to the tree-shaded drive and recognized his own limousine pulling through the tall wrought-iron gates. His driver opened the door for Monsignor Sullivan.

"Cabron! Les voy a cortar los cojones!" Bastard! I'd like to cut your balls off! The general spit the words at the priest; drops of saliva and pisco splattered against the window. "Better prepare your soul, Monsignor. Keep hiding those guerillas, and we'll see if your almighty God can protect you."

Enrique watched his wife bend down to kiss the monsignor's ring. "I ought to arrest you myself," the general said, eyeing the pair of antique, wood-handled pistols mounted on the wall beside him. Instead he downed what remained of his sixth glass of pisco and went to pour another. That much of the powerfully spirited grape brandy would have annihilated a smaller man, but the general could hold his liquor. And he carried his weight well. Only recently had that ever-expanding belly forced him to succumb to the misery of chronic lower back pain. On his fifty-ninth birthday Mariel had given him a black, girdle-type brace. He was wearing it today under his highly decorated dress blues. It wasn't his back that was bothering him at the moment, however. Lucia, his only child, was about to marry a Norte Americano. Rosales felt like taking the damned girdle off and making somebody eat it.

Not only was her fiancé a skinny wimp of an American boy, but his name was Lester and he was a Jr. to boot. Lester wanted to be an art curator for a museum. Lucia insisted he was only sensitive, not a fag, but the general wasn't so sure. When I was his age, Enrique thought, I had the balls of a bull. I made them all take notice.

"Excuse me, sir." The general's aide was a short, nervous young man with sharp eyes. "Excuse me, General Rosales, sir." Enrique had been so lost in thought he hadn't heard Lt. Garcia enter the room. When he turned to find the man standing at attention, he said the first thing that came into his mind.

"Why in hell can't she marry you?"

Lt. Garcia looked confused but was smart enough not to answer the question. Rosales swigged down another gulp of pisco. "What is it, Lieutenant?" He sat down heavily on the long, studded leather couch that had been made by hand long before he was born.

"I'm sorry sir, but I thought you'd want to know." Garcia looked anxious.

Despite the fog of alcohol, Enrique stiffened. It could be only one thing.

"Those sons of bitches. They're going through with it, aren't they?" President Fregado's commission investigating "misdeeds" of the military coup of 1973 had submitted their findings three weeks earlier. Rumors to the contrary, Rosales did not believe the bastards would be foolish enough to indict him personally.

"The announcement will be made on Monday, sir."

"Who are they going after, goddammit?"

"Sir, General Pinochet's trial is set for September 5th. Yours will be right after." The aide looked terrified. It wouldn't be the first time Rosales had shot the messenger.

"I'm sorry, sir," Lt. Garcia added. "If I may say so, sir, I consider it a gross display of contempt for what you have done for this country. You have my dedicated support, sir."

The general's large frame seemed to sink deeper in the old leather sofa. He rested his arms on his knees and held his head in his hands. The aide had never seen his commander in such a posture. Garcia wasn't sure what to do. He was afraid to move or even speak.

Almost three minutes passed before General Enrique Rosales stiffened the muscles across his back and rose to his full height. Garcia was feeling overwhelmed by the man's sheer physical presence when the general spoke in deliberate, confident words.

"This will never come to pass."

General Rosales produced a closed-lip smile, and the lieutenant felt fear shiver through his extremities. He was utterly certain the general would have his way. A knock on one of the doors leading to the garden released the pressure of the moment. With a mere motion of his head, Rosales dismissed his aide.

Turning to see his thin wife slip through the barely opened doorway, Enrique poured himself another pisco. Women weren't supposed to be that skinny, he thought. Too much money to spend. Not enough children.

"Enrique," Mariel said. "Please don't drink any more. The ceremony is about to begin. Lucia is ready. Wait until you see your daughter," Mariel said, appealing to her husband's fondness for his only child. "She's waiting for you in her room."

General Rosales looked at his wife with contempt. He would not tell her about the trial. Her head was filled with nonsense, with flowers and gowns and music and monsignors. He pictured that insolent priest just outside in his own yard, traipsing around in that flowing purple cape before those adoring idiots. It was too much to bear. And to think he was paying for the whole thing.

"I'm not giving my daughter away to any damned American!" he said and pulled back another half glass of pisco. "I'll never see her. I'll never see my grandchildren."

"We can visit any time," Mariel pleaded with him.

"I'll never go to that goddamned country," he bellowed and slammed his highball glass on the dark wood of the bar. The crystal splintered, and shards of glass flew everywhere. "Those crooks killed my father, buried him alive in a goddamned copper mine."

"It was an accident," his wife said, already raising her voice. She felt as if this battle had been warring inside her all day long and she was already out of patience. "You promised me, Enrique. You gave me your word. Now look at you, you're bleeding. There's glass in your cheek."

He swiped his palm across his face, pulling free the crystal slivers. "Maybe my word is only as good as those damned Americans' out there." Rosales was yelling now. "They paid my mother nothing. Nada!"

Mariel glanced quickly through the window to see if her husband's ranting could be heard outside. Fortunately, none of the guests had turned her way.

"We've been through this a thousand times," she told him, her own voice turning shrill. "Not now. This isn't the time."

"I'm not going to stand there and listen to that bastard Irishman preach to me."

Mariel looked horrified and made the sign of the cross. "Dear God in heaven," she said. "You can't speak of a priest that way." Enrique laughed and took another gulp of his drink. When the door to the study opened unexpectedly, he looked up angrily.

Lucia floated into the room, radiant in her grandmother's cream lace wedding gown, its long train rustling across the floor. An ancient lace mantilla fell softly around her face. Her near-black hair hung in loose, thick waves over her pale shoulders.

"Papa," Lucia said. "Es muy bonita, si? Do you like it?"

Mariel ran to her daughter's side and began to fuss with the gown, but General Rosales stood immobilized by the sight of his beautiful girl. She was the most beloved thing in his life, perhaps the only pure thing he'd ever known.

"Everyone's waiting, Papa." Lucia reached out her hand.

* * * * *

"Mulroney asked me to give you this," Hambly said. He handed Clive Bingham a sealed envelope. As his boss was reading the memorandum, Norman's glasses kept slipping down his oily nose.

"We got the okay to alert Rosales," Bingham said brightly. He immediately slipped the paper through the shredder behind his desk. "Admiral Kingsley's been notified to stand by."

"How do you think General Rosales will respond, sir? This has got to be a bit of a shock."

"If it'll keep the economy healthy, the Chileans will go along with anything."

"Yes sir, but according to the security report, Rosales is a loose cannon." Hambly was reluctant to step on Bingham's toes by lecturing him, but it was a fact his boss seldom read the background reports, at least not lately.

"What's your take on it?" Bingham asked. Hambly considered that the go-ahead to clue his boss in.

"He's always been a maverick. When the coup took place, Rosales was green, an unknown. But not for long. The night the military bombed the presidential palace; they rounded up all of Allende's supporters and took them to the Santiago stadium. Thousands of them. Interrogated, tortured, killed. It was quite a show. One of the best acts was Corporal Enrique Rosales, soon to be General Pinochet's aide-de-camp."

"Yes, Hambly. Go on." Bingham nodded his head, encouraging his assistant to continue.

"There was a popular folk singer at the time. His name was Manuel Davi. Rosales was responsible for personally torturing him over a period of days. He was regularly abused, beaten, his hands broken. Then Rosales ordered him to sing his songs of revolution for the captive audience. Finally they fired upon him until he was dead. They used his dead body for target practice."

"So?" Bingham said, growing irritated with his assistant's instruction. "Does this relate?

"Rosales may not be feeling too loyal to his own country right now, sir. Seems the government's ready to indict him."

Bingham could not let his assistant have the last word. "They'll never get away with it," Bingham said. "Those military thugs still have the power. Do you know it's been estimated they killed 80,000 of their own people? Of course we financed a good part of the coup. Had to douse that Communist Allende."

"Yes, sir," Hambly said. "I see what you mean."

"Hell, General Pinochet led the massacre, but they still let him run the army. After all, he brought them prosperity. You know what that bastard said when they found mass graves of unidentified bodies, people who had mysteriously disappeared during his rule? Pinochet reminded them what good economy it was that two or more bodies had been buried in the same grave."

"I see, sir."

"These people care about their money, Hambly. And that's where we come in."

Bingham placed the phone call himself. The sooner this operation was complete, the sooner he was out of there.

* * * * *

High Mass! It was torture, General Rosales thought. His kneecaps, bearing the entire weight of his body, were pressed against the hard wooden kneelers. He could feel his back muscles begin to spasm. This was too much for any man to bear.

Out of loyalty to his daughter and under the spell of her loveliness, he'd done what his wife wanted. He'd given his daughter away to that slimy American excuse for a male. He'd obeyed Monsignor Sullivan's commands during the ceremony even though he'd felt the urge to take a swipe at him. Then he'd taken his seat politely, in the front row next to his wife. But this High Mass humiliation was nothing more than the Church's way to keep its parishioners in their place. And it was going on forever. Que Barbaro! Damn!

Enrique Rosales leaned his backside against the edge of the bench hoping to take some of the pressure off his knees. Mariel noticed immediately and gave him a look just like his mother had during Sunday Mass 50 years earlier. When some activity in the side aisle caused him to turn, he was relieved and delighted to find Lt. Garcia motioning him to hurry. Before he left, General Rosales turned to his wife and grinned in triumph. She looked stunned and insulted that he would leave. But it was an emergency; it was business. Besides, he had to take a piss.

"My apologies for disturbing you at a time like this, General," his aide said when they reached the study. "It couldn't be helped. The CIA is on the phone. Mr. Bingham, sir. Said it was urgent. I told him about the wedding, but he insisted I interrupt you."

"The arrogant sons of bitches," Enrique said, though he reminded himself to make Garcia a captain as soon as all this was over. "Pour me a drink," he said and grabbed the phone.

"What's the problem, Mr. Bingham?" The general's voice boomed through the room.

"I'm afraid there's a bit of trouble developing, General. I thought as

Director of the Department of Security you should be informed. Some evidence has led us to suspect our friends over at the LIFT accelerator. We're not certain, mind you, but there's a possibility a nuclear weapon may be in the process."

"What do you mean, 'in the process'?" Rosales demanded.

"Don't be alarmed," Bingham said. "I felt you'd want to be alerted. We'll know more in the next few days."

Lieutenant Garcia handed Rosales his drink. As Bingham continued, the general gulped.

"The threat of nuclear proliferation endangers the peace of the Western Hemisphere. That includes all of us, General Rosales."

"I'm aware of that," Rosales said. This is bullshit, he thought -- a nuclear bomb being built at the LIFT in the Chilean desert?

"And there are American citizens working at the LIFT. They have to be protected. I'm sure you're in agreement."

General Rosales was silent. He was too savvy, too much of a survivor, to let himself speak. First he had to think this through.

"I'll keep you apprized of the situation, General. Hopefully, no action will be necessary. We understand the LIFT facility has been a boon to the economy in the region, and it's not the President's intention to interfere with that."

Hogwash, Rosales thought. The LIFT employed more foreigners than Chileans. He wanted to tell this son of a bitch what he thought of the President's intention, but managed to hold his tongue by taking another drink.

"By the way," Bingham continued, "the President asked me to tell you he's personally lobbying in favor of the increased foreign aid package to your country. We're confident both houses of Congress will pass it. More important, he'll keep you in mind when the new trade agreement comes up for negotiation in the fall."

Americans were bullies. Rosales knew from experience the best way to stop a bully was to be a bigger bully. He hung up the phone without saying goodbye. There was only so much a man could take, and at that moment, Rosales had reached his limit.

* * * * *

"Therefore my children," the Monsignor said, "I implore you to remember those brothers and sisters who are less fortunate. We are all children of God.

We are all Chileans...."

Mariel Rosales could not understand what was keeping her husband. The Monsignor was almost finished with his sermon. She wanted desperately to look over her shoulder, to search for Enrique, but that would only call attention to his absence. To leave his daughter's wedding -- she didn't care if World War III had been declared. It was inexcusable.

"We must do more than pray for them," the Monsignor was said. "The poor of our country are the true Chileans. They struggle and fight for basic survival, for respect, for the opportunity to live a decent life. They deserve our love and our help...."

Maybe it was just as well Enrique wasn't back yet. If he were to hear what the good Monsignor was saying, Mariel thought. She turned to sneak a quick look. In the moment she caught sight of her husband, an involuntary sound escaped from her lips.

Boom!! Boom!! The roar of the two wood-handled pistols sent every wedding guest screaming, many hugging the ground for their very lives.

"Silencio, padre!" Enrique Rosales bellowed across the lawn. Those who weren't too terrified to sneak a look could see him standing in front of the arched doors of his study, both arms raised into the air, a smoking revolver in each hand.

"Adios, Monsignor," Rosales said laughing. "Nobody's marrying any Americans here today."

"Enrique, please!" Mariel cried. "What are you doing?"

"Get out!" Rosales ordered. "Every last one of you lousy Yankees. Off my land! Now!" The general took aim at one of the banquet tables laden with food and flowers. With two more blasts of the revolvers he shot both the heads off the dripping angels. The ice ricocheting off the sterling silver candelabra made a singing sound that amused him. He shot the angels through the heart.

Guests were scattering across the lawn, many screeching and crying, some crashing through the shrubbery. Mariel saw to her horror that Senora Montt was crawling on the ground, her pale blue silk dress dirtied by bark mulch. Some man lay beside her, his tuxedo tangled in rose thorns.

Mariel heard a cry and recognized her daughter's voice. She turned to see Les and Smiffy Rogers grab their son by the arm and drag him away. Lucia screamed and ran after him, her train catching on one of the potted urns of cascading flowers, her gown ripping as she stumbled and rolled to the ground. Mariel could hear her sobbing beneath her lace mantilla.

"General Rosales," Monsignor Sullivan implored. He was still standing before the linen-covered wedding altar, just beneath the canopy of white lilies and yellow and pink roses. "In the name of Our Lord Jesus Christ I beg you, General...."

"You better beg me good," Rosales yelled back. Taking aim at the Monsignor with one revolver, he took pity and raised the barrel of the gun at the last moment, shooting off the top half of the altar's gold crucifix and all of Jesus Christ's head.

Mariel saw the Monsignor take off for the front gates, his arthritic body moving faster than she could believe. All the other guests were scattered every which way, desperate to escape. Making the sign of the cross, Mariel Rosales realized she was the only member of the wedding party still standing.

CHAPTER 8

They call it "The Big Eye." King Keck, the most powerful optical telescope in the world, sits atop Mauna Kea volcano on the Big Island of Hawaii, the best site planet Earth has to offer.

"Would you like some coffee?" Charlie asked. She stretched her arms to the ceiling, flipped her baseball cap backwards, and took a deep breath. The last hour of the night's viewing was coming to an exhausted end.

"I want to double check the computer printout on that last shot," Selena said. Dark circles around her eyes reflected the eerie blue light of the monitor. "I can't have any variance here. That's important."

Selena felt worn by the emotions of the last few days. Coupled with jet lag, she was more exhausted than she could remember. That didn't count the sheer physical stress of being at Keck.

The air pressure at 13,796 feet was only sixty percent, and the lack of oxygen affected people in strange ways. Blood vessels in the brain and lungs dilated. The heart rate increased radically with the slightest exertion. Gas in the bowels expanded due to reduced atmospheric pressure. The kidneys kicked into overdrive ridding the body of water, and the respiratory rate zoomed, making a person feel lightheaded. Visitors to Keck had been known to faint simply by walking across the floor of the dome. Selena thought Charlie seemed better adjusted to the altitude. But, then, she'd always been good for the long haul.

"Just checked the printout," Charlie said, heading for the lounge door. "Everything looks fine. How about that coffee?"

"Sure. Maybe it'll help."

Once she was alone, Selena allowed herself to feel just how irritable and spaced-out she was. Her head ached and she wasn't thinking as clearly as she liked. She'd already put in five hours of steady work, but she still cursed herself for falling prey to the symptoms. This was no time for mistakes. Despite the discomforts, "The King" offered valuable advantages, like the charge-coupled device.

Phenomenally sensitive, the CCD would register in thousands of shades of gray ninety percent of the telescope's light, then electronically integrate and feed the signals to a computer. By morning, Selena would have hundreds of megabytes of data for analysis, hopefully confirming her previous findings on NEA Hartmann 2009. This she would present to the asteroid conference in Chile in just three days.

Looking back over the last five years, Selena remembered how the research seemed like a journey that would go on forever. At times it felt as though she were running on empty and had taken the wrong exit to find gas. Now she could see how her hunches had steered her in the right direction after all. She recognized there had been reassuring cues, Burma Shave signs, all along the highway. Still, she knew she had a vested interest in the outcome of her research. That could be dangerous. There was too much at stake.

Selena realized this night's viewing was over. While stars produce light, her asteroid was like the planets. It merely reflected the sun. Its radiance, unable to compete, had disappeared at the first hint of daylight.

Charlie returned to the control room without coffee. The fake fur of her jacket's hood practically covered her face.

"You look like an Eskimo," Selena said.

"Security's locking down," she said, handing Selena her jacket. "Major blizzard on the way. Everybody goes down the mountain, at least as far as the dorm. No exceptions."

Selena slumped onto a stool. "What about tomorrow night?"

Charlie shook her head. "It doesn't look good." Seeing how disappointed Selena was, she added, "We've got Wednesday to finish up."

"I wanted to run some things downstairs," Selena said, propping her head up with her hand. A second later she was chewing on a cuticle.

"No go," Charlie said. "This storm's gonna be a doozey. They're predicting winds over a hundred miles an hour. The whole mountain's liable to start swaying."

Selena was fairly certain she'd gotten the data she needed, but she wouldn't know for sure until she checked it in the lab. Now that would have to wait.

"Do you have our disc?" she asked Charlie. "Did you make a copy?"

Charlie nodded yes and patted her big leather shoulder bag. "Come on," she said. "You need some sleep. You look awful."

Selena slid off the stool and, wrapping her arms around Charlie, she rested her cheek on the top of her friend's head.

* * * * *

"You're going there, aren't you?" Charlie asked. After five hours of sleep they'd met in the dorm cafeteria. The plan was to fly to Oahu for the day and visit Charlie's brother, a biology teacher at a high school on the outskirts of Honolulu. Samuel and his wife had just given birth to their first daughter, and Charlie was anxious to see her new niece, Eve. When Selena begged off, Charlie guessed immediately.

"I don't think you should go alone," she continued. "I'll call my brother, tell him I can't make it."

"I'll be fine," Selena insisted. "You give Eve a kiss for me, okay? And take pictures." Selena had made up her mind. The visit to Makapuu Point where Nik died might be upsetting, but maybe it would help to put all the doubts to rest. She had to find a way. Nothing else seemed to work.

"Any word from Katya?" Charlie asked.

Selena shook her head. "I checked my voice mail again this morning. She was supposed to call last night."

"They said this might happen." Charlie reached up and removed Selena's hand from her mouth to stop her nail biting.

"I put a call in to the tour company," Selena said, hiding her fist in her lap. "I know I'm being silly, but I don't care. I left a message."

"Hey, you're a mother," Charlie said. "Silly comes with the territory. You're entitled." Charlie checked her watch and the face of Mickey Mouse smiled up at her. Katya had given her the watch years ago, after a trip to Disneyland. "We better get a move on," she said. "I don't want to miss that flight."

* * * * *

Charlie left Selena at the Budget car rental counter and went in search of a mailbox. Passing a gift shop in the crowded Honolulu terminal, a huge, stuffed polar bear caught her eye. One of the bear's hands looked like it was scratching its white, fluffy head. Charlie couldn't resist. The new baby will love it, she thought — if it doesn't scare her to death first.

"Where's a mailbox?" Charlie asked the sales clerk. He pointed toward the exit marked "Tour Buses." Slinging her large brown bag over her shoulder, she wrapped both arms around the broad bear and headed in that direction.

"You're as big as my Sam," Charlie told the stuffed animal. She could hardly see around its floppy pink ears. "I hope you don't shed." Propping the stuffed animal on top of the mailbox, she pulled two computer discs, each sealed in a separate envelope, from her leather bag. Returning one, she checked the address and postage on the other, then slid it carefully into the mailbox slot, embraced the bear, and walked out the exit. Her brother Samuel was just pulling up in his white minivan.

After loading the polar bear into the back seat, Charlie climbed in the front and gave her brother a big smooch. Buckling her seat belt, she noticed someone waving madly from inside the terminal, running in her direction. It's that hysterical young woman in the business suit, Charlie thought. The one who lost her puppy. Damn. Charlie pulled her baseball cap low and pretended not to notice.

"Drive, little brother," she said. "Let's get out of here."

* * * * *

With her arm resting on the open window of the rented Mustang, Selena drove east. She had tried to eat her Big Mac and fries, but it all tasted like cardboard. Besides, she was suddenly frantic, every atom of her being focused on what she would see and feel when she reached Makapuu Point.

An hour later she came around a high promontory and saw the moon-shaped beach of white sand glistening below the steep cliffs. Multi-colored gliders dotted the air. From here, the graceful scene was so benign, so charming, it was difficult to imagine the horrible death.

Selena parked behind an open air Jeep covered with "SURFERS DO IT STANDING UP," and "SURF NAKED" stickers. She made her way down to the edge of the cliff and stood with her hands in the pockets of her jeans, her body slightly bent into the wind. To her left the hang gliders were taking off in a rainbow of primary colors. If it's true, she thought, at least he died doing what he loved.

Selena walked farther along the cliff feeling sad and a little frightened. If only I could see his face, she thought, just once more. She was glad she'd come, though. Being there made her feel some final closeness with Nik.

Following the curve of land, she strolled until she reached a pile of massive boulders marking the end of the cliff. A narrow dirt path wound through the sun-warmed rocks, leading to a stand of trees that blocked the view of the next bay.

Not ready to turn back, Selena climbed the boulders and followed the path into the wooded area. She could hear the savage roar of the surf below and ventured closer to the edge of the precipice, far enough to see the next beach stretched warm and lazy in the afternoon sun. Almost directly below Selena eyed a small, rocky cove. Protected from the surf, it lay just around the point of rock, inaccessible to the tourists enjoying the tame beaches on either side.

Selena moved closer to the cliff's edge and looked down. Under an overhang she could see three boys playing, digging at something in the sand, their voices blocked by the deafening surf. How on earth did they get down there, she wondered?

One of the boys was jabbing violently at something, but she couldn't make out what. Grabbing tightly to a branch, she leaned farther out. A glint of silver caught her eye as the taller boy in the red baseball cap stabbed relentlessly at a mound in the sand. He backed away holding his sore arm. Selena saw the other two boys jump up and down excitedly.

Unsettled by a gust of late afternoon wind, she felt her foot slip in the sandy soil of the cliff's edge, sending pebbles falling below. She stepped back quickly before the children looked up. When she again peered over the precipice, the two smaller boys were tugging at their secret treasure while the other sawed away with his knife. It was then Selena realized. They had found a huge dead fish, its large, pale outline barely visible against the sand.

Feeling her hold slip again, Selena backed away from the edge to rest. She saw sneaker prints in the sand just to her right and followed them to a rocky overhang. From there she viewed the steep path of their descent, narrow and gravelly with little to grasp along the way.

From her new vantage point Selena noticed the boys had succeeded in gutting the fish. The taller poked around its innards while the smaller two used longer pieces of driftwood to keep a safe distance. When the boy in the red T-shirt snagged something on the end of his stick and began waving it in the air, Selena had to dig her fingers into the gravel to keep from falling.

"Oh my God!" she cried out. Her feet slid from beneath her and sent stones and dirt tumbling, pelting the boys on the head.

"Hey!" the older boy hollered, pointing to her. "Cut it out. Whadya doin'?"

Selena's eyes never left the other boy's stick. On its end, a piece of yellow cloth fluttered in the sea breeze. She recognized it immediately. It was the same yellow as the Dacron wings of Nik's glider.

Securing her footing, she called, "What have you got down there?"

"Nothing," one boy said.

"It's a shark," one of the others said.

"Shut up," the tall boy yelled, and looked up, shielding his eyes from the sun. "You can't come down here. It's too steep. You'll never make it."

She wasn't listening. Her mind was filled with the memory of Nik. He had stopped by on a Sunday to show off his new, yellow bird, had insisted upon assembling the whole thing in the back yard, explaining to her and Katya in detail how each piece worked. Katya wasn't the least bit interested and behaved rudely. She'd never liked her mother to date, and Nik had been no exception. Remembering how she hadn't chastised her daughter for fear of making a scene, Selena felt a sickening jolt of guilt, then anger. I've hesitated in too many ways, she told herself. For far too long.

Searching the rocky ledge for something to hold onto, Selena called to the boys. "I'm coming down."

* * * * *

Selena could hardly believe the size of it. The shark must have been ten or twelve feet long. Standing over its hacked-up carcass, her eyes scanned the length of the creature. She was surprised at the white, clean-looking innards. Her nose wasn't fooled, though. She could smell the already decaying flesh baking in the Hawaiian sun. A jagged piece of aluminum tubing had ripped through one of the fish's internal organs. About midway down the belly she saw the bright yellow swatches of Dacron, chewed and shredded, but undeniably the same color as Nik's glider.

Then it was true after all, she thought, feeling the weight of sadness descend on her. He was dead. With her arms wrapped tightly around her, Selena took some deep breaths and walked the few feet of sandy cove. She couldn't help but picture the ferocious shark tearing at Nik's body, devouring it limb by limb. She tried to calm down, told herself he was already dead by then, had already faced the worst.

"Look at this," the boy in the tattered red T-shirt hollered. Selena turned to see him poking at a long, fat tube of slimy, pale yellow flesh. Moving closer, she saw that it ran in a circle, up and down the length of the fish.

"Oh, my God!" Selena cried. She covered her face with her hands, but she couldn't keep from looking. There, inside the shark's flabby wet stomach, was part of a human hand. The fingers were white and bloated with seawater, distorted but recognizable. A buzzing fly landed on the wrinkled piece of flesh and Selena could feel her stomach churn. She backed away, turned and walked to the water's edge.

"Hey," the taller boy hollered. "Do that again."

"I didn't do nothin'," the younger one answered.

"Just gimme that." He grabbed the long stick of driftwood and poked at the shark's insides. "Look," he said. "Down there. Underneath. Get it."

Selena saw it, too. The boy in the red T-shirt hesitated, stepped back from the smelly fish, but she ran impulsively to the shark and fell on her knees beside it. Reaching under the slimy yellow gut, she pulled out a gold wedding band, wet and glistening in the sunlight.

"Hey! That's mine," the older boy said. "I found it first."

Selena hurried back to the water's edge and, crouching down, rinsed off the ring. Turning it slowly, she searched the smooth surface of the inner band.

"D. H." she read out loud. "1948." She had to read it again before she let herself sit back, let her body relax against the sand.

"Hey, gimme that ring," the older boy said over her shoulder. He held out a dirty hand.

Selena, smiling with relief, gave it to him. It wasn't Nikolai's ring. It couldn't be. She'd never seen him wear it, and those weren't his initials. The person in the belly of that fish couldn't be Nik. He couldn't have killed himself in that gliding accident.

Her elation lasted only a few moments. Where was he, then? What had happened to him? Her confusion quickly grew into fear. Biting down hard on a raw cuticle, she winced. I've got to let the CIA know about this, she thought. I've got to find Charlie.

* * * * *

Charlie felt like she was hallucinating at a Las Vegas sideshow, but she knew it was just her state of mind. From her perch at the end of the Kona Kapula hotel bar, she had a full view of the weekly luau.

In the harbor, torch-lit outrigger canoes carried ukulele players and hula dancers. On the hotel beach a giant Chinese lion figure spouted firecrackers as sun burnt tourists applauded from their picnic tables, too stuffed on roast pig and sweet potatoes to move. Fireworks were due to start any minute.

It was only nine p.m., but her brother and sister-in-law had gone to bed after an early dinner out, eager to claim whatever sleep they could before the baby woke them. The night's viewing at Keck had been cancelled, but Charlie couldn't sleep; she was used to keeping observatory hours. Besides, she was depressed. After rocking Eve to sleep, she'd come face-to-face with a truth she'd managed to avoid. It looked like she would never have a child of her own.

A little Hawaiian girl dressed in a traditional grass skirt, her face almost buried in leis, walked past Charlie's bar stool.

"Aloha," Charlie said. The child looked up, her big, dark eyes distressed, and then kept right on moving. She's on a mission, Charlie thought. To the girls room.

Signaling the bartender, Charlie ordered her third Blue Hurricane. It had seemed like the appropriate drink, considering the weather and her mood. What the hell, she thought, removing the pink umbrella and downing the last few drops. I sure as hell don't have to worry about three o'clock feedings.

"Aloha," a voice said behind her. "What a surprise to find you here."

Startled by the soft petals of an orchid lei brushing against her cheek and settling on her shoulders, Charlie swiveled on her bar stool to discover the young woman who'd lost her puppy. Oh God, Charlie thought. That's the last time I'm going to be kind to strangers.

"I'm sorry I was such a baby the other day," the young woman said. "You must let me buy you a drink. I don't know what got into me. I was so sad."

"It must be catchy," Charlie said. "But I don't think I need another cocktail."

"By the way, my name's Lia Gibson." She took Charlie's hand in both of hers and held it. Charlie thought she looked younger than the other day, and stunning, like a Ralph Lauren model in her backless, white linen dress. Her long, auburn hair fell softly over one shoulder.

Lia motioned to the bartender. "Two more, please," she said sweetly. "We'll be over there." Carrying Charlie's heavy brown shoulder bag and the drink, she led the way to a far booth.

"There," she said once they were settled. "I couldn't compete with the racket from that waterfall behind the bar."

"Any word on your dog?" Charlie found her eyes lingering on the soft curve and hollow of the young woman's bare shoulder.

Lia threw her arms out in celebration. "They found her," she said. "In Cincinnati of all places. Can you believe it?"

"That's great," Charlie said.

"She'll be on the next flight here." Lia's dark eyes widened with her smile. "And she's flying first class this time. But what's the matter with you? You look suicidal."

"Sorry," Charlie said. "I'm feeling sorry for myself." Finishing the last sip of her drink, she popped the red cherry off its stem with her teeth, and pulled the fresh cocktail closer. Lia reached across the table and unhooked Charlie's lei from the collar of her blue work shirt. When the back of her soft hand accidentally brushed Charlie's cheek, she let it linger for a moment.

That was just an accident, Charlie told herself, reaching for her Blue Hurricane. When she looked up, Lia's eyes were still on hers.

"You shouldn't be so hard on yourself," Lia said. "I wish everyone was as nice as you."

Charlie shrugged. Embarrassed, she rested her elbow on the table and propped her chin in her fist. "Who could possibly not be nice to a beautiful young woman like you?"

"Oh, it's not that," Lia said. "I guess I'm just disappointed."

"What's the matter?" Charlie leaned a little closer.

Lia didn't answer at first. Instead she took another sip of her drink. "My father was supposed to meet me here, but he's been delayed because of business. As usual." Lia seemed to force a smile. "We're going to rent a house on the North Shore for a week."

Charlie thought she saw sadness cross the girl's delicate features just before Lia dropped her head. "What is it?" Charlie asked. She placed a tender hand on Lia's arm. "Why are you so sad?"

When Lia looked up her eyes were wrinkled and her lip quivered as she failed to fight off tears. "It's nothing really," she said, wiping her eyes with a cocktail napkin. "I just can't seem to drink anything since...since my mom died a year ago. Dad and I were going to spend that day together."

"That's gotta be tough," Charlie said, patting Lia's outstretched hand. "When my mom died it made a complete crybaby out of me."

Lia looked up and smiled, her eyes locked on Charlie's. "You know, you have beautiful hair," Lia said. "I love the gray."

The first bang of fireworks over the bay startled them both, but as Charlie sat back in her seat, Lia squeezed her hand.

"I think I'll order another drink," Charlie said, pulling away.

"I'll get it," Lia insisted. "I'm going to the ladies room for a minute. I'll tell the bartender."

A brilliant burst of silver and red sparks opened like a flower in the night sky. Charlie felt dazzled by it, and confused. Was Lia coming on to her? She wasn't sure, but the fireworks were suddenly exciting, and Charlie realized she wasn't feeling so depressed after all.

"Aren't they great?" Lia said when she returned. She was standing beside the booth, her hand resting on Charlie's shoulder. "I've always loved fireworks."

"Me too," Charlie said.

"Listen. I've got a great idea," Lia said. She dropped a room key on the table. "I've got the penthouse suite all to myself tonight. I bet the view of the fireworks would be fantastic. Wanna see?"

* * * * *

Selena sat down and propped her feet on the balcony railing of her motel room. The hush and roll of the night surf just below should have calmed her, but she couldn't relax. What good are cell phone, she thought, when they don't work half the time? Finishing the small bag of salted peanuts she'd gotten from the vending machine down the hall, she took a sip of ginger ale. That would be dinner for tonight.

She had climbed the steep cliff from the beached shark, hurried to her car, and driven to the nearest phone booth. First she checked the observatory. The sun would be setting soon over blue skies on the island of Oahu, but the Keck observatory was still locked down, a blizzard expected to hit the heights of Mauna Kea that evening. Next, Selena put a call through to Bingham at the CIA. He wasn't available, and she had no phone number to leave for his return call. She tried Charlie at her brother's, but no one was home. Maybe they've gone to dinner, she thought, and decided to find a room for the night, someplace with a phone.

She stopped at the first beachside motel with a vacancy sign, hoping to relay the information to Bingham, contact Charlie, and then get some badly needed rest. Instead, she found herself stuck in a small room saturated with the sour smell of cigarettes, pacing the floor, waiting. Samuel told her she'd just missed Charlie. Selena asked for a return call, no matter how late. Where could she be at this hour? Selena wondered. Even Bingham had failed to call back.

At least you reached someone at New World EcoTours of San Francisco, she told herself. When there had still been no message from Katya on her voice mail, Selena phoned the travel agent at home. The woman assured her it wasn't unusual for calls from the children to be late, sometimes by a week. It was the jungle after all. Selena found the woman's blasé attitude irritating. She might not be so calm, Selena thought, if it were her own daughter.

The can of ginger ale was flat now, but she finished it anyway and tried to think. None of it made any sense. The happy postcard from Nik followed by his suicide? The death of Marfa Ivanovna the same week? Someone else's wedding band in the shark's belly with Nik's glider? Maybe the KGB or whatever they called themselves these days was responsible. They'd be aware of the value of Nik 's research, the potential for its application. I should have taken some of the flesh from that hand in the shark's belly, she thought. For DNA testing. But what good would it do? Bingham would say sharks travel in schools, and Nik could have been eaten by another shark altogether. The evidence wouldn't prove anything conclusive. Still, Selena couldn't help but think maybe Nik was still alive. It was almost painful to feel the hope grow inside, but at one in the morning she felt eager with nervous energy, desperate to do something, anything.

Looking up at the night sky, Selena searched out and quickly found the constellations Great Bear and Little Bear. As a child in New Mexico she had spent many hot, summer nights in the backyard. Her father would be working late at the lab at Los Alamos, and the smell of desert sage made her mother melancholy for her home on the island of Mykonos. It was on those nights she would tell her daughter the Greek stories of the stars.

Selena's favorite was about Callisto, a beautiful Greek princess and an expert huntress. Zeus, the king of the gods, fell in love with Callisto, but when the queen of the gods Hera found out, she became jealous. Banished to live alone in the forest with the wild beasts, the princess gave birth to a beautiful baby girl, Arca. Further enraged, Hera made the princess shaggy with fur and gave her a face with a muzzle. When the princess begged for mercy, she found her voice had turned to a roar. She had become a great white bear.

Her baby girl, not recognizing her mother, screamed and ran away, out of the forest, where a kind farmer's wife adopted her.

When Arca grew up and became a great huntress, she came upon Callisto with her bow and arrow. The princess ran to hug her little girl, growling with happiness. Arca would have shot her mother dead, but Zeus reached down and swung Callisto by the tail up among the stars. So mother and daughter might never be separated again, he changed Arca into a little bear and tossed her into the heavens, too.

Selena gazed up at her favorite constellations and smiled wistfully, then sighed. Lately she felt lonely for her mother almost as much as when she was a little girl. If only she were still here, Selena thought. But she knew it wouldn't be the answer to her problems. Nobody's mother was. They were only people, like the rest of us. Like me, Selena thought, remembering Katya.

Leaving the balcony, she paced the short length of the room, then turned and walked back to the sliding glass doors. Why hadn't Charlie called? And where in hell was Bingham?

CHAPTER 9

Stuck behind a snowplow, the drive up the mountain to Keck took almost three hours. Selena and Charlie wanted to use every minute of viewing time and went right to work. By six in the morning they were in the lab analyzing the results.

"This can't be right," Selena said. She stared at the computer print out. "It negates all our findings at Palomar. Something's terribly wrong."

Dumbfounded, Charlie paced the floor. "Keck can't be wrong," she said. "Both night's viewing here confirm the same orbit. And it's way too close to home."

"We were tired," Selena said. "Could it be our error?"

"No." Charlie stopped pacing and stared at Selena. "Maybe the storm damaged the telescope. If it's off by a fraction, that's all it would take."

Selena shook her head. "Nobody's reported any difficulty. We'd know." Nervously, her little finger went to her lip. Charlie noticed, but didn't bother to stop her. "There's only one other possibility," Selena said. She pushed the eject button on the computer and pulled out the disc. She held it before them. "Could somebody have tampered with the discs?"

Both women were shocked by the idea but knew it wasn't as far fetched as it sounded. With the Star Wars bill coming to a vote, impressive government contracts were at stake. Anything was possible.

"But how?" Charlie said. "When? Did they change the telescope's hard drive, too?"

"If someone got to our disc, they could have infected everything with a virus. As soon as I inserted the disc, it would have changed our data throughout the system."

"Who?" Charlie asked. With the same idea in mind, she and Selena stared at each other.

"The discs were with me all the time. In the dorm when we slept," Charlie said, shaking her head as the possibilities lessened. "My room was locked. No one got in."

"What about last night? What was her name? Lia?" Selena stared at Charlie.

Charlie felt something rise up inside her in protest, but she walked immediately to the phone. When she reached the desk clerk at the Kona Kapula hotel, she was informed Ms. Gibson had checked out very early the morning after the fireworks. When Charlie had woken that morning she'd found a note saying Lia had gone for a jog, that she would call Charlie later at the observatory. Charlie checked her messages. No call.

"There's only one way to know for sure," Charlie said. "I mailed the other disc back to the mainland before last night. It should arrive at school this afternoon. I'll have to meet you in Chile."

Selena nodded. Looking at the computer printout on her lap, she felt the urge to pray. If this information was correct, Hartmann 2009 was on a collision course with planet Earth. That was the last thing she wanted to announce at the asteroid conference in two days. It would mean certain passage of the Star Wars bill.

"All right," Selena said, checking her watch. "But there's one more thing I want to check." Partially unzipping her yellow insulated body suit, she reached into her pant's pocket and pulled out Nik's postcard.

* * * * *

In the women's room at the Juan Santamaria airport in Costa Rica, Katya Hartmann sat fully clothed on a toilet seat. She'd been crying for the last fifteen minutes and was embarrassed to come out, hoping the woman with the baby would leave. Katya had been listening to the mother talk to her baby while she changed the dirty diapers.

The whole bathroom stinks now, Katya thought. The hell with this. Putting on the headphones of her tape player, she pushed the play button, adjusted the volume to high, and bolted from the stall holding a wad of toilet paper to wipe her runny, black mascara. She was surprised to find the mother of the baby was only a girl, not much older than herself. The fat baby smiled at Katya, and she felt tears surface again, so she stuck her tongue out at the kid and made a quick exit.

The tour's return flight to Los Angeles had been delayed for at least another hour. Strolling the busy terminal, Katya stopped at a frozen yogurt shop and ordered a Dutch fudge double scoop with jimmies. With her black, Grateful Dead backpack hanging off one shoulder, she worked her way down the main corridor, licking the melting cone. At a souvenir shop she stopped to look at magazines and was surprised to find *Art in America* toward the back of the store.

"Excuse me, Miss. Excuse me," the short, busty sales clerk kept repeating, but Katya could only hear the Rollling Stones belting out *Satisfaction*. "Miss," the clerk said coming up from behind. She jabbed her finger into Katya's shoulder. Emotionally raw from crying, she jumped and turned in a snarl, yanking the headphone off her right ear.

"What?" she said.

"You can't eat that in here. You'll have to take it outside."

"Oh, give me a break," Katya said.

"It's not allowed," the clerk said and pulled down the hem of her pink nylon sweater. She stood with her hands on her broad hips. "Didn't you see the sign?"

"Oh, Jesus," Katya said. She made a face, but turned to go, working her way through the crowd of travelers. Near the entrance she saw Naomi and her new friend, Gwen. They were holding up an "I Love Costa Rica" T-shirt.

"She ought to wear one of these," Naomi said and laughed, not noticing Katya. "Just change it to 'I Love Federico.'"

Gwen grabbed the shirt, stretched it across her chest, and pushed her adolescent breasts out as far as she could. She swiveled her hips as she pronounced each syllable with exaggerated passion.

"Kat-y-a Loves Fed-er-i-co."

The two girls laughed while Katya, unnoticed, fought the urge to mash her ice cream cone into Naomi's face.

"Miss. Excuse me, miss." The salesclerk sounded angry. She had followed Katya to the front of the store. "You have to eat that outside." She pointed to the Dutch chocolate cone. It was melting, dripping off her hand onto the floor. People stared.

Naomi and Gwen turned to see a big dollop of chocolate mush hit the tile. They laughed and pointed.

"You know what your T-shirt should say," Katya told Naomi. "Fat Naomi loves candy bars." She pushed her way through the crowd towards the front of the store, the cone still melting.

Naomi followed. "It's too bad Federico already has a girlfriend," she said, announcing it to the whole store. "And it isn't you!"

Katya's face reddened with humiliation. Everyone had seen the beautiful young woman arrive at the gate and plaster herself all over Federico. Their kiss had gone on forever, right in front of the whole tour group.

"She was gorgeous, wasn't she, Gwen?" Naomi said.

"He was crazy about her, too," Gwen said.

If the plane to LA hadn't been delayed, I would have been gone, Katya thought. Federico must have been counting on that. Either that or he just didn't give a damn.

The salesclerk was jabbing at Katya's shoulder again, then shoving her in the direction of the store entrance. Katya felt her anger intensify to a point she recognized, a place where she didn't care anymore. Swinging around to yell, Katya smeared frozen yogurt all over the woman's tight, pink sweater. The slurpy scoops bounced off her breasts and flew across the store, landing at the feet of a customer. Katya threw the empty cone on the floor, made a hateful face at the sales clerk, and then turned away. With both hands she grabbed Naomi by the neck and began pushing her back, out of the store. The salesclerk was screaming now, and Naomi was hollering, her eyes buggy, trying to fight back.

"Cut it out, Hartmann," Gwen yelled, yanking on Katya's arm. "Stop it. You're such a loser."

Katya pushed harder until Naomi fell backward, into the passing traffic of the terminal, onto the floor. The sudden, fierce beep of a motorized cart made her look up to see a black man driving too fast, straight for her, only yards away. He pounded at the brake and jerked so abruptly the sole passenger, a gray-haired woman with a cane, flew off her seat, onto the floor next to Naomi. She screamed, and then yelled something in German. There was a flash of light as a Japanese man took pictures.

Everyone was yelling at Katya now. The driver hollered as he rushed to pick his passenger off the floor. The salesclerk pointed and screamed something about a troublemaker. But all Katya heard were the words out of Naomi's mouth.

"You're sick," Naomi said. "My mom told me you needed a father and she was right." Strangers backed away as Naomi struggled to get to her feet.

"Just shut up," Katya yelled down at her. She tried to sound mean but she really wanted to run and hide.

Gwen helped Naomi to her feet. "That's why you flirt with my dad. It's disgusting."

"I don't know what you're talking about," Katya said. She hefted her backpack higher on her shoulder and started to walk away, but Naomi's words spit at her from behind.

"I know who your dad is. I heard your mom arguing in the kitchen. I was in the backyard, under the window. She said she didn't want to tell you yet."

Katya felt her insides lock up, her chest harden until it hurt. She spun around to face Naomi, to make her shut up.

"You're making this up," she yelled. "You don't know anything."

"Oh yeah?" Naomi said, brushing herself off. "His name is Nikolai. That's what she called him. That's who your father is, stupid. Everybody knows but you."

Katya's throat was so tight she couldn't breathe. She couldn't answer back.

"Even I know, stupid," Gwen said, taking Naomi's arm. "Come on. Let's get out of here."

The beep of the motorized cart began, and the German woman yelled something at the driver as they pulled away. People were moving on. The salesclerk was wiping her sweater at the cash register.

Katya couldn't move; she couldn't swallow. In the midst of all the commotion, she felt sealed off without air. She couldn't hear anybody or anything; she couldn't think. She was alone within an echo chamber where Naomi's words reverberated, over and over again.

* * * * *

Selena's words were heated, as if Charlie were the one who didn't believe her.

"I already told Bingham about the postcard. He didn't care. When I finally got through about the shark, it was the same thing. He doesn't take any of this seriously."

Selena didn't trust the CIA for a minute. She'd learned that lesson at an early age, when her father lost his job at Los Alamos. He'd been terminated only a few years after her mother died because he dared question the nuclear weapons research. He ended up working in New Jersey for a chemical company. He made a lot more money, but bitterness grew inside him. Selena never knew whether it was because of the loss of his Olga or what the government had done to him.

"Damn it, Charlie," she said. "I still don't believe the suicide. Something's going on here. I can feel it."

"Are you telling me the woman who once declared emotions to be dangerous and untrustworthy is now listening to her feelings?"

Selena wasn't paying attention. The muffled, eerie sound of wind outside the observatory made her shiver. Turning the postcard over, she ran her finger across the curling stamps then slid her nail under the peeling edge and broke the seal of dried-out glue. Four of the five stamps came off easily. She rubbed and scraped until the last one was gone.

What she saw before her was unmistakably a mathematical formula, tightly written, in a precise and careful hand. Selena knew instantly this was not one of Nik's quick scribbles or disjointed notes. Nik had meant to hide the formula on this postcard.

Suddenly too warm, she unzipped her bodysuit, took her arms out of the sleeves. Charlie pulled up a chair. The laboratory's computer system wouldn't be programmed for Nik's level of research in superconductivity, but its astronomy software included fairly complex physics, and because the observatory was affiliated with the University of Hawaii, the software was user-friendly. It was designed to answer questions like, Why? How? and What? for students. It might help Selena answer some of the same questions that had plagued her.

She placed the postcard on the table and carefully punched in the formula. She worked backwards, deciphering each component of the equation to discover its purpose. From Nik's discussions, she knew she would recognize the formula if this was really it.

"What was he trying to hide?" Charlie asked. "What was he working on?"

"Unidentified Superconducting Objects," Selena said. "USO's. He wanted to recreate superconductivity at temperatures near or even above room temperature. Because superconductivity is so expensive to maintain, its commercial applications are limited. At first they had to use liquid helium to produce the extremely low but necessary temperatures."

"I remember from physics class," Charlie said. "We learned that liquid helium, like good whiskey, is expensive."

"Exactly. It's also difficult to handle and requires bulky apparatus. So they worked to find so-called 'high-temperature' compounds which used liquid nitrogen."

"And liquid nitrogen only costs as much as milk."

"But Nik was trying to make a superconductor work at room temperature, for everyday applications. He was trying to find the recipe for a ceramic USO."

Selena's face brightened in the blue glow of the screen. The computer was churning out the components of the formula. It appeared a temperature of 340 degrees Kelvin was related to a series of materials.

"This has got to be it," Selena said. They waited as the computer suddenly went into overdrive, regurgitating the information, sputtering to produce a response. The words "Ytrium-barium-copper-oxide, a metallic oxide used in ceramics," appeared on the screen. The 340 degrees Kelvin and these components had to be elements of the recipe.

Selena felt certain. Nik had succeeded in creating a room-temperature superconductor. This was monumental, she knew. It would change the world as we knew it. Suddenly the puzzle began to fall in to place.

* * * * *

"Are you a student?" the greasy-haired young man sitting next to her asked. "Are you going to the conference?"

"No," Katya said. She pulled her left arm off the armrest, held it tight to her body. She didn't want to even touch the nerdy-looking geek sitting next to her on the plane. His fingernails were too long and he had body odor. Gross! Little did he know that her mother was running the whole damned conference. But Katya wasn't going to tell him. She turned up the volume on her tape player and looked out the window.

After Naomi and Gwen left her in the airport, Katya took off in the opposite direction. There was no way she was getting on the same plane with them. There was no way she was going to spend the next week at Naomi's house with her freaky family. To think everyone in the neighborhood knew who her father was. She never wanted to go back there again. Why had her mother kept it from her? And Charlie, too. She hated them both. And why did it have to be him, that Russian guy? Katya refused to believe it, but she was going to find out. She was going to walk right into her mother's precious asteroid conference whether she liked it or not. Let her mother be embarrassed in front of her friends. See how she likes it.

* * * * *

Selena and Charlie hurried past a group of waiting passengers in the Honolulu terminal, half of them watching the lounge TV. The news program made Selena come to a halt. A reporter was holding a microphone to the crafty face of Senator Ralph Whiting of North Carolina.

"We can't just sit here unprepared," the Senator was saying. "One of those dang things is headed our way right now. We've got to be ready to defend ourselves, and this program will do that AND it's gonna provide jobs."

Selena shook her head and scrutinized the faces of the people watching. How could they know what to believe, she worried, then hurried to catch up with Charlie.

"Listen," Selena said when they reached her gate. "When you get back to LA, call the tour company. Keep after them, will you? I will, too, but it might be hard while I'm in transit. And here's a phone number at the LIFT. Let me know as soon as you learn anything — about Katya or the disc."

"You bet," Charlie said. She'd been quiet ever since they'd discovered the discrepancy in the Keck results. She was furious to think that young woman could have gotten to their work. What was worse, Charlie felt she had let Selena down.

"If you can't reach me by phone, send e-mail. I'll check often. I have to run," Selena said. The strap of her carry-on bag dug into her shoulder and she hefted it to the other side. "Here," she said, searching a side pocket of her briefcase. "Take my keys. Remember where we parked?"

"How could I forget?" Charlie said. "Floor 5, Aisle D, Red. I'm going to steal that car just as soon as you get everything fixed."

Selena gave her a big hug. "Take care of yourself, will you? Everything's going to be all right."

"Yeah," Charlie said. "It better be."

Selena took off for Gate 7 and Charlie headed across the terminal. She hadn't gone far when she heard Selena call out.

"Hey! How was the baby?" In all the confusion and excitement, Selena had completely forgotten about Eve.

"She's gorgeous." Charlie said. "Looks just like me."

Selena waved, but Charlie wasn't smiling. She turned a corner and was lost from sight.

* * * * *

"She's just a kid," the security guard on the phone told Jean Lévesque. "Says her mother's running the conference. What do you want me to do? Put her on a bus with the rest of them? Should I try to reach Dr. Hartmann to verify?"

"No," Jean said. "Don't do anything. Where is she now?"

"She's walking around in the lounge." The guard looked out the two-way glass of the LIFT airport security office. Wearing unlaced hiking boots, Katya jerked back and forth to the music only she heard, her vintage summer dress hanging two sizes too big and swaying across her suntanned legs. "She's not a friendly type," the guard said. "Looks like one of those punk rockers."

"Listen to me. Put her in my office immediately. Hold her there. Don't let her out. Don't let anyone in to see her. And don't even mention this to anybody else. Do you understand?"

"Sure, but what's the big deal."

"None of your fucking business," Jean said. "Just do as I say."

"Yes sir."

"I want all calls to Dr. Hartmann, all calls, every single one, routed to my office, to my personal line. Immediately. Do you understand?"

"Yes sir."

Twenty minutes later Jean Levesque drove up to the back door of the LIFT air terminal. He personally escorted Katya Hartmann into the back seat of a limousine with darkly tinted windows.

* * * * *

Charlie's overnight bag hung from one shoulder, and her big leather bag swung from the other. With both short arms wrapped around a cardboard box of late birthday presents from her brother, she could only dangle her briefcase from her fingertips. By the time she got to Floor 5, Aisle D, Red, of LAX's parking garage, Charlie's arms felt like they were about to fall off. Talk about going for the burn, she thought.

She slid her dangling briefcase onto the hood of Selena's black Porsche, and then let her overnight bag slip off one shoulder onto the cement floor, balancing the box of presents on top. Her brown bag was stuffed to capacity with last minute trinkets she'd picked up in Honolulu. Charlie fumbled blindly through the contents. She could hear the keys jangling at the bottom.

"I just put them in here," she mumbled to herself.

Finally unlocking the door, Charlie reached down to pick up her overnight bag. A small pool of liquid darkened the cement between the front tires. Damn, she thought. I guess beauty and function don't always go hand in hand. Last time that happened it was the brake fluid. I'll have to stop and have it checked.

With her keys in her teeth, she slid into the low, bucket seat. Selena must be too tall for this little car, she thought. It fits me much better. Checking the rearview mirror, she brushed her frizzy bangs off her forehead, and made a hopeless face, as if the situation were more than she cared to deal with.

Remembering the brakes, she pumped them a couple of times. They seemed to work fine. She put the car in gear and turned the key.

The explosion was instantaneous and so powerful Charlie never felt a thing.

CHAPTER 10

Each day he was led to this carpeted, basement room with cement walls. Each day his kidnappers attempted to convince him he must cooperate. Each day he refused.

Dr. Nikolai Potapov leaned over the scale model of the LIFT accelerator in Chile and angrily drummed his fingers on the Plexiglas cover. A large, rugged-looking man, his Hawaiian tan was still dark despite the days of being held prisoner. The light from a solitary half-window caught the scattered gray strands in his beard.

Again today they left him alone in this subterranean cell and told him to wait. That first day he'd distracted himself with architectural drawings displayed like works of art depicting a dream city of the future. Then he began to study the engineering plans rolled and stored in cardboard boxes in the corner, cast off upon completion of the project. Nik searched for a way to escape. He found nothing.

Pacing the room, he held the image of his kidnapper's sickly smile. In hindsight he could see how flawlessly the scheme had been implemented. The memory only fueled his anger. He was familiar with the tyranny of force, had experienced it in Russia, but never expected to endure it again, not like this. He swore he would never be part of the work going on here. They could never force him to share his formula.

Nik knew his high-temperature superconductors would utterly transform the world. The extent of the change was unfathomable: by using superconducting wires to transmit and store electricity, billions of dollars would be saved in wasted energy. His formula would levitate trains, allowing them to travel without noise or friction at unheard-of speeds and minimal expense. Electric motors one-tenth the current size would power ships and cars. Supercomputers as big as a loaf of bread would do the work of room-size computers. Nuclear fusion, the mightiest known force in the universe, would become possible and permit interstellar travel.

With cheap, high-temperature superconductors, we as a civilization would be able to do more things and do them faster than we had ever before imagined. The potential applications were limitless. And dangerous. With my formula, Nik thought, superconductor infrared sensors in space could precisely detect a target on Earth as small as a human being.

* * * * *

"I just got a call from counter terrorism," Norman Hambly told his boss. "If you'll turn on your TV, sir, there's a news report you might find of interest. CNN." Bingham reached for his clicker.

"This is Theresa Diaz with a news bulletin from Los Angeles. Authorities are investigating what may be a terrorist bombing at Los Angeles International Airport earlier today." Bingham turned up the volume.

"The explosion left a huge crater in the American Airlines parking garage. One woman is believed dead, and four others injured in the blast. Investigators are beginning the painstaking process of piecing together the evidence from what they believe was a car bomb. A police detective on the scene said the investigation could take weeks."

Hambly interrupted. "Dr. Hartmann took the plane to Chile, sir. Her assistant went to LAX alone."

"Very good," Bingham said.

Ms. Diaz continued. "A motive is as yet unknown. However, twelve different terrorist groups have called claiming responsibility for the bombing. A federal agent of the Bureau of Alcohol, Tobacco, and Firearms told our reporter on the scene that the Iranian fundamentalist group Hezbollah has used a similar modus operandi in the past."

Bingham hit the power button and leaned back in his executive chair. "Those bastards take the rap for everything," he said.

* * * * *

Nikolai Potapov struggled to understand. What was Pierre Lorillard's plan? What would a man like Lorillard want to do? Nik believed the key was in Pierre's character. He was a man of immense vision, a man whose only religion was what he called progress, the forward movement of life. In discussions with Nik, Lorillard had ridiculed those who fought to curtail scientific investigation in areas like DNA or fetal tissue research. They were as foolish as the Prohibitionists, Lorillard said. And their efforts would prove just as futile.

But the man was unpredictable in an unnerving sort of way, Nik thought. He remembered the climb up the mountain, Lorillard's trick to push Nik to his limits. And then there was the surprise birthday gift.

They'd been sitting by the pool at Blenheim, an ancient stone estate in Geneva. It belonged to a Malaysian businessman who had invited Pierre to make use of the "summer cottage" while attending the CERN anniversary celebration. Roos Coons, Lorillard's business partner in the LIFT, was talking to Pierre while Nik baked on the lounge chair. He decided to go for a swim and dove into the cool, blue water, coming up for air at the far end of the pool.

That's when he saw the butler approach from the main house. He was carrying a crystal champagne bucket, sunlight igniting the faceted surface of the glass. Another servant paraded down the long, manicured grounds and placed a sterling silver stand for the champagne bucket to the right of Pierre's chair, and handed him a long, rectangular package, gift-wrapped in burnished gold paper and tied with a large red bow.

"What's all this?" Nik asked. He climbed up the pool ladder and dripped his way back to the chaise lounge.

"Happy birthday, my friend," Pierre said. He gave Nikolai the package as the butler popped the cork on the bottle of 1988 Dom Perignon. Roos watched with seeming delight.

"How did you know it was my birthday?" Nik asked. "I'd forgotten myself until yesterday." He threw his towel aside and sat on the edge of the chaise with the present balanced on his knees, eagerly tearing off the wrapping paper. Inside he found an ornately carved box of dark, oiled wood. He opened it, but looked bewildered.

Trying not to sound puzzled, Nik said, "It's a rifle." Carefully lifting the gun from its bed of black velvet, he held it up for all to see. The sun glinted off the polished metal of the sights.

"It was custom made by an old gunsmith up in Alberta," Pierre said proudly. "The length of the pull should fit your arms and shoulders. It belonged to my brother, Bertrand. I've got one myself, just like it."

99

Roos took a sip of champagne and pulled a cigar from his breast pocket. The butler quickly produced a lighter.

"That's a honey of a rifle, Nik," Roos said, stoking the cigar and puffing smoke all around his head. "I used to trade hunting stories with one of my patients at the clinic. When old Joe came down for his last treatment, he gave me his favorite rifle. Sort of a thank you and goodbye gift all in one. He passed away two weeks ago. The rifle's a beaut, mind you, but nothing like that baby. We'll have to go on a wild turkey hunt someday."

"To tell the truth," Nik said, "I'm not a hunter. I don't know a thing about shooting a gun."

"I'm going to teach you," Pierre announced. He stood up, moved closer to Nik. "We're going to a valley in the Laurentians. Bertrand and I used to hunt that territory when we were kids. I built a lodge there." Then, with surprising tenderness, he added, "It was my favorite place on earth." An awkward silence followed as Pierre looked out over the trees.

Lorillard suddenly strode over to Nik and grabbed the rifle from his hands. Lifting a shell from the case, he loaded the gun, then peered through the sights, aiming at a pigeon. When the shot rang out, the unexpected blast was deafening. Nik remembered watching the bird, mangled and bloody, hit with a thud on the stone patio. He was shocked and looked to Roos, who also seemed disturbed and puzzled by the unnecessary killing. Neither one spoke a word.

"In the fall we'll hunt moose," Pierre said. All emotion was now purged from his voice. He handed the gun back to Nik and walked back to the house.

Yes, Nik thought, remembering that day, Lorillard is a visionary, but he's unpredictable to say the least. And dangerous. Closing his eyes, Nik tried to imagine what Pierre had planned for the formula.

"Good morning, my friend."

Startled, Nikolai spun around and found himself face-to-face with his captor.

"I've been told," Lorillard said, "you refuse to share your work with me. Could this be true?" He seemed to find this humorous.

"You're a fool. I'll have nothing to do with this," Nik said. He grimaced in disgust, and then stalked across the room. From the beginning he'd suspected there was something not quite right with the LIFT project. Now he knew just how wrong it was.

"I wish I could enlighten you as to my plans for the formula, Doctor Perhaps some day, hopefully soon. I don't intend to use it for military purposes.

My ultimate goal will benefit mankind to a degree even I cannot imagine."
Lorillard walked to the corner window and gazed out at the blacktop and the
chalky, dry terrain. His eyes squinted from the sunlight and the sheer effort
to contain his excitement. He continued, not looking at Nik.

"We've been tapped into your computer for the last year. The magnetic
compounds are here, in my laboratory, ready for immediate, on-site production
and testing."

"This research is far too important to be owned by a single company,"
Nik said. "Especially one that condones kidnapping."

Different motives are involved here," Lorillard said. "I can't explain
everything right now."

"Does Dr. Reisman know about this?" As director of the LIFT accelerator,
Reisman had been in charge of its development from its inception.

Pierre Lorillard ignored the question. He was losing his patience. He turned
from the window. "I can assure you, whatever is needed to make you work, it
will be done. We'll start immediately." He walked toward the door.

"I won't cooperate."

"We shall see, my friend," Pierre said, then added in a tone of apology,
"We offered you a great deal of money. None of this would have been
necessary."

In the silence after Lorillard left the room, Nikolai stiffened with rage.
The bastard, he thought. The incredible arrogance of the man.

* * * * *

On the fourth floor of the Chilean Office of National Security in Santiago,
General Enrique Rosales stared, as if for inspiration, at the light-reflecting
crystal of his office chandelier. He was dictating a letter to his aide, Lt. Garcia.
Rosales pronounced each carefully chosen word with patriotic fervor.

"This trial is a violation of my constitutional rights," he said. "The judges
are controlled by the Marxists. I am not going to prison while there is no
justice."

Lt. Garcia finished writing and looked up proudly at the general. "That's
very good, sir."

"The bastards. Tell them this," Rosales said. "Do you want to force another
coup d'etat? Yes, put that down. Let them think hard."

"Yes sir," Garcia said, writing furiously. "Shall I release this to the press
immediately?"

"A military man does not belong in prison," Rosales insisted. "Tell them that, too." His back had been aching badly since the near wedding of his daughter, Lucia. Today he could feel sciatica running the length of both legs.

"Go on," he said, motioning Garcia to hurry. "Tell them what General Enrique Rosales has said."

* * * * *

Clive Bingham had spread the satellite photographs of the LIFT accelerator across his desk at CIA headquarters. He wasn't looking at them, though. He was staring out the window, oblivious to the squirrel insolently leaping from limb to limb.

Twenty-nine years in the service of my country, he thought. What do I have to show for it? Rachel and John are gone, one to California, the other London. Eunice and I rarely see them. The arthritis in my elbow is getting worse, he thought, rubbing his casting arm. He passed his hand over the top of his thinning hair. Eunice kept reminding him that the latest studies indicated baldness meant he was seventy percent more likely to have a heart attack. I just want to get the hell out of here, Clive thought. I want to spend more time on the lake. Before Eunice's prophesies come true. But first I've got to wind up Operation Blue Whale. Clive Bingham pressed the button on his intercom.

"Hambly, bring me that psychological profile on Lorillard again."

"Yes sir," Hambly said, then produced three consecutive sneezes. As if germs might travel through the wires, Bingham yanked his hand away.

"Something's going on down there besides building a proton accelerator," Bingham said before his assistant closed the door. "What in hell is Lorillard really up to? If he's not making a nuclear bomb, then what?"

"That seems to be the question, sir," Hambly said, but he knew it was academic. The threat of nuclear proliferation would be used to justify the operation. If no evidence was found, it would be planted.

"Hell," Bingham said as if he could hear Hambly's thoughts. "The U.S. paid for most of the research that made that damned collider possible anyway." Bingham strode to the window and rested his hands on his hips. Timing was of the essence. Up until now it had been in the United State's interests to allow the completion of the LIFT accelerator. Once they went online, however, and Lorillard announced the success of the first experiment, the world would sing his praises and it would be too late to intercede.

"Aha!" Bingham cried. Hambly jumped, thinking his boss had discovered the answer.

"You're back, you little bastard!" Bingham rapped on the window at the scampering squirrel. "You can't win, you stupid, hairy scavenger." Relishing his certain victory, Bingham chuckled, then remembered the business at hand.

"I want you to call Rosales in Santiago," he said. "Tell him we're going to have to move presently, maybe next week. I don't want to talk to him. Just tell him I'll give him forty-eight hours notice."

"Yes sir," Hambly said and pushed his glasses up his nose. He reached in his back pocket for a well-used handkerchief. "Anything else, sir?"

"Get me Mulroney. I want him to call Admiral Kingsley at the Pentagon. Time to move those aircraft carriers into position off the coast. They'll need three days to reach their destination. They'd better get started."

When Bingham was alone he opened the right hand drawer of his desk. From under a pile of papers he pulled out a color photograph of a lakefront fishing lodge nestled on the edge of a pristine wood. A private pier lead to a small powerboat. On a yellow stickum attached to the bottom of the photo was a note: "For Sale - Owner Anxious - $150,000 Firm."

* * * * *

"We'll visit your mother in a little while," Jean said. She was another spoiled American brat, he thought, but a spunky bitch, and kind of cute in a weird sort of way. He opened his desk drawer and, pulling out his gun, stuffed it in the back waist of his pants. Katya was too busy poking her nose in to the security room electronics to notice.

"I'm hungry," she said.

"What does that mean?" Jean said. "Feed me?"

She glanced over her shoulder at him. "What's your problem?" Had this guy forgotten, Katya wondered, that her mother was running this conference? She rolled her eyes and continued down the row of monitors, her finger trailing a smudge line across each screen. They were all numbered, each one displaying the activity in a different room: people working in a lab, men and women entering the building, secretaries at computers, empty hallways. Only one screen was turned off.

"What's in this room?" Katya asked. Not bothering to look at him, she missed the smirk of delight that spread across his face.

"I'm going to show you in just a minute," Jean said. He stuffed a red bandana in his back pocket and grabbed a piece of plastic cord with a noose at one end.

Katya was busy looking at the largest screen. It was centrally positioned with a row of switches above, all flipped up except one. The picture on the monitor looked like a floor plan, each room outlined in green except one. That room blinked red. Katya reached up and flipped the single down switch to the up position. "OPEN ACCESS" flashed twice. The red room turned green.

"Neat," Katya said and reached for another switch.

"Get your hands off that!" Jean yelled. "Shit!" He hurried over to re-flip the switch. She continued to ignore him until he grabbed her arms and cinched them tightly behind her back.

"What in hell?" she said, furious, then cried out from the unexpected pain.

* * * * *

General Enrique Rosales stood behind his desk, the phone plastered to his bright red ear.

"Tell the president I will not retract my statement," he said. "The day they touch me or one of my men, the rule of law will cease. I cannot be responsible." He slammed the phone down as Lt. Garcia knocked and hurried in.

"Excuse me sir, but there's a special delivery letter. You have to sign for it personally. Garcia escorted the postman into the office and directed him to place the letter on the general's desk. As he signed, Rosales recognized the handwriting on the envelope. His wife had refused to see him since the day of Lucia's wedding. The letter was written on fine linen paper in black ink.

"It is clear to me after your behavior last week that you are incapable of rising above the crudeness of your background. I write to inform you that your daughter will live with me from this time forward. She does not wish to see you. You are never to set foot in my ancestral home again. If I were to pass you on the street, I would not recognize your existence. As far as I am concerned, from this day forward and for the rest of my life, you are dead. Mariel Banderas Rosales."

Enrique Rosales stared at the letter before him. The "crudeness" of my background, he thought. He crumpled the paper in his large hand. So even my family has turned their backs on me.

"Garcia!" he hollered. Framed in black onyx, a photograph of himself,

Mariel, and Lucia rested next to the general's gold nameplate. He grabbed the weighty frame and heaved it across the room. Lt. Garcia walked in as the dangling chandelier crystals shattered and broken glass rained down.

"Yes sir," Garcia said, covering his head with his arms.

General Rosales didn't notice. He stormed to the arching window, and clasping his hands behind his back, he laughed. So they refuse to recognize my existence. We shall see.

"Garcia," he ordered. "Arrange a meeting with special forces. For this afternoon. I'll show them crudeness."

* * * * *

The door to Nikolai Potapov's room flew open and banged hard against the wall. Before him stood his interrogator, his kidnapper: Jean Levesque. But today he was holding a gun to the head of someone else. Blindfolded, she wore a light summer dress and brown hiking boots. Her ears and nose were pierced with rings, her skin darkly tanned. She must have been terrified, but she held her head high. It was Selena's daughter.

"Katya!" Nik said, then demanded of Jean, "What are you doing to her?"

Katya froze at the words she'd just heard. She recognized the voice, the accent. It was him. If Naomi was telling the truth, the man standing right in front of her was her father.

Nikolai's mind was stupefied. What was going on? Had Selena brought her daughter to the conference? Where was Selena? Nik felt a sour fear rise in his gut, as if something very important were at stake, something his body knew, but his mind couldn't grasp. His hand ran through his coarse, thick hair as he struggled to understand.

"This pretty little thing is a surprise for you, doctor," Jean said. "Guess who she is. You want to tell him?" he asked Katya, grabbing hard at her thin arm. She murmured a frightened sound, and pulled her shoulders in tight.

"Tell him," Jean demanded, yanking her closer. "Tell him who he is."

"I think...I think," she said, half scared, half angry. "I think you're my father."

"Louder," Jean insisted. When she didn't answer, he pulled her tied arms painfully high behind her back.

"My father!" she cried, tears and rage choking her.

"Stop it!" Nik cried and angrily started for Jean.

"Stay back," Jean ordered. He cocked the gun and raised it higher, closer to her head. Nik stood in helpless, terrified shock and stared at the girl. This was his child? Selena's? Could this be true? It was impossible to grasp.

Levesque grabbed Katya around the waist and pulled her up against his chest.

"Katya!" Nik cried.

"Stop!" she begged, fighting desperately to break free from Jean's hold. "Help me! Help!"

Hearing the desperation in her voice, Nik remembered the day they had taken his son away, his inability to stop them. At that moment, he knew with certainty he would do anything to save Katya. He must. He started again for Levesque.

"That's far enough!" Jean warned and dragged Katya back against the door. Nik stopped abruptly, only a few feet away. "Your kid's gonna keep me company until you've finished. Call her Miss Motivation," he said and laughed. "I'd advise you to work fast." With a sinister grin he backed out the doorway. "Lorillard's waiting for you at the lab," Jean said. "Better put your thinking cap on if you care about his little piece of candy." Jean laughed then pushed Katya out the door. He slammed it behind them.

Nikolai could hear her cry out. "Stop it! Help me!" Then her young voice was muffled. He ran to the door, but there was only the sound of silenced struggle. Suddenly he could not contain the fury he felt. He banged desperately on the door, kicked and yanked, vainly struggling against the lock, but he knew it was no use.

He had to think clearly. There had to be a way. But even in the desperate moment, he could feel a new, terrifying joy begin to fill his soul. A daughter? His child? Katya? The fear and anger returned, even stronger. She was with that beast.

CHAPTER 11

Through the reading glasses perched on the end of his large nose, Roosevelt Coons looked at the *New York Times* front-page photo. Before a packed ballroom at the Plaza Hotel, he was accepting the Goodson Humanitarian Award for his generous support in the battle against cancer.

Roos Coons folded the newspaper and placed it on the white linen tablecloth next to his empty breakfast plate. Slowly rising, he shuffled his ungainly body through the French doors onto the sunlit tile patio of Zambarano.

A Spanish-style hacienda on the coast of Chile, Zambarano was built in 1888 for the patrones whose peons worked the surrounding land. Now it belonged to Pierre Lorillard, Rossevelt Coons' partner in the LIFT accelerator.

"Don't forget your vitamins and pills, Mr. Coons," Calvin said in his slow, southern drawl. He held the unfinished papaya juice in one hand and five pills in the other. Calvin was an elderly black man, stooped and rather slow moving, and he'd been with Roos for thirty years. "Gotta take care a that heart a' yours, sir."

Roos smiled and took all the pills in one gulp. At eighty-two, the flesh on his face hung in soft jowls, and his bulbous nose was red with broken blood vessels. He looked like a friendly, if sad, basset hound.

As a young man, Roosevelt Coons had served in the Marines at Guadalcanal, then returned to his hometown of Eutaw, Alabama, where he went to work for Abel Vaughan, the owner of a farm supply store. One day a lovely young woman came in to buy supplies for her uncle's pecan grove. Roos had never felt so tongue-tied and awkward in his whole life. As he later told it, from that point on all he could think of was huggin' and kissin' and sloppin' sugar. He and Miriam were married a year later.

While Roos was learning the business from Abel, he was learning a thing or two on his own about banking. He started with a $100 loan from the Hibernia Bank on Courthouse Square. He told Mr. Coleman he wanted to buy a washing machine for his wife. Instead, he held onto the money and a week later walked across town to the Bank of Eutaw. There he borrowed another $100. The next day he returned to the Hibernia Bank and paid Mr. Coleman back, early and with interest.

A few weeks later, Roos Coons visited the Hibernia Bank and took another loan, which they gladly gave him, this time for $250. He used the money to pay back, early and with interest, the loan from the Bank of Eutaw. A month later they gladly lent him $300. Back and forth he went over the next year until he had the trust and respect of both banks. That was the beginning of Coons MeritMarts.

The sea breeze carried the sound of the squawking gulls as Roos looked out at the magnificent Spanish tile pool that cantilevered from the cliffs of Zambarano. The brilliant Chilean sun dazzled the aquamarine water of the private bay just below.

Calvin interrupted Roos' train of thought. "It's nine o'clock, Mr. Coons. I believe Mr. Lorillard's expectin' you."

"Thanks, old buddy," Coons said. "I'm moving slower 'n a swamp today."

Roos lingered in the comfort of the warm sun. That Lorillard sure is a strange coot, he thought. He's a cold fella, and slick as goose grease. 'Cept when it came to that Russian fellow. Roos' mind wandered to that day after the CERN anniversary celebration, when the three of them had flown from Geneva to New York. That was only a week ago, Roos thought, shaking his head, and that handsome young Russian fella was still alive.

They had flown through the night on Lorillard's Gulfstream V jet, each enjoying his own stateroom. During breakfast, Pierre's good-humored but loud voice filled the plush cabin.

"You should have seen Nikolai on the mountain the other day."

The slippers on Pierre's small feet left a trail in the deep gray carpet as he rose from the couch and crossed the room. He stood behind Nikolai, placed his hands on Nik's shoulders.

"He's turned into quite the climber. His style reminds me of my brother Bertrand."

"You mean your brother out in Vancouver?" Roos asked. "Isn't he an artist?"

"That's Michel. He's a flake. Believes in this meditation garbage and magic crystals. A wasted life. Bertrand wasn't like that — he could do anything and make it look effortless. He was supposed to take over the business after the war, but he was killed. In an accident. He'd been home on leave."

A crease of pain lined Pierre's face. He turned to look out the window of the jet.

"My father didn't care about anything or anybody after Bertrand was killed," he said. His voice was hard now, and bitter. "Michel wasn't interested in business, so I stepped in."

"I'm sorry about your brother," Roos said, looking even more hang dog than usual. He'd never known Pierre to speak of Bertrand or to be so emotional. The intensity of his partner's feelings surprised Coons. He recalled having heard a terrible story about the accident, but couldn't remember the details. Roos was gratified, however, to see Pierre feeling such affection for Nikolai.

"Yes, my brother was special." Pierre said. "And sometimes, this fellow reminds me of him."

Roosevelt Coons gazed at the surf crashing against the cliffs of the Chilean coast. Now he remembered the story. The 'accidental' death of Pierre's brother had been at Pierre's own hands. Lord knows, nobody must have blamed the child, Roos thought. He'd been only sixteen or so at the time.

Bertrand had taken his little brother out on the town, introduced him to various manly activities, including a good deal of liquor and the local brothel. On the way home, Bertrand had insisted Pierre drive the car his father had just given Bertrand for his twentieth birthday. Those boys never made it home in one piece.

It was in the fall and the car evidently hit an early patch of ice. Pierre couldn't control the vehicle. It skidded right off a bridge. Fortunately the young boy's window had been open, probably because he'd been so drunk he was woozy and welcomed the cold air. Pierre managed to swim out of the car and reach the surface, expecting his brother to do the same. But Bertrand never made it. Pierre went back for him, over and over again, until he nearly died of hypothermia. Some people passing by dragged the boy to safety. The coroner said the older brother had died instantly from a broken neck.

No charges were ever filed, possibly because of the father's position and wealth. It would not be an easy thing to overcome, though, and Roos had hoped Pierre's affection for Dr. Potapov would bring things full circle, would help to heal the wounds. But now that young man was dead, too.

Roos wondered how much of Pierre's lifetime drive and ambition had been caused by the 'accident.' He'd heard it said that if Lorillard were riding in a canoe, he'd paddle downstream. Roos knew the business Lorillard took over after his brother's death consisted of one travel agency in the city of Montreal. Today it was the undisputed giant of the entire travel and entertainment industry with hotels, resorts, casinos and restaurants. Annual revenues now totaled $12.8 billion. Through the years, Lorillard had remained the sole stockholder. But despite all his success, Pierre was still paddling downstream.

Calvin returned to the patio and opened the gate leading onto the long stretch of lawn. "George called, sir. The helicopter's ready and waiting."

* * * * *

Pierre Lorillard had sent his personal black jet monogrammed with a metallic gray 'L' to pick up Dr. Hartmann in Santiago. As the plane circled the LIFT airstrip, Selena saw the immense project laid out below. The LIFT accelerator was located 120 miles from the coast in the most desolate region of northern Chile, the Salar de Maracunga. The 15.7-mile circumference of the huge underground ring was marked by a "berm." Looking like a gopher mound from the air, in fact it represented massive amounts of earth excavated while digging 150 feet down. The berm created a border for one of the most magnificent architectural structures Selena had ever seen.

From the circle of the ring, an intricate web of structural supports rose to create an open-air dome covering the entire LIFT area. It looked like a spider's web of steel. At the center, ten stories off the ground, an office control pod shaped like a spinning top and serviced by a cylindrical glass elevator capped the dome. From the air the elegance of the LIFT design was remarkable. It was a five-mile-wide network of silver veins joined at the heart, the control pod. The symmetrical lacework of tubing spanned the perfect circle, throwing its spidery shadow across the flat roofs of the huge buildings below.

Heat waves, performing an exotic dance of welcome, levitated around the jet as it pulled to a stop. A silver limousine crawled onto the tarmac. Within moments, Selena emerged into the thick heat and glare of the desert and walked briskly to the car, not waiting for the chauffeur to open her door.

Despite the newly paved blacktop and freshly planted palm trees, the outskirts of the facility looked to Selena like a deserted Arizona subdivision. The geometric shapes of a dozen buildings, some of them massive, rose from the monochrome of sandy, flat landscape. Few people moved through the heat of outdoors. Even the limousine with its dark, tinted windows looked vacant as it snaked quietly through the empty streets.

Through the cool glass of the limo, Selena looked up to see Roosevelt Coons' helicopter hover above the control pod. Then, with amazing agility, the pilot guided the Agusta A109C through the lacework dome.

Just as the helicopter landed Selena's limousine pulled up to the landing pad behind the LIFT administration building Kronos Hall. She saw armed guards turn their backs and cover their faces against the blowing desert sand until the rotors finally whirred to a standstill and the dust settled.

From the safety of the basement security office, Jean Levesque viewed the two arrivals. Standing impatiently before the static and noise on the monitors, he pulverized his chewing gum, the skin across his mutilated ear pulling tight each time he clenched his right jaw. When Dr. Selena Hartmann got out of the limo, he stared without blinking.

She was wearing a white blouse and a pair of linen slacks, wrinkled from the trip. She carried a green canvas duffle bag and a briefcase. Nice ass, Levesque thought. He watched Pierre Lorillard greet her, and Roosevelt Coons amble slowly towards the car with a big, sloppy hello. You'd think they were old friends, Jean thought. What a clown. When the three of them pulled off in the limo, Levesque flipped a switch, and their conversation came through the security room speakers. He turned up the volume.

"Welcome to the LIFT, Dr. Hartmann," Pierre said. "It's an honor to have you. I've been following your work for some time."

She noticed Lorillard's smile lingered as he absorbed and evaluated her appearance.

"I know you must be tuckered out from your trip," Roos said. "But we thought we'd take you on a little driving tour of the compound. You know us boys," he chuckled. "We gotta show off some for the pretty new girl in town. Then we'll let you clean up for this afternoon's presentation."

Her neck was stiff and her stomach upset from too much bad coffee. "That's fine," she said.

"I must offer my condolences about your friend, Nikolai Potapov," Pierre said. "I was quite fond of him. He spoke of you with high regard and affection."

"Yes," Roos said. "I still have a hard time believing that fine young man committed suicide."

"I don't believe it," Selena said matter-of-factly. Pierre looked at her as if he must have misunderstood.

"His death was a great loss for me, too," he said.

"I'm not convinced mourning is in order," Selena said.

Lorillard stared. "I'm sorry. I don't understand."

"Neither do I," she said, then abruptly changed the subject. "Pierre, I was expecting a message from my assistant. How can I check to see if it's come through?"

Pierre dialed the car phone. "Hello, Jean. Dr. Hartmann is expecting an important phone call. Do you have anything?"

Jean's voice came over the speakerphone. "I'll see, Mr. Lorillard."

In the security office at Kronos Hall, Jean Levesque put Pierre Lorillard on hold, then proceeded to hum a few lines of "Your Cheatin' Heart."

"Hello, Mr. Lorillard," Jean said. "I checked, sir. There was a call for Dr. Hartmann from someone named Katya. Should I read it to you, sir?"

"Yes," Selena said, leaning closer to the speaker.

"It says, 'Called to say hi. Everything's fine. On my way home. Will call later. I love you, Katya.' That's it, Dr. Hartmann," Jean said.

"Thank you," Selena said. She looked puzzled. 'I love you'? That didn't sound like Katya. Maybe the trip had done her good. Maybe she wasn't so angry anymore. Selena noticed Pierre watching her reaction and explained, "That's my daughter. I've been anxious to hear from her."

In the security room Jean Levesque laughed. "I'm kinda anxious to hear from her myself," he said. "As a matter of fact, I think I'll pay her a visit this afternoon."

As they passed the administration building, Selena again noticed the name carved over the front entrance: Kronos Hall. That was some mythological character, she thought, but couldn't recall the details. Something to do with a god who swallowed babies, certainly not what I want to think about now.

* * * * *

"Will you look at these," Jean said, marveling at the pastel drawings and oil paintings Katya had created. Her work lay strewn around her "guest" suite at Zambarano. "They're pretty good. Where'd you learn to paint like this?"

Katya looked at him with loathing. She didn't bother to answer. Instead she pulled her white terrycloth robe tighter, covering her blue, knit bikini. For the past two days she'd lived like a princess in a castle, a prisoner confined to a secluded but elegant suite of rooms, the guest compound located on the north side of Zambarano.

For amusement there was a television, videotapes, all the books she could read. For exercise there was a private pool on the patio just outside the French doors of her living room. But all Katya cared to do, all she was able to do, was paint and draw, desperately trying to burn off the anger and fear and frustration she felt, trying to figure out what she could do, how she could escape.

She knew she could easily climb the vine-covered wrought iron fence that enclosed the patio. Jean Levesque had warned her, however. Twelve feet past the gate, an electric fence had been installed. If she tried to leave, her body would be hit with enough volts to stop her dead.

"How about painting something for me?" Jean asked. "I'd like to see how you do it."

Katya stared at him with cold contempt. He had come to see her several times and would hang around, making awkward attempts to be friendly. She thought he was attracted to her and she found that repulsive. As lonely as she felt, she despised this man and didn't bother to hide it. Still, she was terrified inside. The sight of his mutilated face made her shudder.

Lorillard had given orders the girl was to have whatever she wanted, but no visitors except Jean. Her food was brought on a tray and left in a silent waiter. A guard would knock three times a day to let her know the meal was there, then leave without a word.

After a first night of obstinate pacing, Katya had broken down and sobbed, then used the only thing she knew to survive, her art. She spent her time trying to draw and paint the exquisite orchids she'd seen in the rainforest, but the delicate beauty of their shapes had been replaced with sharp, jagged edges, and their lavenders and pale yellows had deepened to savage reds and raging purples, their black centers descending into desolation.

"Better yet," Jean said. "How about doing one of you? Maybe in that black negligee?"

Katya jerked the ends of her bathrobe sash, pulling the knot tighter and tighter.

"What black negligee?" she asked and looked away.

"The one you wear every night."

"How do you know what I wear?" This was impossible, Katya thought. Was he peeping through the windows?

She had bought the Fifties style negligee at a Salvation Army store, stuffed it into her luggage when her mother left the room. After seeing the eco-tour's "accommodations," she decided it would be a waste to wear it.

Jean's eyes lit up with sinister delight, but he refused to speak.

"Are you watching me? How could you know?"

"I have my ways," he said.

Katya pulled the collar of her robe tight around her neck. Her stomach buckled with nausea at the thought of him watching her. She had never felt so violated. She hated him.

"Hey, look at this one." Jean held up a particularly bleak and wrathful picture. "How about letting me have this painting?"

"It's not a painting," Katya said. She marched across the room, pulled the drawing from his hand, and started tearing it up in his face. "It's a pastel. Or don't you know the difference?"

Jean was left with only handful of paper. He went to grab what was left of the picture, but she pulled it farther away, out of his reach. He lunged and grabbed for her, got hold of her arm.

"Give it to me," he said, laughing as if it were all a childish game. He yanked her tight against him.

Katya couldn't stand being touched by him. She tore at the painting, ripped it into tiny pieces and crumpled it. She threw it on the floor, stomped on it.

Jean only laughed harder. "You'll just have to make me another one," he said, not letting go.

Katya started screaming and squirming, but it did no good. He had her in his grip. The futility of her attempts to break free only made him laugh harder.

"Let go of me!" she screamed, then twisted her head as far as she could toward the hand he rested on her shoulder. With bared teeth she went for his fingers, then bit down hard.

"Aghhh!" Jean spun away from her, grabbing his hand in pain. Suddenly he swung and hit her full force on the face with the back of his bleeding hand. The impact sent her sliding across the floor, into the sofa. Katya lay sprawled on her back, her robe falling open around her body. Jean stood over her, his eyes and mouth twisted with hate. She was petrified. What would he do next? The smile that crept across his eyes terrified her.

"Maybe I ought to go see your father about this," Jean said. "Let him know what a bad little girl he has."

Katya tried to hide her confusion. What was Levesque doing? What was he saying to her?

"You don't know what you're talking about," she said, almost spitting the words at him.

Jean snickered and started to walk towards her, but she scrambled to her feet, backed away, her eyes never leaving him. He started to run around the couch, like he was playing chase, joking, then stopped suddenly and laughed.

"Maybe I'll just have to punish your old man, since I can't catch you." He shrugged his shoulders, then walked towards the door, laughing at the shock on her face.

"Maybe you better do a nice drawing for me," he said, holding up the single torn piece of pastel still clutched in his hand. "Maybe then I won't have to visit your dad."

When Jean slammed the door behind him, Katya covered her face as if she could hide from what she'd just heard. Jean Levesque threatening to hurt her father? Why was this nightmare happening to her? Falling on the couch and clutching a pillow to her face, she broke down and sobbed. She cried so hard, it surprised her. Where was all the sadness coming from? She'd never had a father and she'd always believed it was okay. Why the tears now? She told herself she was just frightened, she wanted to go home. At that moment she would have given anything to be safe in her own house, with her mother's arms wrapped around her. She missed her mom more than she'd ever thought possible.

Rising from the couch, she pushed the hair back off her face and walked onto the patio, sitting beside the pool. With her shoulders slumped, her feet dangling in the cool water, she wondered. Who was he, this Nikolai Potapov? Levesque said she was being held as insurance until her father completed his work. Then she would be allowed to leave. As much as Katya wanted to, she couldn't believe Levesque would ever let her go.

Seagulls squawked in the sky overhead and Katya cringed. Suddenly she felt very frightened she would never get out of this place. Now, with her father so close, she realized she wanted to more than ever before.

CHAPTER 12

Magnified against the stage wall, the diagram of the LIFT accelerator held the attention of the entire auditorium. In his excitement, Dr. Henry Reisman swung the pointer light around the circumference of the ring, spittle flying from his dentures as he explained.

"The LIFT will put the energy of a rocket behind two particles, then send them on a demolition derby with death. The protons will shriek off in opposite directions and create the ultimate, subatomic pandemonium."

He must be in his 80's, Selena thought, looking at the stooped shoulders under Reisman's white lab coat. But he's jumping around on the stage like Michael Jackson. She noticed he had a nervous habit of adjusting and readjusting his hearing aid by turning his finger in his ear, as if he were screwing and unscrewing a bolt in his brain.

"The LIFT," Reisman continued, "will do for physicists what microscopes do for biologists or what telescopes do for astronomers. It will allow us to see into nature, to probe beneath the surface of things."

Behind the draped table on the right side of the stage, Selena slid a black high-heel off her size ten foot. Relief was immediate. She tried not to sigh into the microphone, but caught Roosevelt Coons smiling at her from across the stage. Returning her attention to the presentation, Selena noticed Reisman's bushy gray eyebrows were raised in perpetual alarm. It wasn't amazement, though. From what she'd heard, suspicion was more likely. He was a disappointed man.

After supervising the construction of the Stanford Linear Accelerator, he ran Fermilab in Illinois, and later became Director of the Superconducting Super Collider in Texas. When funding for the SSC was threatened, Reisman testified before congressional hearings as to the value of the research, but the SSC budget was cut severely, and finally eliminated. Reisman grew disheartened. It was then his wife left him. She said he only loved his work; he would hardly miss her. She'd been right.

But now as Director of the LIFT accelerator, he would live to conduct the first experiments, to discover what the universe was like milliseconds after the Big Bang. He would finally be recognized by not only the scientific community, but by the world.

"Once we've pushed the particles to nearly the speed of light, we'll force them to collide," Reisman said. He hammered his two fists together. "They'll literally smash each other to bits. That's our goal, to pulverize the proton down to its essence, expose the hidden particles of the subatomic world."

Selena watched the audience. The presentation was the opener for the asteroid symposium and an effective public relations ploy. Pierre Lorillard had begun with a brief speech, introduced Henry Reisman, and then disappeared. Representative Chapman wasn't due until tomorrow, but press turnout was already more than Selena anticipated.

She noticed both Roosevelt Coons and the audience of astronomers looked like they were mesmerized by a startling science fiction movie. Reisman himself stood under the black banner of "Lorillard Industries Future Technology" like a kid beaming with excitement at his new toy. It was a thrilling time in physics, she thought, and then remembered Nik. Turning his turquoise ring around her finger, she closed her palm over the stone. Nik's life's work had contributed to the LIFT technology. He would be missing so much.

"It will take approximately three million trips around the track for the protons to build up sufficient speed," Reisman said in conclusion. "The collision will generate a fireball of energy greater than the simultaneous output of all the power plants on earth, compressed into a space smaller than a single proton."

Applause reverberated through the hall, and Reisman quickly adjusted the volume of his hearing aid. Behind the draped table Selena rose, keeping one bare foot on tiptoe for balance. She was anxious to wind up the presentation because she wanted to try Charlie again. So far, she'd gotten only the answering machine. Could she be on her way? Why hadn't she called?

"Our hosts have agreed to take questions," Selena said. "Let's start right here." She pointed to a young man in a maroon CALTECH sweatshirt.

"Mr. Coons," he said. "You're American, but your partner, Pierre Lorillard, he's from Canada. The accelerator's in Chile. Who's going to benefit from this proton smasher?"

"That's a mighty good question," Roos said, rising slowly from his seat. His Alabama accent slowed and softened his words. "As you may know, young man, Coons' MeritMarts became quite a success." He scratched a wiry eyebrow. "We sold enough masking tape last year to wrap the face of the earth twenty layers deep." The audience laughed. "So I made sure all the medical benefits from this super collider here could be used at bare bones cost."

"But what about the other research?" the student insisted. "It's estimated superconductor technology will be a ninety-billion-dollar business."

"That end of the deal belongs to my partner, so you'll have to ask him." Coons shook his head and chuckled. "But watch out. He's got a reputation for being eccentric. Unlike myself, of course." The audience laughed as Coons took his seat.

Selena had to admit there was a certain endearing hokeyness to the man, although she couldn't help but distrust anyone who'd made so much money. He also carried the nasty smell of cigars with him. Ever since Selena quit smoking, her nose had become so sensitive she didn't know if it was a curse or a blessing. By now both Selena's shoes were off, and there was no need to stand on tiptoe.

"Yes, Professor Atkins," she said, pointing to a fellow faculty member.

"Mr. Coons," Atkins asked, "Do you really think this particle accelerator will lead to weapons in the fight against cancer?"

As he rose to address the question, Coons' crusty, large hand fumbled for the gold pocket watch hidden in his vest.

"Son, this proton collider makes about as much sense to me as shooting a twelve-gauge shotgun at my grandfather's watch just so's I can figure out what makes the darned thing tick. But I have to tell ya, when my Miriam was taken from me seven years ago, those last years we had together...." He hesitated for a moment, his thoughts seeming to go someplace private. "Well, they were the most precious in my life, and they would never have been possible if it weren't for science. And for Dr. Henry Reisman here." Coons looked around, his face lit with an affectionate grin, but Reisman had left the stage.

Roos shrugged and continued. "Henry used one of these crazy proton colliders up at Fermilab to shoot beams of neutrons into her tumor. That's what kept her alive. Now Miriam and I weren't blessed with children, and it's my belief the Good Lord had other things in mind for my money. So when Dr. Henry told me about the LIFT and introduced me to Pierre, well, ya know, folks, I'm old enough to realize it ain't a joke. You really can't take it with you!"

It sounds wonderful, Selena thought, but there were many who felt Reisman had milked Coons to build the LIFT. With the proton collider completed, Reisman could make one last play for the precious Nobel. Lorillard's involvement was another matter. He had started the project and used Reisman to recruit Coons and his money, but his motives were self-serving, not philanthropic. Lorillard Superconductor, Inc., would benefit immensely from the ongoing research.

Before Selena could conclude the presentation, the photographers began flashing pictures and calling out questions, mostly about the potential asteroid collision.

"Dr. Hartmann," a man from the *Los Angeles Times* called out. "What's the word? Is it headed our way?"

Selena thanked Roos Coons, made some quick concluding remarks about the symposium, and then quickly left the stage, ignoring the reporters' questions. She wasn't prepared to share the answers she'd found at Keck. At least not yet.

* * * * *

Nikolai Potapov found himself staring out the barred window of a small laboratory in the LIFT control pod, eleven stories up. His eyes rested on the horizon, miles across the flat desert, but he saw nothing. He could only think of the young woman, of Selena's daughter. His daughter.

Lorillard had set the ground rules. Any attempt to escape or communicate with others would mean immediate punishment of Katya. If Nikolai cooperated, they would both be allowed to go free when the formula was completed and thoroughly tested. Katya would be 'found' in Santiago, the unharmed victim of a failed ransom attempt by guerilla forces. Nik would be given a new identity, a position at a prestigious university, and allowed to continue with his work. That is, unless he wanted to stay at the LIFT. But Lorillard had given his word. No one would be harmed.

Nik didn't really believe any of it. Still, he could not contain the sense of hope there might still be happiness after all the years of mourning and bitterness. With just the thought of his son, Nik's chest grew hollow and sick. The familiar pain would never leave him, he knew. The sorrow had become a part of his body, of his internal system, of his breathing. Like a terminal disease, it had infiltrated his cells and destroyed his life.

It wasn't my wife's fault, he thought. If anything, I was more responsible. She wanted to go on with life, to stop the suffering. I couldn't. But there was more to it than that. We were dead to each other even before Yuri's death.

But now the joy, the excitement just to be alive. Why didn't I go to Selena earlier, when I first arrived in the States? All those years in Russia I had thought of her. And this last year was the loneliest of my life. I felt I had lost everything, my son, my marriage, my work, even my country. Nik told himself he had been afraid to presume after fifteen years. But there was more to it, he knew. He had been afraid of caring again, afraid of more loss.

Nikolai blinked and focused his eyes on the bars that secured his window. He could not risk harm to Katya, but the thought of giving Lorillard the formula for room-temperature superconductors sickened him. What choice did he have? If only he could plan an escape. He grimaced at the remembrance of Jean Levesque. I must hurry with the work, he thought. Katya is with that animal.

* * * * *

The Magnet Test Laboratory, a fifty-thousand-square-foot building, was the final quality control stop before the superconducting magnets were installed in the proton accelerator. Dr. Henry Reisman stormed through the rows of newly compounded magnets, hurrying to catch up with Lorillard.

"But will they hold when we start ramping?" Reisman demanded. "We must be certain."

Pierre Lorillard's voice echoed off the walls of the immense building.

"They're ready," he said, slapping his hand on the glossy black surface of a fifty-five-foot-long dipole magnet tube. "It's time."

Lorillard knew that the world was full of naysayers who felt they must mind other people's business. He understood that once the LIFT had completed a successful experiment, the international community would jump on his bandwagon, but until that time, his project was in danger.

"We've got to perform a few more tests," Dr. Reisman said agreeably. "It won't take long."

"We must go ahead, Henry," Pierre insisted. "I didn't get where I am today by being overly cautious."

Reisman adjusted his hearing aid once again. He couldn't believe what Lorillard was saying.

"You don't understand," Henry said. "When you drive a car around a corner it's harder to steer if you're going fast, right? These magnets must be extremely powerful to keep the speeding particles on course. If one is faulty, it could 'quench.' It would lose its superconductivity and create a disastrous chain reaction. There's no point in taking chances now."

"Carpe diem, my friend," Lorillard said. "Seize the day." Reisman was the one who didn't understand. The more time spent testing and re-testing only gave the U.S. more opportunity to meddle. If you wanted control on sharp corners, the smartest thing to do was to accelerate.

"But this is science, not business," Reisman said. If the magnets fail, we'll have to retrace our steps and start again."

"You've examined the specifications," Pierre said calmly. "You've told me that theoretically there's no reason why the magnetic compounds won't work, isn't that true?"

"Yes, but..." Henry said. His throat tightened and his voice became strident. He began to spit his words. "What if we're wrong?"

"Henry, this is going to win you the Nobel," Lorillard said. "Begin final installation immediately."

"But, Pierre...!" Henry was almost shrieking.

"It should be completed within thirty-six hours. No more talk. I want it done. Do you understand?"

Gurgling sounds of distress continued to come from Reisman's throat, but he had nothing else to say. What could be done? The fools of the world didn't realize the importance of his work, and once again they were going to interfere.

* * * * *

Selena stood at the entrance to the Kronos Conference Center still worried. At least you know Katya is all right, she told herself. After skipping the group tour of the control pod to catch up on some details, Selena tried another call to Charlie. Still no contact. And no one at the school had seen her. Their presentation was scheduled for the day after tomorrow.

As Pierre Lorillard's limousine pulled up to the steps, she wondered. Why hasn't Charlie called? If she doesn't get here in time, should I tell the truth, that Hartmann 2009 is on a collision course with Earth? The press will have a hay day; the conservatives will go wild. I'll single handedly ensure passage of Star Wars. The thought made her shudder and she was glad to put it away.

Selena took a seat inside the dark, cool limo next to Roos Coons. She noticed Lorillard seemed excited and confrontational, the way little boys act when they're attracted to little girls, she thought.

"So tell me, Dr. Hartmann," Pierre said. "Do you believe we're alone in the universe?"

Selena perceived an air of braggadocio about Lorillard, a 'dare me' gleam in his small eyes. It was a challenge she found hard to resist.

"It's not a matter of belief," she said. "At this point it's all speculation. I'm interested in finding out for certain." He's looking for intellectual combat, she thought. And he's confident he'll win.

"What about the SETI project?" Pierre asked. "They were searching for a message from another planet. Don't you agree with your fellow scientists? A signal could be out there, just waiting for us to be receptive."

Roos chimed in. "Don't you figure we pretty well got our hands full already? You know, when you go prayin' for rain, you gotta deal with the mud."

"They've listened to tens of millions of different frequencies," Selena said, playing the devil's advocate. "They've used a computerized analyzer, sorting the information in seconds. But they haven't come up with anything. Not one knock on our door."

"Yet!" Pierre said. "But there are billions of possible frequencies that might carry a signal. They haven't even scratched the surface."

"SETI examined 700 stars," Selena said. "They found nothing but cosmic silence."

"That leaves over 399 billion stars to go." Pierre grinned triumphantly. "I'd say the odds are in our favor."

"It's still only speculation. I'm interested in facts."

"But what about life?" Pierre insisted. "Is it out there?"

Selena crossed her legs. Lorillard's eyes followed the shimmering line of her hose. "It sounds like you're convinced," Selena said. "I'm certainly not. I assume you're familiar with the Fermi Paradox? If they're out there, then why haven't they been here already?"

"I don't have to tell you the standard response to that," Pierre said.

"Somebody better tell me," Roos said. With a befuddled expression, he looked back and forth between the two of them.

Pierre held out his hand to Selena. "Be my guest," he said.

Selena thought he looked pleasurably excited, almost sexually, at the intellectual sparring match. She explained to Roos. "If we're as inconsequential to aliens as the ants are to us, the theory goes, why would they bother? How many ant civilizations did you investigate on your last picnic?"

Pierre could hardly wait for her to finish. "What makes you so sure they haven't?"

He looks like he just won King of the Mountain, Selena thought, as they arrived at the accelerator entrance.

"Why are you so interested in the search for life on another planet?" she asked.

"It's the most profound question I know," he said. "Are we alone? If we are, what does that mean? Is our little blue planet the only one that can sustain life in this mighty universe? I think it's highly unlikely, don't you?"

"I can certainly understand your eagerness to find out," Selena said. "I suffer from the same impatience."

Donning hardhats, they entered the massive elevator. Pierre was suddenly mumbling to himself about the hat, sounding irritated by the necessity of wearing one. Selena noticed security was tight.

"There's no potential military use for an accelerator." Selena looked directly in Lorillard's eyes as the high-speed elevator plummeted. "Little threat of terrorists. Why so many guards? What are you afraid of?"

"When those beams of protons start smashing into each other," Pierre said, his forehead uncharacteristically creased and moist. "We want to be sure there aren't any scientists or technicians in the tunnel. There's no room for accidents at the LIFT."

"But why do they need guns?" she asked, pressing her point. Lorillard looked older, she thought, and wondered if it was the light. Just then the elevator doors opened, and Pierre rushed out, ignoring her question. He hurried over to Dr. Reisman who was enjoying the attention of a small group of reporters. Together they proceeded down a fifty-foot corridor, their footsteps echoing in the underground chamber.

"Well, what do you think so far?" Roos asked her.

"Extraordinary," Selena said.

"Wait until you see one of our detectors," Pierre said over his shoulder. He looked torn between his excited pride and whatever was making him anxious.

"How did they actually dig the tunnel?" Selena asked.

"They used a monster boring machine," Roos said. "Sorta like a dentist's drill, only fourteen feet across. Ouch! Just clawed right through the rock and shale, then spit it out."

Selena noticed Pierre was being unusually quiet. She had the distinct impression he didn't like being underground. They stopped briefly at the entrance to the fourteen-foot-wide circular tunnel of the accelerator. Two tubes of long, glossy black magnets were horizontally suspended along the far wall. The cylinders stretched in both directions as far as she could see, one tube on top of the other. It was an eerie place, she thought, but the air was dry and remarkably scent-free. Reisman turned to the left. They followed the curve of the tunnel until they reached the entrance to an underground hall.

"The beams will travel through the magnets a distance equivalent to 180 round trips from the earth to the sun," Reisman said.

"Those must be numbers you can relate to," Pierre said, as if daring her not to be impressed.

"And this is where the protons will collide," Henry said, stepping into the cavernous hangar and pointing to the far wall. Selena looked up in a state of absolute awe. Rising five stories before her stood a monstrous bulls eye of a machine. Every inch of space in the enormous circular structure was intricately wired. It looked like an elaborately veined and multi-colored cornea. Electronic, optical, and energy-sensing devices encircled the 'eye' of the detector. Each part was tailor-made to pick up specific information from particles that would exist for less than a billionth of a second. Selena was familiar with impressive astronomical equipment, but the detector was like nothing she'd ever seen. Its sheer size alone was difficult to comprehend. The intricacy of the device was mind blowing.

"They tell me that baby weighs as much as a battleship," Roos said.

"The detector will catch the colliding particles, record their speed, direction, and type," Dr. Reisman said proudly. "Our physicists will analyze the information later."

This was quite a toy they'd built for particle physicists, Selena thought. She knew there was a certain amount of jealousy going around. At least the U.S. government was no longer threatening to wipe out the budget for small science by using all the funds to build the Superconducting Super Collider in Texas. A lot of scientists were happy about that.

"What about radiation?" she asked. "Is that a danger?"

"The only significant radiation will be the showers of fast-moving particles from the collision," Reisman said. "The detectors will absorb most...."

Selena literally jumped in her skin as an appalling alarm shrieked through the detector hall. She saw Pierre Lorillard panic, his eyes darting, hunting for danger. He ran towards the door. Roos Coons mouth hung open. Only Henry Reisman remained unfrightened. He was too busy being furious. Selena couldn't hear him because of the alarm, but he was giving someone hell. And his words seemed to be directed towards Pierre. When the alarm ceased as abruptly as it began, Reisman's shrill words trailed into the warp of silence.

"....told you it's too soon, you fool!"

Pierre Lorillard stared, his forehead and eyes still stretched in panic. He said nothing. On the loudspeaker a computerized voice reassured them in electronic monotone.

"The situation is secure. All cause for alarm is over. The situation is secure."

"I think it's time to move upstairs." Lorillard sounded more than anxious. Turning abruptly to a nearby uniformed guard he said, "Call security." He sounded irritated. "Tell them to have George prepare the helicopter."

Roos looked at Pierre with raised eyebrows. It always amazed him how readily Lorillard ordered Roos' own pilot around. What was the matter with the weasel now? Roos wondered. He's bein' a bit of a crosspatch, if you ask me. Ever since we came down here to the ring. As a matter of fact, the same thing happened before, last time we were down here. Then Roos remembered the car accident with Pierre's brother. How he had gone back down, over and over again, to try to save Bertrand. How his brother had stayed in the car, deep under the surface of the water. Maybe Lorillard just didn't like being underneath anything, Roos thought. Maybe that's why he always liked to be on top.

"Dr. Hartmann," Pierre said, taking charge. "Mr. Coons and I will show you to your visitor's cottage. It's late. I'm sure you must be tired."

You don't know the half of it, Selena thought. She was anxious to get back to her room and check her e-mail. There had to be a message from Charlie by now.

CHAPTER 13

"Dr. Hartmann?" The young woman with the camera hustled up the stairs right beside Selena, shooting one frame after another. "Any word for us, Doctor?"

The press contingent must have doubled over night, Selena thought as she entered Kronos Conference Hall. The reporters continued to call to her, pressing for an answer.

"Are we headed for a collision?"

"How close will it come?"

"My presentation is tomorrow afternoon," Selena answered without slowing down.

"How about a comment on Mr. Lorillard, then," a young man said, brushing his hair off his forehead, pen in hand.

"He's a powerful man. And a gracious host." She pushed through the glass doors. The reporter stayed right behind her.

"Half the buildings around here are named after Kronos. Any chance Lorillard has an over-inflated ego?" the reporter asked.

"You'll have to help me," Selena said. "My Greek mythology is slipping."

"Kronos, King of the Universe. A real doozy. Killed his father then married his sister and ate five of their babies. She hid the sixth one and gave him a stone to swallow instead."

"Kronos and Lorillard. Colorful guys," Selena said, the story coming back to her. There was something else to it, she knew, but was too harried to think of it just then. Making her way through a crowd of astronomers, she hurried up the stage steps, leaving the reporter in her wake.

Time was running out. She had sent Charlie three e-mails, two last night and one again this morning. Still no response. Could she be on a plane to Chile, disc in hand? Wouldn't she have written or called first? The presentation was scheduled for tomorrow afternoon and Charlie knew that. Could something have happened to her? Surely, Selena told herself, I would have been notified. But what if the disc had been tampered with? Could Charlie be in danger? Selena shuddered, told herself no, she was just too keyed up.

The relentless questions from the press weren't helping matters. Even her call to Katya hadn't gone through. Selena shook her head as she assembled the papers on the table. The operator said the phone at Naomi's house was temporarily out of order. On top of everything else, the shark incident in Hawaii continued to haunt her. She would put another call through to Bingham. As soon as she had a chance.

Standing behind the draped table on stage, Selena looked out at the slowly filling auditorium and quickly bit the ragged cuticle of her index finger until it bled. She was beginning to feel her efforts were star-crossed. Grinning to herself, she recalled Charlie had made some dire astrological predictions in Hawaii. The details eluded her, but no matter. Selena would have dismissed them anyway.

Selena took her seat and reviewed the day's scheduled presentations. That afternoon Pierre Lorillard was flying her to his estate on the coast for dinner with Representative Chapman. She was looking forward to learning the latest lineup of votes on the Star Wars bill, and what their chances were to block passage. It was going to be close.

* * * * *

The brush laden with black oil paint streaked across the face of the lavender orchid, obliterating its loveliness. Katya was destroying her work, ravaging it in her desperation.

"I hate him. I hate him." With each word she made another black slash. "He's never going to touch me again."

Ever since Levesque's comment about the black negligee, she knew he was watching her. After searching in vain for cameras, she'd hidden in the closet to undress, hadn't even touched the black negligee.

Katya dropped her paintbrush into the jar of turpentine and fell back into a chair, her paint-covered hands dangling off the upholstered arms. Jean Levesque would be back soon, probably tonight. She had to do something. She couldn't cry anymore. She wouldn't let herself.

If this Nikolai Potapov was really her father, if it was true Jean Levesque might try to hurt him, then what did Levesque intend to do to her? She couldn't just wait and see. Katya pulled herself upright in the chair. She had to try to get out of this place. She had to escape. But how? She'd tried calling the guard who delivered her food, but he either couldn't hear her or refused to respond.

Washing up at the kitchen sink, Katya wondered how Levesque managed to get through the electrified fencing when he came to visit her. He must turn the power off at the main house, she thought. That means I could get out of here. But I'd have to fight him. I know I'm not strong enough, unless I can figure out something to help me. I've looked all through this place for some sort of weapon, a knife, a fireplace iron, anything that could do some damage to that pig.

Katya reached for the can of turpentine. It was almost empty. Pouring some on a rag, she began to rub at her hands. The smell was obnoxious, she thought, her eyes resting on the warning label, printed in bold red letters: "DANGER! Combustible liquid and vapor. Keep away from heat, sparks, flame. Causes severe skin and eye irritation. Harmful or fatal if swallowed." Suddenly she had an idea.

If she could just get Jean Levesque to visit again. With the thought of being free, of leaving this prison, Katya tried to see over the wall, pushing up onto the tip of her toes like a child reaching for an ice cream cone. Oh God! To see her mother again.

But the vision of Levesque's ugly face quickly doused her hope with fear. God, what if it didn't work? What would he do to me? she wondered. Leaning against the counter for support, she took a deep breath and tried not to imagine.

Should I do it? she wondered. Or would it be a totally stupid move?

* * * * *

Unable to sleep most of the night, Nikolai Potapov had risen early to work on two projects: his superconducting formula and his escape plan. Either could hold the key to saving Katya and himself.

He felt certain there was a specific, immediate application Pierre had in mind for the superconducting formula. The most obvious use would be for the LIFT accelerator. Therein lay the danger.

Nik rose from the computer and strode to the control pod window. The sun had just come up on the wide expanse below, but already the desert looked parched and hot to the touch.

He knew that in the accelerator the electromagnetic force must be exact. If painstaking care were not taken, the consequences could be disastrous. Was there a way he could fool Lorillard and safely alter the formula? Searching for a loophole, he went back to the basics and reviewed cause and effect.

By passing electric current through a superconducting wire, magnetic fields were produced. These powerful, superconducting magnets would be used to propel the proton beams around the underground racetrack. But when electricity passes through a wire, it encounters resistance because wire is a substance, and all substance consists of atoms, always in motion, vibrating about chaotically and colliding. The faster the atoms gyrate, the higher the temperature produced because the electricity must force its way through the dancing atoms of the wire, using up some energy that turns into heat. As a result, the wire grows hot and only some of the electricity manages to get through.

At extremely low temperatures, close to 'absolute zero,' the atoms in the wire stop cavorting. Instead, they line up in an orderly fashion against the wall, like shy boys at a cotillion. They no longer resist. Hence, none of the passing electrical energy is lost to heat.

Nik crossed his arms on his chest and scratched his beard. The LIFT magnets must carry an incredible amount of current to exert the necessary force. So long as they remain superconducting, they provide no resistance to this current and therefore produce no heat.

Walking across the room, Nik considered the alternative. If the magnets should "quench" or 'go normal' and lose their superconductivity, the sudden resistance would produce dangerous amounts of heat. The magnets would....

"Good morning, doc."

The door slammed and Nikolai turned to find Jean Levesque grinning at him.

"Just thought you'd like to know how your little girl is doing," Jean said. "And I brought you some photos of an old friend." Levesque threw an envelope onto the lab counter. Several photos slid out, partially revealing the emaciated body of Marfa Ivanovna.

* * * * *

When Selena finally received e-mail from Charlie at lunchtime, she at first felt immensely relieved, then immediately choked with frustration. She decided she must look at the Keck results once more. It was futile, she knew, but she had to try anyway. Besides, she wanted to check the status of the bolometer project at the superconductor lab. She could use their mainframe to do the Keck calculations.

The Lorillard Superconductor Laboratory was an immense hangar of a building. Various workshops flanked both sides: a machine shop, a maintenance room, a welding shop, storage rooms, and a conference room. The central stretch of lab space was divided into three large work areas. Up above, a mezzanine provided office space. The lab was a scurry of activity, but when she found the work area for the superconducting bolometer, no one was around.

"Hi, I'm Mick." The voice came from under a workshop table. Selena watched a prematurely balding young man with one earring crawl out on his hands and knees. "Dropped my contact," he said. He gingerly held the lens on the tip of his right index finger. "The main technician's at lunch. I'm his assistant."

Standing up, the young man rinsed the lens in his mouth and reinserted it as Selena introduced herself.

"I know who you are," Mick said. "I saw a newscast of your testimony before Congress. Very good stuff."

"Thanks," Selena said. "I hope it does some good."

"You better put one of those on," Sadler said, indicating a row of hooks strung with white lab coats. "Company rules." He rolled his eyes.

Selena slipped on a lab coat with the familiar Lorillard 'L' over the breast pocket. You could never forget whose show this was, she thought.

Mick gave her a brief but thorough review of the SCB project. The two-foot-wide rectangular mechanism would fit under the Hale telescope. Its sensitive superconductive filaments were framed by steel-encased electronics that would feed the data to a computer.

"It's a beauty," Mick said. To Selena, it looked like a work of art.

"Can I plug into your mainframe?" she asked. "I've got some calculations I need to look at. My laptop can't handle it."

"Sure," Mick said, showing her the connection.

While setting up, Selena noticed a steel double door marked 'OFF LIMITS' along the back wall.

"What's that all about?" she asked.

"Another lab," he said. "Word is they're working on SQUIDS. Top Secret bullshit. Very high security. Listen, I'll just be over there. Holler if you need me."

"Thanks," Selena said. Her screen lit up, but before she submerged herself into the complexities of the orbit of Hartmann 2009, she brought up the search menu and typed in SQUIDs, then hit enter and scrolled the information on the screen, most of which was familiar to her.

Superconducting Quantum Interference Devices were the most sensitive detectors of any kind available to scientists. While only about two microns wide, they consisted of several complex layers of thin superconducting film and operated on a quantum-mechanical phenomenon.

At extremely low temperatures where electrons couple together, they form waves. These waves can be thrown out of sync by even the weakest magnetic fields. SQUIDs are such supersensitive magnetic sensors that they can measure these fluctuations. Similar to radar on a submarine, the SQUID will scan an area with a rotating, sweeping sensor, and map the spatial variations. After one sweep it feeds a computer and creates a two-dimensional image, producing a contour map that effectively reconstructs the region.

Best known for their medical diagnostic applications, SQUIDs were also used to detect minute interior defects in metallic structures, such as airplane wings. Geologists relied on them to prospect for petroleum. One of the most promising uses was in geophysics research to determine subsurface composition in inaccessible locations.

The article went on to indicate that like other superconductor applications, SQUIDs had their limitations. Low-temperature SQUIDs were expensive and lacked mobility. High-temperature SQUIDs created thermal noise and gave less precise measurements. What was needed was a SQUID with super sensitivity and a low noise factor that could operate at a high temperature allowing for mobility at less expense.

And that's exactly where Nikolai's formula would fit in! Selena thought.

* * * * *

This was perfect, he thought. Lorillard would have to agree. Jean Levesque relished the thought of Nikolai Potapov's sad face when he told him the bad news about Dr. Hartmann. Holding the receiver between his shoulder and good left ear, Levesque punched in the number eighty-nine.

"What is it?" Pierre's voice blared through the phone. "I'm busy here with Dr. Reisman."

"I think you better come over here, sir. There's something you need to see right away."

"This better be good," Pierre said and slammed down the phone.

Jean dragged his mouse across the computer screen and within moments the printer produced four pages of e-mail, the last one addressed to hartmann@caltech.edu from charlie@caltech.edu. Jean's eyes squinted in anticipation.

"We've got a problem with that woman," Levesque said as Pierre stormed into the office.

"What woman?" Lorillard demanded.

"Hartmann. Here. Read this. Start with the first one."

Jean pushed the pages of e-mail into Lorillard's hand, then crossed his arms and waited. Pierre scanned the pages.

"....waiting to hear from you. Did you find the disc? Let me know....increasingly suspicious of Lorillard's involvement with Nik's....he'd be highly motivated to get his hands on the formula...evidence I found in Hawaii....don't think Nik committed suicide...never made any sense...."

"....receive my last e-mail? What's your arrival time....Let me know ASAP about the findings on the disc. Did they corroborate our initial results from Palomar? Were we right? Did someone tamper with the disc in Hawaii? I've got to know before the...."

"....decided I have no choice but to reveal all the findings, even the conflicting evidence....know what this will do to the Star Wars vote, but what if I'm wrong and Hartmann 2009 is on a collision course with Earth? Please contact me...."

Jean watched Pierre's face as he read the words, but Lorillard showed no emotion. Jean had told him the woman was trouble.

"Take a look at this one," Jean said, handing the final sheet to Pierre. It was another e-mail, only this time addressed to Selena.

> *Sorry not to get back to you sooner. I'm afraid I can't make it to Chile in time for the conference. You'll have to go ahead without me. Good luck. You're going to need it.*
>
> *The mailed disc definitely confirms our Keck results. Completely. No one could have tampered with this disc, Selena. It appears Hartmann 2009 is headed our way. I encourage you to announce this at the conference. I know it's not what we hoped for, but the Keck telescope isn't wrong.*

The letter was signed Charlie.

Turning his back on Jean, Pierre walked quietly to the window.

"She thinks she's found evidence the Russian didn't commit suicide," Jean said.

"She can't make that announcement," Pierre said, ignoring Jean. "Star Wars will certainly pass. I can't have it."

"We've got to take care of her," Jean said.

Pierre turned and gave Levesque a look of contempt. The man was too full of hate to grasp the situation. Someone had skewed Hartmann's research with this conference in mind. Who? He would have to find out.

"Dr. Hartmann has proven valuable to me," Lorillard told Jean.

"We've got all her research," Jean said. "Somebody else will take over where she left off."

"Why are you so anxious?" Pierre asked.

"She's gonna make trouble. You don't want that. Not now." Lorillard seemed to be struggling with the decision and blaming Jean. What's the big deal, Jean thought.

Pierre turned slowly and walked to the door.

"All right," he told Levesque. He didn't sound pleased. "We must be absolutely certain it looks like an accident. I can't afford to upset Dr. Potapov any more than necessary."

Jean's jaw flexed upon hearing the words. Lorillard was always protecting the Russian. But this time he was too late.

"Do you understand me, Jean?"

Levesque stared at his boss' obstinate expression. Lorillard was waiting for an answer.

"Yes sir," Jean answered bitterly.

CHAPTER 14

Pierre was late when he picked Selena up at the guest cottage. He seemed a jumble of emotions, one minute distraught, the next excited, as if something bad was threatening to spoil the special occasion he'd planned.

"Come along now. We don't want to miss the sunset at Zambarano." Selena hurried into the limo with her briefcase. "Bring it, if you must," he said. "But no one does paperwork in heaven, Doctor."

Despite the pleasant words, his smile was strained. In the flex of his jaw and narrowing of his small eyes, she saw his effort to suppress what looked like anger.

"Is something wrong?" she asked. Lorillard chuckled as if the possibility were ludicrous. He changed the subject.

"Another guest this evening will be General Enrique Rosales," he said. "From the Chilean Army. Perhaps you've read about him. I thought you might find some local color entertaining."

"Is that a warning?" Selena said. Again Lorillard laughed.

"You're a very clever woman, Dr. Hartmann." He held her eyes. "And remarkably beautiful, I might add."

For a moment Selena thought she saw remorse, perhaps resignation, in his pressed lips. She nodded and considered asking him some other clever questions like, What do you plan to do with the SQUIDs? and What do you think really happened to Nikolai Potapov? But the limo was already pulling up behind Kronos Hall, and Roos Coons was waving to them.

"Here's the weasel now," Coons said as the car came to a stop. They walked together toward the chopper. "And here's our lovely California rose. What about Representative Chapman?"

"He's arriving later this evening. At Zambarano," Pierre said. He turned to look when a door slammed.

Selena saw a tall, thin man with a streak of white hair over his forehead strut into the late afternoon heat. He carried a briefcase.

"Please take your seats," Pierre said. The testiness in his voice had returned. Coons continued talking to his pilot and the strange man with the white-streaked hair took a seat up front. Selena got in the back. The man looked over his left shoulder, leered at her, then smiled.

"Jean," Pierre said sternly. "I'll send the copter back for you." Selena watched the man look around the aircraft as if he were counting seats. It was then she noticed the scarring on the right side of his face. He seemed puzzled, but grabbed his briefcase and got out without saying a word. Selena thought he looked angry.

"Report to me as soon as you arrive," Pierre called out. The man didn't look back or respond. When he turned onto the sidewalk, Selena saw the scarred side of his face once again. He stared at her for a moment before entering the building. She realized what really frightened her wasn't the damage to his face, but his eyes. They looked menacing even when his other features were expressionless.

The copter swooped up through the latticework of the LIFT web and headed for the coast, Pierre in front with the pilot, Selena and Roos in the back. She felt uneasy, but wasn't sure why. Something was disturbing her, and it wasn't the jostling air currents as they rose to fifteen hundred feet.

"Roos," Pierre hollered over his shoulder. "Is Dr. Reisman going to be joining us for dinner?"

"Nope. That guy can't see the eggs for all the feathers," Roos said, shaking his head. "He's all work. And more mule-headed since Nancy left him. That's probably why she hightailed it outta there in the first place. I've talked to him, but he can be deaf in more ways than one."

Pierre wasn't disappointed. He knew this was Reisman's pathetic attempt to stand up to him. Henry would fight Pierre about going on-line every step of the way. He's like a nervous mother with a new baby, Lorillard thought. But he'll serve my purposes for a while longer, unlike that fool, Jean Levesque. I'll tolerate no more from him. Not after this afternoon.

Pierre had been on his way to pick up Dr. Hartmann when he decided to stop and visit Nikolai. He found him gagged and tied.

"What's the meaning of this?" Lorillard had demanded of the guard. "Untie him! Immediately, I tell you."

As soon as Nik was free, out came a torrent of abuse. "The man is nothing but a vicious dog!" Nik yelled. "I want her out of there. Do you hear me? Now! Katya must be here. With me! I won't give you anything until I know she's all right."

When Jean Levesque showed Nikolai the photos of Marfa Ivanovna, when he taunted him about Katya, about what he might do to her, Nikolai went berserk. He attacked Jean, started throwing things in the laboratory.

"Get Lorillard," Nik hollered to the guard as he lunged for Jean. He grabbed him by the throat, wild with rage, still yelling. "Now! Get Lorillard over here!"

Jean used his army training to eventually incapacitate Nikolai with a sharp blow to the neck, then ordered the guards to tie him up and gag him. Levesque gave strict orders: Lorillard was not to be disturbed.

Remembering the shock of finding Nik that way, Pierre scowled. Jean Levesque had more than served his purpose. It took the sound of Roos Coons' deep holler to bring Lorillard back to the present.

"Hey, George," Roos yelled to the pilot above the sound of the rotors. "I don't suppose it'd be all right for me to smoke one of these now?" He reached into his breast pocket and pulled out a cigar.

"No," Selena said. "It wouldn't be all right."

George Parker shook his head. "Absolutely not, sir."

"Good grief," Roos chuckled. He put the cigar away. "My Miriam used to get all in a pucker every time I smoked. Now they won't let me do it in the LIFT. And down at the clinic the nurses give me a regular tongue lashin' if I light up." Roos was shaking his head in playful despair when Lorillard cried out.

"There's my Zambarano. Off to the right," he said, pointing enthusiastically. "Dr. Hartmann, can you see it?"

* * * * *

Selena was escorted to a suite of rooms on the west wing of the estate and left to freshen up and rest before dinner. Surely Naomi's phone would be working by now, she decided. Kicking off her shoes, she felt the cool smoothness of the saltillo tile as she walked to the phone.

Selena stood at the desk and waited for the call to go through. An old, wooden ceiling fan turned lazily over a huge wrought iron bed nestled between potted palms and ferns. It's been a week since I've had a good night's sleep, she thought.

"Damn," Selena said, and slammed down the receiver. A recorded message was telling her the line was temporarily out of service. "Why in hell don't you fix it?"

She went to the bathroom to brush her teeth and told herself to relax. You've got to keep it together until tomorrow, she thought, until the presentation is over. She was too keyed up to sleep now, and decided to explore Zambarano.

From her private patio she walked along a stone path through a trellis to the rose garden. Calmer, she sat for a while on a black wrought-iron bench breathing the sweet fragrance of the flowers. A lustrous green lizard slithered out from its hiding place and sunned itself not far from her big toe. Selena let her head fall forward, felt the warm sun bake the tight muscles of her neck. She had to make up her mind. Time was running out. Despite Charlie's advice, Selena was not convinced she should reveal the Keck results.

Walking down to the cliffs, she sat on a stonewall overlooking the bay. Lorillard's yacht, *Grand Tour*, was anchored just offshore. She wondered if Pierre had named the boat after an astronomical phenomenon. "Grand Tour" to an astronomer meant space flight that uses gravity assists from other planets. The design of the yacht was so streamlined, Selena thought, it looked like it could take off for the moon.

The view of the coast was sublime, but Selena found it unnerving. It reminded her of the place where Nik's hang glider had crashed. She sighed and tried to clear her head of the painful thoughts. After the presentation she would be free to deal with Nik's disappearance. For now she had to stay focused and calm. She had to think.

There must be another explanation for the new orbital calculations. Selena did not believe they were accurate. If only she had more information, she'd know what to do. She wished Charlie were with her, but she knew in the end the decision must be her own. Maybe Pete Chapman will have encouraging news on the Star Wars vote, she thought. That could make the decision easier.

Looking out across the water, Selena couldn't help but feel the magic of Zambarano. She'd experienced it right away, as soon as they'd arrived. Pierre understood beauty, there was no denying that. His home was utterly elegant yet comfortable and relaxing -- a place where she could go barefoot, a place to be in love. Sun-warmed air, the smell of the sea, the charm of the gracious old buildings, it was how she imagined her mother's island in Greece. A place of calm, as if life were a harmonious passage, something to be savored, not hurried.

Turning to view the grounds, Selena noticed a large balcony on the second floor of the east wing. Several astronomical telescopes were positioned for viewing. She remembered Lorillard's obsession with the subject of astronomy and the existence of extraterrestrials in particular.

Farther north of the main estate, Selena saw a smaller house that looked like a private guest compound. A path led from the arched entryway of the cottage down to the sea. Flowering vines climbed the stucco walls, gracing the tile roof. How lovely, she thought. She felt drawn to the area and for a moment considered exploring the guesthouse, but the strong sun on her face and shoulders was beginning to burn. She decided to return to her rooms. She would nap, if only for a few minutes.

* * * * *

When Jean Levesque arrived from the LIFT, he met briefly with Pierre Lorillard, and then went to the Zambarano security room. Standing before a monitor, he watched Dr. Selena Hartmann lie fully clothed on the top of her bed. She appeared to be dreaming, struggling with something in her sleep.

Rolling onto her side, she clutched the pillow beneath her head, then woke with a start and sat upright, looking frightened and confused. She reached for her watch on the bedside table, and then hurriedly undressed. Dropping her clothes on a chair, she walked naked to the bathroom.

Through the glass doors of the shower, Levesque watched Selena soap her body. She appeared reluctant to leave the shower, but in a few minutes, dried herself and walked into the main room. Dressing quickly in black silk slacks and a sleeveless shell of pale citrus green, she combed her hair and applied makeup. At seven-thirty Selena draped the matching black jacket over her shoulders and left.

In the security room, Levesque quickly pressed some buttons on the security console.

"Let's see how our little princess is doing," he said. The monitor picked up the interior of the guest cottage. There on the screen was Katya, in full view.

Dressed in the black negligee, she stood at her easel, painting. Candles were lit throughout the room. He could see her long legs and the silhouette of her body through the sheer black fabric. Levesque had never seen her look so sexy. He flipped off the monitor and hurried out of the room.

* * * * *

A fire burned in the massive stone fireplace of Pierre's wood-paneled study, warming the cool evening air. Selena found the four men, cocktails in hand, awaiting her arrival.

"If you aren't a sight for sore eyes," Roos said.

"Indeed," Pierre said. "Tres magnifique." Next to him stood the imposing, uniformed figure of General Rosales.

"Please, señora," the general said. "Call me Enrique."

Looking at the man's stiff bearing and his chest of medals, Selena thought 'Enrique' would stick in her throat. The lethal smell of hard liquor permeated the air around him. She greeted the three men and turned to Representative Chapman. A short man in his early fifties, he wore a bow tie and looked like an intellectual caught unexpectedly in the maelstrom of politics.

"Hello, Selena," Pete said and gave her a welcome hug and kiss on the cheek.

"Selene, Selene," Roos Coons said. "She was the Greek goddess of the moon, I believe."

"My mother chose the name. She was Greek."

"And have you passed those wonderful genes onto somebody else? It'd be a darned shame not to, ya know."

Selena laughed. "Is that a proposition, Roos?"

"No," he answered. "But I'll make it one if you think I got a chance."

"I have a daughter. Her name's Katya."

"Ah, now there's a sweetheart of a name. From the Greek word katharos," Roos said. "It means 'pure.'"

"That's quite a knack you have," Selena said.

"Well, I'm glad you're impressed. When I was a salesman, people got a big kick out of it. Made me sound awful smart at the same time."

I like this man, Selena thought. He lacks pretension and he makes me laugh. She heard General Rosales' gruff baritone rise above the other voices and turned to see Pete Chapman's look of disgust as he backed away.

"A pollutant?" Rosales said, sticking a cigar between his teeth. "No es posible, señor. Esta es pure gold." He beamed with proud satisfaction.

"It's also a carcinogen, General," Chapman said. "Not just to the smoker, but to anyone in the room. In my state, it's illegal to smoke in public places. I'm proud to say I sponsored that bill."

139

"Illegal?" Rosales said, pulling out his lighter. "You Americans try to control everything. Even in somebody else's country."

Roos Coons stepped into the fray. "I got my hide tanned earlier today for just the same thing," he said. "I tell you what, General. After dinner you and I'll slip away and enjoy some of that pure gold on our own. Whaddya say?"

General Rosales looked at Coons like he was an idiot and shouldn't butt in.

"Let me show you what I've got for us," Roos said and handed Rosales a cigar. "Take a look at this." General Rosales downed what remained in his glass then grunted at Chapman, but was sufficiently distracted to let the moment pass.

Relieved, Pete Chapman changed the subject. "How is your clinic doing, Mr. Coons?"

Roos took another drink and cleared his throat. "I was hoping you'd ask, sir. I'm about to build a new wing. Sure would like you and your photo people to come by for a visit."

Once the subject of the clinic was introduced, there was no stopping Coons. Pierre was talking to Rosales now, and this gave Selena an opportunity to survey her surroundings.

She was standing beside Lorillard's desk, an ancient oak piece, six feet across and powerful in its simplicity. His library was extensive, she noticed. She searched for anything that might be informative. On a small table beside a reading chair were several books. One in particular caught her eye. It was a Russian publication that had created some controversy over the last year: *Is Mankind Heading For A Raw Materials Disaster?* Selena looked up to see Pierre staring at her pleasurably. She took advantage of a lull in his conversation.

"Is this another of your interests, Mr. Lorillard?" She held the book up, flipped through its pages.

"I'm a businessman, Doctor. It pays to be informed; wouldn't you agree?"

"You're damned right," General Rosales said. Selena didn't answer.

"Dr. Hartmann," Pierre said excitedly. "I'd like to show you one of my favorite possessions. I think you'll appreciate it. Come with me. All of you. Come."

He lead them from the study to the main foyer and out to the interior courtyard of the estate. There, on a pedestal beneath the open and darkening skies, lit from both above and below, stood what appeared to be a sculpture of nature, an exquisite stone with some otherworldly beauty.

Its shape was irregular, in some places angular, in others rounded. Almost five feet high, it took on different forms from different perspectives, sometimes looking eerily human in its expression. In the light it was iridescent and mottled with green olivine and darker nickel-iron. Black graphite traced detailed veins through silvery shards. Yellow crystals were ablaze beneath the surface. Parts of the stone were dull and deep, sucking in the light, while others glittered reflectively.

"It's a pallasite meteorite," Selena said, almost whispering. She moved around the pedestal, entranced by the rock, touching it with fascination. "A stony-iron class. It's the most magnificent specimen I've ever seen."

Representative Chapman was fascinated. "What's the significance of this piece?"

"Meteorites," Selena explained, "are fragments of asteroids that passed through the Earth's atmosphere without being destroyed. The stony-irons are the rarest type, rich in minerals. In the future we should be able to mine these asteroids, use them as natural resources."

"What do you mean, rich in minerals?" General Rosales asked. He sounded skeptical. "My father was in the copper business."

"In the early history of the solar system," Selena explained, "some asteroids were heated to the melting point, just like planet Earth, causing them to differentiate into mineral zones. Heavy elements like iron and nickel sank to the center. The lightest minerals floated to the top."

Pierre stood back watching Dr. Hartmann's expression, enjoying her delight as well as her authority. He felt the urge to possess her. She was as magnificent as his specimen, he thought. A remarkable woman. And she makes me laugh.

"When Earth differentiated," Selena continued, "it carried down nearly all the noble metals, such as gold, platinum, osmium, iridium. These are rare in the earth's crust." Selena noticed General Rosales was now paying close attention.

"The asteroids, however, were constantly subjected to collisions in space with other asteroids, breaking them into pieces, exposing their cores. What we see before us is the glorious remnant of such a collision."

Roos had seen the stone many times before and was enjoying Selena's talk more than the rock.

"Where?" Selena asked, looking at Pierre. He knew exactly what she meant.

"Here," he said. She looked amazed.

"The Atacama Desert, near the central area of the LIFT. It's the reason I chose that site."

Selena remembered. There had been an important meteorite find in the region in 1822.

"What good are they?" General Rosales asked, wanting to be convinced. "It's just a rock from space." Crudely, he motioned with his glass for the butler to bring another drink.

"These can be quite valuable," Selena said. "Thirty times the value of gold and more." Selena knew there were wealthy people who collected meteorites, but this specimen was incredible. She'd never seen anything like it. The color, the radiance, the patterns. It belonged in a museum of art more than geology.

General Rosales walked up and peered at the stone in disbelief.

"Jewels from space," Pete Chapman said, keeping his distance from Rosales.

"I've been a collector for some time," Pierre said. "Some of my specimens are worth millions of dollars, but this is my favorite."

"I can see why," Selena said.

"Mighty nice," Roos said, enjoying the evening air and looking at Selena. Coons had never been that excited about material possessions of any kind.

"I'm anxiously awaiting the results of your research, Dr. Hartmann," Pierre said. He enjoyed their discussions; a worthy opponent was difficult to find. "I especially enjoyed the article on the limitations of precisely tracking the orbit of NEA Hartmann 2009 with available infrared technology. I hope your expectations of the Keck telescope were fulfilled."

Selena had been spellbound by the meteorite, but she quickly turned and stared at Lorillard.

"My expectations were more than fulfilled," she said. "Where did you say you read that? That article was never published."

"I'm afraid I don't remember," Pierre said. He looked momentarily uncomfortable. "I really don't know." Pointing to his brain, he said, "Age, you know. The memory is the first thing to go."

"My memory's been shot to hell forever," Roos said. "Least that's what Calvin, my helper, says. I have to take his word for it 'cuz I can't remember." Roos chuckled at his own silliness. Selena thought Pierre laughed a little too heartily.

"Well," Pierre said. "Why don't we bring our drinks into the dining room." He held out his arm for Selena.

CHAPTER 15

Jean Levesque entered the guest quarters without knocking. Sultry Spanish guitar music permeated the atmosphere. He saw Katya standing behind her easel on the other side of the room, lost in a fog of creativity. The candles flickered as a breeze billowed the sheer black negligee around her young body.

Jean watched Katya pause and step back, holding her brush up as if conducting an orchestra. When she saw him, she smiled. Levesque felt elation, right between his legs.

"Having a séance tonight?" he asked, grinning. "You look like a witch with your wand there, like you're casting some kinda spell."

"You haven't been to see me." She began to paint again.

"Does that mean you missed me?"

Katya said nothing, just continued her work.

"What you up to?" he asked. "Something new?"

"You wanted a painting, remember? I'm going to give it to you."

"Oh yeah?"

"Why don't you come see for yourself?" she said.

The smile never left his face as Jean worked his way around the couch and past the coffee table to see what was on the other side of the small easel. Despite his curiosity, he could hardly take his eyes off Katya. She seemed charged with a fierce intensity, magnificent in the candlelight.

He was standing right beside her now, their arms touching. She raised her head. Her dark eyes focused all their power on him. He could not believe the desire he felt for this young woman and he forced himself to turn away, to look at the painting. Her gaze remained on his face as his expression changed.

The painting was the face of the devil, scarred and ugly, looking venomous and evil. The devil's right ear was mutilated and deformed, just like Jean Levesque's. At first Jean looked surprised, almost hurt, then disappointed, but within seconds he was smirking. His nasty laugh wasn't far behind.

Katya's knees were shaking so hard at that moment she didn't know if she could go through with it. The alternative at this point, however, was dealing with an aroused and angry Jean Levesque. There was no turning back.

* * * * *

From the long dining room table Selena looked out through arched, floor-to-ceiling glass panels to a patio overlooking the sea. A magnificent Rodin sculpture, ponderous yet elegant, graced the night air. It was positioned so all the dinner guests could enjoy the beauty of its curving, pensive form backlit by the setting sun. Zambarano was enchanting and seductive, she thought. She felt the desire to surrender to it, but knew that was impossible.

General Rosales sat directly across from her, Pete Chapman on her right. Wine was poured and the appetizer served right away — lobster delicately flavored with cilantro and a hint of lemon in white sauce.

"I'd like you all to be the first to know," Pierre Lorillard said from the head of the table. His face took on a look of controlled pride. "I'm going online with the LIFT accelerator. Final magnet installation is taking place as we speak."

"Congratulations, señor," General Rosales said. He took another stiff pull on his drink. Sitting down, the buttons on his uniform were stressed to the popping point.

"Holy smoke," Roos said. "Maybe I should evacuate my patients first."

"I don't think that's necessary," Pierre said, smiling indulgently at his partner.

"That's sooner than planned, isn't it?" Selena asked.

"Why wait?" Lorillard said. "All is in order. I'm not one for dawdling, Doctor." It's unfortunate, he thought, seeing Selena's warm brown eyes in the glow of the candelabra. She, too, has fallen prey to that perennial human malady of restraint dictated by fear. They call it caution, but its real name is cowardice.

"This will be quite the media event," Pete Chapman said. "You didn't by any chance push this up to coincide with the Star Wars vote?"

"I know we're on opposite sides of that issue, Representative. Surely you can't fault me for doing what's good for my business?"

Rosales finished his drink and slammed his glass down. "You're damned right, senor." He sneered at Chapman.

"How is the vote lining up?" Selena asked Pete. "Anything encouraging?"

"I'm afraid not," Chapman said. "It's going to be extremely close. The size of government contracts involved with this bill means there's lots of special interest money to buy votes — for their side, that is."

Selena looked disappointed, but tried not to show her confusion. She hadn't really expected better news, but now the weighty decision was unavoidable.

"There are still one or two fence sitters, though," Chapman said. "I'm counting on your presentation tomorrow to push those votes our way."

"Star Wars?" Rosales laughed. "Now you Americanos can pass laws against smoking in space."

"I see you're aware of Edward Teller's missile defense program, General." Chapman's tone was antagonist. "We call it his, 'I've Got a Bomb For Every Problem' campaign."

"Edward Teller. Father of the hydrogen bomb," Rosales said, nodding his head vigorously. "Smart man."

"Yes, but now he wants to put all those idle bomb experts to work again. This time to blow up menacing space invaders."

"Space invaders?" Roos said.

"The economic pressure to adapt military technology to peaceful uses," Chapman said, "makes it an easy switch. Replace human enemies with rocks from space."

"Which reminds me," Selena said to Pierre as the main course was served. It was a fish dish with a red sauce drizzled around the edge of the black and gold plates. "In the superconductor lab today I heard rumors you're working on SQUIDs. What do you intend to do with those?"

"They have many uses, Doctor," Pierre said. "Unfortunately I'm not at liberty to divulge the conditions of specific contracts."

"Renata sure can cook," Roos said, looking at his plate. "You know, Pierre stole her from a restaurant in Tuscany. 'Course my granny always said I was gonna dig my grave with my teeth." Roos placed his large hand on his ample belly. "Talking 'bout graves, Pierre, I'd like to get back to this LIFT business. When exactly do you plan on starting up this pinball machine?"

"Within the next week to ten days," Pierre said.

"Well, keep me posted, will ya?"

"Brilliant publicity stunt for Lorillard Superconductor Laboratory," Chapman said. "The ultimate fireworks display of sorts."

"Let's certainly hope not," Pierre laughed. "I don't expect a spark of trouble. Speaking of the lab, I heard an interesting story about superconductors the other day. Evidently some scientists wanted to know for sure: were superconductors really perfect transmitters of energy? So in England in 1956 they conducted an experiment. First they sent an electrical current through a superconductor ring. Then they waited to see how long it would take for it to run out of juice, so to speak. After two and a half years, there was absolutely no loss of energy. The experiment could have continued indefinitely, but for an insurmountable obstacle. Anybody want to guess?"

Selena almost answered, but stopped herself in time. This was a story she'd heard Nikolai tell Katya.

"Doctor?" Pierre said. "Do you know this story?"

"I'm not sure," Selena said. "Why don't you tell us."

Pierre nodded. "You're too gracious, doctor, but as you wish. It seems the experiment could have lasted forever, except the supply of liquid helium used to cool the superconductors was stopped by a trucking strike."

"Intolerable," General Rosales said. "Liberal fools."

Representative Chapman couldn't resist. "I suppose here in Chile you'd have them all shot, General?"

"We would not allow progress to be stopped on such important research, señor."

"And who defines 'progress,' General? Who defines 'important?' That seems to be the question."

I do, Pierre Lorillard thought.

* * * * *

Katya kept her gaze locked on Jean Levesque's face. He was snickering at the painting propped on the easel. It was his likeness painted as a scarred devil. He continued to stare at the picture as Katya bent her shaking knees and reached for the jar she'd placed on the table right behind her.

"Aren't you the sweet angel," Jean said, looking up from the painting. At that moment, Katya swung her arm, hurling the liquid turpentine right at his face. He must have caught a glimpse of something in her eyes, because Katya saw the flash of instinct take over. He moved with astonishing speed. The liquid splashed across his shirt and neck but missed his eyes.

She bolted backwards. He grabbed for her but fell to the floor and clutched the skirt of her nightgown. She was above him, struggling to get away. She could hear the fabric ripping as she pulled harder, desperate to reach the doorway. Now he had her by the leg. Her other bare foot was slipping, and when he jerked hard, she fell beside the coffee table, knocking two of the dozen candles off the table to the rug below.

Jean continued to pull her towards him, inch by inch, but she grabbed the leg of the heavy marble table and resisted, fighting to free herself, kicking him with her other leg.

"You're gonna spread your wings and fly for me, angel," he said, laughing as if it were all a game. "We're going to take a little trip to heaven, you and me."

"Leave me alone," she cried, but knew it was hopeless. He'd never let her go. She could see down the hallway to the front door of the cottage. If only she could get loose from his grasp, she could run out into the yard and hide in the darkness. She felt Levesque grab hold of her free leg.

"I've got you now," he laughed. Wrapping both his arms around her, he began to pull her closer. She could feel the silky fabric of the nightgown slipping on the shiny wooden floor. She was sliding closer to him no matter how hard she pulled on the leg of the table. She couldn't hold on much longer. He was too strong.

In the moment before her grasp broke loose, she cried out and reached with one arm, swung it wide across the top of the coffee table, pushing the still-lit array of candles towards Jean. She swiped hard and sent them flying towards his face. She missed, but the turpentine on his shirt flared. The blaze spread to the liquid on his neck. He screamed, grabbed his neck and rolled over on the floor, beating his flaming chest.

Katya scrambled to her feet and ran for the door. In only a moment he was up and after her, holding one hand to his neck and tearing the charred shirt off with the other. Just before she reached the door he grabbed her again and threw her to the floor. Before she could get away, he was on top of her.

The rage in his eyes was the most hideous, terrifying sight she'd ever seen. His shirt was off now, and his bare, scarred chest was pressed against her. He smelled like burnt flesh and hair. Katya couldn't breathe. She struggled to suck the air in, but it wouldn't come. She felt she would suffocate.

Jean reached for the strap of her nightgown and tore it down, exposing her breast. He leered at her, and in the horror of that moment, she panicked, too frightened to scream. Her eyes couldn't blink. When the shrill sound of a smoke alarm pierced the air with an unrelenting screech, it shocked them both. They looked up to see the Oriental rug in flames.

Jean suddenly bent his head back and yowled like a wild animal in heat, then looked at Katya and kissed her hard, forcing his tongue down her throat, cutting her lip with his teeth. Two guards crashed through the front door with fire extinguishers. Levesque looked at them with disgust, then, wincing with pain, he rolled off her.

As the guards extinguished the fire, Katya crawled away from Jean, out onto the patio, away from the smoke. He got to his feet and leaned heavily against the wall.

"Sir," one of the guards said. "You're needed at the airport. The dinner guest will be leaving soon."

"Just get out of here," Jean raged.

When they were gone, he remained at the front door, seemingly impervious to the pain from his burns. Katya stayed curled in a dark corner of the patio, on the far side of the pool.

"I'll be back for more," he said. "I liked that. Right now I've got some business to take care of with your mother."

Her mother? What was he going to do to her mother? As Levesque turned to go, Katya saw the sick smile in his eyes.

"Wait! Wait!" she screamed, running after him. But it was too late; he was gone.

"Mommy! Mommy!" Katya beat on the locked door until her strength was gone. She slumped on the floor in tears. What would he do to her mother? Oh God, she pleaded. If only I could reach her.

* * * * *

At the distant, but shrill sound of a smoke alarm, all conversation in the dining room had stopped. They looked around, concerned.

"What in tarnation is that?" Roos asked, just as Arthur entered the room.

"I'm sorry, sir. There appears to have been a small fire in the guest cottage. Nothing serious. It's being taken care of right now. I assure you, everything's under control." As if on cue, the sound of the alarm ceased.

"Thank you, Arthur." Pierre's eyes lingered on Selena. She showed no reaction.

"Excuse me, sir," Arthur said. "Dr. Hartmann has a phone call. I indicated you were dining, but the party said it was important."

"Who is it?" Lorillard asked.

"A representative of Eco-Tours, sir. They said it was very important. An emergency of sorts."

Selena looked puzzled, then concerned. "It must be about my daughter," she said, already rising from the table.

"Arthur will show you to the phone," Pierre said.

I don't understand, Selena thought. Katya's back in Los Angeles. What could be the problem?

"Daughters," General Rosales said. He placed his hand across his chest. "They will bruise your heart worse than any lover." Feeling a cigar under his jacket, Rosales pulled it out and began to light up.

"You're not going to do that here?" Pete Chapman said. He adjusted his bow tie and cleared his throat indignantly.

"I told you, General," Roos said. "We'll go off to the study in just a bit. Then we can be bad boys if we want."

"A good meal deserves a good smoke," Rosales said after puffing hard on the cigar until it was fully lit. Smoke billowed across the table. General Rosales emptied the last of his drink and held the glass in the air. A waiter quickly filled it. "A toast," he said, bowing in Pierre's direction. "Gracias, señor."

Chapman sat bolt upright in his chair and fanned the air with his napkin.

"I'm sorry, General, but I'm allergic to tobacco smoke. Even if I weren't, I'd find your behavior offensive." He began to cough.

"You Americans have become too soft," Rosales said. I'd like to squash you like a snail, he thought. "You're always trying to boss other people around, señor, but you're in Chile now. In my country. I make the rules here."

Chapman was choking, his face red, his eyes watering.

"Representative, you better come with me," Roos said, taking him by the arm. "Let's get some fresh air." He led Chapman towards the atrium.

Pierre was beginning to feel anxious about Dr. Hartmann. The next few minutes were essential to the smooth outcome of his plan.

"General, I'm afraid I'll have to ask you to put that out." Lorillard motioned impatiently to one of the waiters to bring an ashtray.

"Hold back there," Rosales said when the waiter approached.

"General," Pierre said. "Dispose of that. Now." The man was a baboon, Lorillard thought. After his third drink all civility left him. Evidently he'd been drinking a good bit lately. Rosales felt the haze of liquor leave his head. Who in hell did he think....

"Thank you," Pierre said as the waiter took the cigar. "Tell me, General. How is your wife? I'm sorry she couldn't make it this evening."

The bastard, Enrique thought. He knows why she isn't here. Rosales stared long and hard at Lorillard. Enough of the Norte Americanos. Enough of foreigners telling him what to do in his own country. Lorillard had crossed a line.

When Selena entered the dining room, her face was ashen. Chapman and Coons walked in right behind her. Roos immediately noticed something was wrong.

"What is it?" he asked. "What's the problem?"

"My daughter's missing. She never made it back to Los Angeles. They've traced her to the Santiago airport. I don't understand, but she must have been coming to see me. She must have gotten lost on the way." Selena's voice trailed off. "Or something's happened to her."

"Now don't you worry," Roos said, putting his arm around Selena. "I'm sure she just got confused. They'll find her, lickety split for sure."

"I've got to get to the Santiago airport as soon as possible. I can help look for her." Biting hard on her raw cuticles, Selena felt the familiar hollow panic invade her. It was happening again, just as it did with her mother. She had to do something. She had to hurry if she was going to prevent disaster.

Arthur had been standing quietly by the door.

"Call my car immediately," Pierre ordered. "And alert the airport. Dr. Hartmann can take my plane. And see to her belongings."

"Yes sir," Arthur said.

"What about your presentation," Pete Chapman said, coughing. He was standing as far away from General Rosales as the room permitted. "It's tomorrow afternoon."

"Maybe she'll be back in time," Roos said. "Could be back by morning."

Selena smiled gratefully at Roos. At the moment his optimism was comforting.

"Ask them to reschedule for the following day, late afternoon. That'll give me the most time. Hopefully I'll be back even sooner." Selena was fighting off tears, telling herself she had to be strong, everything was going to be all right. She would find Katya.

"When did this happen," Roos said. "How long has the child been missing?"

"That's just it," Selena said. "I had a phone message from her yesterday. She said everything was all right. She was headed home to Los Angeles.

Now they say she's been missing for days. I don't understand."

"Don't you worry," Roos said. "We're gonna find that little lady. I promise you."

"The car is here, sir." Arthur handed Selena her briefcase. "I've alerted the airport. The pilot is preparing for takeoff."

CHAPTER 16

The man with the white streak of hair greeted Selena. Jean Levesque explained he would fly her to Santiago in Pierre's Metroliner II, a smaller plane used for mountain climbing expeditions. The jet Chapman had arrived on was unexpectedly being serviced, Levesque told her, sounding irritated by the complication.

She stashed her briefcase under the co-pilot seat and strapped herself in. Within minutes they were taxiing down the runway. Jean operated the aircraft with smooth confidence, but Selena still felt uncomfortable. She told herself it wasn't because of his appearance, but rather his manner, which she found severe and cocky. At the moment, however, all she wanted was to get as close to Katya as possible and she was prepared to fly with anybody who could get her there.

They hit full throttle and she felt the growing pressure against her chest as the craft thrust forward. Usually she liked flying, but tonight she just felt anxious, almost afraid, as they rose higher and higher, then banked to the east.

"I smell something," Selena said over the sound of the propellers. "What is it?"

Jean quickly checked the gauges. Everything was fine.

"Exhaust from takeoff," he said. He'd lost almost all his sense of smell from the electrical shocks the Iranians administered to his nose, but he wasn't about to admit it to this bitch.

"We're going to fly over the LIFT," Jean said. "At night it's really something."

"The last thing I'm interested in right now is sightseeing," Selena said.

He stared at her. "It's on the way," he said. With his head turned, the light from the control panel strangely illuminated his mutilated ear, and his eyes looked even more menacing. The skin of his neck looked raw, like a fresh burn.

"What happened to your neck?" she asked. "You should put something on that."

"It's all right," he said defensively. "I tangled with a hot tamale, but I'm not done with her yet."

"What are you talking about?" This man sickened Selena, but then, nothing seemed normal anymore. Again, she wished she had Charlie with her to search for Katya. Or Nik, she thought.

"Looks like weather up ahead," Jean said.

Selena could see no clouds in the immediate area, but she noticed a splotch on the radar screen. They were heading right for it, but they'd have to change course soon and turn south. They leveled off at 2500 feet. The full moon was rising to the east, and she remembered Charlie's warning. A 'sinister aspect,' Charlie had said. Something about a lunar eclipse in Leo, directly opposite my sun? Maybe she was right, Selena thought. This was becoming a most sinister night. Where was Katya? What was happening to her right now? Selena's mind began to run wild with the possibilities.

In the darkness ahead she could see a circle of illumination curving toward the east. That would be the LIFT. It looked like a perfectly round pool of reflecting crystals in a sea of desert darkness, and as they flew closer, she could see the shape of the dome, its delicate branches of light spreading from the central womb of the pod.

In the far distance to the east Selena saw the sky brighten in a jagged vein. Darkness returned, and with the sharp crack of thunder, she gripped her armrest and dug her fingers into the woven upholstery. Jean noticed. He laughed at her fear.

"The storm's over in the mountains, far away. It's not gonna get you," he said.

The arrogant bastard, she thought, and she started to tell him just that, but the sight of his scarred face made her swallow hard. She told herself to stop being silly about the lightning. There was nothing to be afraid of. She knew she was more likely to die from an asteroid impact than in an airplane crash. If she lived to be seventy, she had a one in 7,000 chance of seeing an asteroid hit the Earth, but only a one in 20,000 chance of dying in a plane crash. Then why was she so frightened?

"So you're one of those space watchers like Pierre?" Jean said. "He thinks there are whole civilizations out there waitin' to make contact. I think he's nuts, myself."

"Shouldn't we be changing course soon?" Selena asked. "We're still heading due east."

Jean stared straight ahead. She saw his eyes pinch. "When I'm ready," he said.

The hostility in his words reached right inside her. It's impossible to talk to this man, she thought. His face continued to make her uneasy. Far ahead she saw lightning slash. Out of sheer nervous energy, she found herself again trying to communicate.

"Small aircraft like this can trigger lightning. It can reach 100 million volts."

Jean snickered. "Is that right?" he said. "I guess you're a pretty smart lady. Is that why the Russian likes you so much?" He turned to watch her reaction.

The question took her by surprise. Where was it coming from? Did he mean Nik?

Angry, she answered. "I don't know what you're talking about."

"Yes you do. Nikolai Potapov. The two of you," he said, smirking.

"What do you know about Dr. Potapov?" Jean ignored her. It must be through Pierre, Selena thought. She told herself she had other battles to fight tonight, but she couldn't let it go.

"Are you in the habit of being rude?" she asked. He looked pleased. Selena unbuckled her seat belt. "I'm going to take a look around back." She pulled her briefcase out from under the seat. Jean turned to watch as she bent down to pull her briefcase out from under the seat. Her hips swiveled through the narrow passage between the pilot's seat and her own.

In the semi-darkness of the cockpit he checked the altimeter and adjusted the throttle, his mind flashing on Potapov's face when he learned of Selena's death. Lorillard couldn't protect the Russian forever. Pierre was making a fool of himself; he was being duped. The Russian would never join his plan. To involve him in the secret project would be making a terrible mistake. Not that Jean gave a damn about that whole thing, but he knew Pierre did. He knew it mattered to him more than anything else, and if Jean didn't protect Lorillard, nobody would. He'd have to do something about the Russian as soon as he returned. Tonight, however, he would take care of this passenger. He had a plan.

When they arrived at Santiago airport, she'd rush off thinking she was going to meet a tour representative at the Espresso Bean coffee shop near American Airlines in the main lobby. Jean would check in at the tower, and there he'd find a florist's box. Inside would be a bouquet carefully wrapped and sealed in cellophane, the message card deeply imbedded in the flowers. Levesque would use a hypodermic needle to inject a stream of pine-scented toxaphene, a highly toxic insecticide, into the cellophane, and then pay some kid to make the delivery. One close-up whiff of those blossoms and the poison would enter her bloodstream, right through that sensitive nose of hers. The remaining gas would quickly dissipate.

Reaction time was less than an hour. The symptoms were convulsions, vomiting, auditory hallucinations, congestion in brain and lungs, coma, and then death. Oh yes, and the piece de resistance? The card in the flowers! It would be signed, "I miss you. Love, Nik."

Jean surfaced from his vengeful reverie and decided he'd like to find out a bit more about this woman and the Russian. Might as well have some fun with it, he thought. She won't be alive to squeal for much longer.

They had passed the east end facility of the LIFT and were nearing the foothills of the Andes. He banked the plane, heading it due south, and set the automatic pilot.

There were only four double seats in the front half of the cabin. The back half was packed with climbing gear in overhead compartments and chests bolted to the floor. Selena was sitting in one of the seats on the right, looking out the window, wondering where she had gone wrong.

It seemed to her she had really tried, but for all her efforts to prevent loss, she had failed. She had struggled to manage it all, to control the outcome for the better, but now her attempts seemed foolish. Like some ill-fitting outline, her tracing paper hopes didn't match the real thing. Instead of coming together, the game plan had shuffled beneath her. The edges would never line up.

This is how I felt, she realized, a few years after Mom died when Dad lost his job at Los Alamos. He became caught up in his misery, and nothing I did could make it better. Selena had tried to keep it together then, but inside she began to doubt, she began to wonder if the world wasn't there to defeat her. Maybe, unlike other people, she didn't work well in the scheme of life. And maybe it would always be that way.

These are old fears, she told herself, foolish doubts conquered long ago. But Nik's loss, the Keck results, now Katya missing, and tonight, this hideous man, what did it all mean? Everything was falling apart, just when she had been foolish enough to dream. Would it always come back to this?

Selena looked from the window to see Jean enter the cabin. She dismissed her thoughts, put them far away, and stiffened in her seat. She nodded to him, and returned her gaze to the window. He walked behind the seat next to hers and leaned against the headrest.

"How's it goin'?" Jean asked.

"I'm fine," she said coolly, not anxious to resume a conversation. "How much longer?" Selena looked up to see Levesque grinning down at her. The tips of his fingers were rubbing the vinyl trim of the headrest, over and over again. Like her own, his cuticles were bitten and raw. She turned away.

"What's the matter?" he asked, focusing his gaze on her breasts. "Don't you like my company?"

"No," she said. "I don't." Leaning forward to look out the window, she blocked his view.

"That's too bad," Jean said. He walked around and sat down beside her. "I guess you'd like it better if Dr. Potapov were here instead."

"I'd like it better if you'd go do your job and fly the plane," Selena said. He was sitting close to her now, leaning over the armrest that separated them.

"Maybe I can make you feel better," Jean said. "Just because the Russian isn't here...." Suddenly he reached out and roughly took hold of her left breast.

Selena pushed his arm away, jumped out of the seat, and backed away. Jean looked up at her, still grinning. She knew it meant trouble. Don't make him any angrier, she told herself. There must have been some sort of rivalry between him and Nikolai, perhaps over Pierre. Don't damage his bruised ego any more.

"I don't feel well," she said. She kept moving away. "I think I'm getting airsick. I think I'm going to throw up."

"Oh dear," Jean laughed. "Poor baby." He rose from his seat and lurched towards her. Selena turned and tried to run but he grabbed her, held her by the jacket, then pulled her back against him, placing one arm securely around her waist. She could feel the heat of his breath against the back of her head. He reached around with his other hand, dug under her blouse, and squeezed her breast hard.

"Let go of me, you bastard." She struggled, swinging her head violently from side to side. He held her arms pinned close to her body while his hand moved across her chest, grabbing at the other breast.

She cried out in pain, twisting, struggling harder.

"I wonder how Dr. Potapov would feel if he saw us?" Jean said. "Is this how he does it to you?"

Was Nik alive? Is that what he was saying? Between her fear and his tight hold around her body, Selena had difficulty breathing. She told herself to think straight. Levesque was incredibly strong. He could hurt me, kill me, if he wanted to. His hand was moving all over her now, down the front of her, between her legs. She could feel his wet mouth against her neck, his teeth on her skin. She squirmed and twisted, but she couldn't break free.

"So you got a thing for a stinkin' Russian, huh?" Jean said. His lips and tongue were all over her ear. "How about a kiss for a soldier who almost gave his life for your fucking country." Selena felt the anger rise in her until she could no longer control it, no longer play it smart. She moved quickly, without thinking, and raised herself on one foot, at the same time jamming the heel of her right shoe up behind her, between his legs.

"Ahhghh!" he cried out, and doubled over quickly, releasing his grip. She tore around the seat, ran towards the front of the cabin.

"Uuughhh," he moaned, still doubled over. "You fucking bitch!" he yelled. Selena looked at him just long enough to see the loathing on his face.

Dashing for the cockpit, she tripped on the doorframe and fell against the controls, knocking the yoke of the automatic pilot off. Her head smashed against the floor in front of the co-pilot's seat. She pushed herself up quickly and crawled towards the door, unlatching the hook that held it open. Just before she slammed it shut, she saw Levesque. He was standing upright now, holding onto the seatback. As she scrambled to her feet she heard him laugh.

"You don't really think you can hurt me, do you?" he hollered through the door. "That's been tried before."

Selena searched for a lock; when she couldn't find one, she jammed her feet against a box secured to the floor and leaned back, bracing the door closed with her weight. She looked up to see red lights on the control panel blinking wildly. She was gasping for breath. From behind the door, she heard Jean curse. It sounded like he was in the back of the plane.

"We're losing altitude!" he cried out. "The engines are burning up!" She listened to him race from one side of the plane to the other.

Lorillard! You bastard!" Jean cried out. "You did this! You tried to get rid of me along with her!"

Selena searched through the windshield but could see nothing in the darkness. Suddenly Jean was pounding on the door.

"Let me in! We're going down, you stupid bitch!" He shoved against the door with incredible force, bulldozing his way through. Selena flew forward against the glass.

He dove frantically for the controls, grabbed the steering yoke and pulled hard, tried to level the plane. The oil pressure lights were blinking madly. The high temperature indicators were already on.

"Someplace to land!"

Selena pushed hard against the dashboard, fought the force of the plane's descent. She managed to brace her forearms against the corridor walls, and moved, inch by inch towards the back of the plane. She looked back once and saw Jean trying to buckle his shoulder harness. Through the windshield she could see the treetops rise up to meet them. Too frightened to scream, she dove for the first cabin seat just as the nose of the plane hit.

The powerful drag of the trees pitched her forward, the side of her body smashed against the front wall of the cabin. Climbing gear from the back broke loose and hurtled through the air. The nose of the plane lurched upwards. When the tail hit, she was thrown back against the first two seats, her outstretched arm wedged between the seatbacks, the center armrest jabbing severely into her ribcage.

She saw the left wing of the aircraft light up as it sliced through the trees. When the tip of the wing hit the ground its aluminum skin peeled back, then the entire wing ripped from the body of the plane. There was a deafening sound of destruction as the metal limbs were torn and crushed all around her.

Her arm, stuck between the forward seats, held her, kept her from being flung with the full force of the impact. When her body finally broke free, she was tossed to the side, her arms flailing in front of her face like a rag doll. Gear from the back of the plane, coiled nylon ropes, backpacks, and boots, came crashing forward and showered down on top of her.

With the final forward thrust, what remained of the plane rolled over onto its right side. Curled in a ball, Selena landed on a window and blacked out.

CHAPTER 17

Slowly, Selena regained consciousness. She opened her eyes and tried to focus. In the darkness she saw movement, specks of light dropping. Like stars floating down to earth, she thought. Moments passed before she understood -- it was snow, falling peacefully in the moonlight, falling through the gaping hole in the plane.

Painfully, sensation returned. She felt the bone of her back against a hard ridge. Her toes prickled, and the bottom of her feet felt warm. Underneath the heap of her body, her arms began to ache. She tried to move but pain shot through her chest, forced her to fall back. She gasped, then lay still. My rib, it's broken, she realized. Maybe more than one.

A moan penetrated the muddle of her mind. She tried again to move, slowly this time, using her legs to ease the pressure on her ribs. She managed to get to her knees and braced herself against the spin of nausea. When it settled, she raised her head. The skin on her face felt heavy, lifeless. As her aching head cleared, she surveyed the remains of the aircraft. One slow bit at a time, she took it in.

The tail section of the plane was completely gone, and the body rested on its side. The left wing had been torn off. Mountain climbing gear and debris were everywhere. A seat dangled from the far wall. She felt a cold wind rush in from the direction of the cockpit.

I'm alive, Selena thought. In that last moment before blacking out, she had been certain it was all over. What if the plane had burst into flames, had exploded, and .... No, no, she told herself. It's all right. I'm alive.

Again, she heard the moaning. Still on her knees and holding her ribcage, she pushed gingerly on the glass of the small window and turned her body to

159

search. Another moan, and she felt the cords in her neck tighten, felt the terror spread through her limbs. She breathed harder as the memory surfaced in random images. He was still alive.

Through the corridor she could see a thin slice of the cockpit. Everything was tilted on its side, exposing jagged edges of torn metal. Silhouetted by the dim light of outdoors, she could see what looked like the back of Jean's head, and one leg and an arm hanging limp from his body. He'd been thrown against the windshield. A few flakes of snow settled on his dark hair. He appeared to be unconscious, but she could hear his breathing.

Brushing the hair off her forehead, she felt warm liquid. She saw the blood, but remained oddly distant and not alarmed. Her sensations were buffered, her thoughts slow and methodical, and she realized she must be in shock. Her professional training took over. She knew what she had to do. If I'm going to survive, she told herself, I've got to remain calm; I've got to stay warm. Very carefully, she propped her feet around the frame of the small window and slowly stood up. Still, he did not move.

The sharp, cold air blew through the tunnel of the cabin as Selena searched the maze and tangle of debris for something warm to wear. The door to an overhead bin hung open with a red blanket inside. To lift her arm and reach for it would be painful, but she had no choice. On her toes and holding her ribcage with one arm, she stretched to catch the corner of the red wool and she pulled. The pain surged sharp and long down her body as the blanket fell to the ground. Finally, she managed to wrap it around her shoulders.

Selena moved towards the corridor to the cockpit. She steadied herself by pressing against the curved wall of the plane's interior and reached for one of the headrests that jutted into the center of the cabin. She could see part of him now. He appeared lifeless and she could no longer hear his breathing. Still feeling removed and protected by layers of foggy distance, she noticed her teeth were chattering.

Suddenly Jean's leg jerked in a spasm and Selena bolted back, almost lost her balance, and grabbed her painful ribs with one arm. Even through the haze of her shock, it wasn't long before her terror turned to fury. She could feel it rise up in her, overwhelm her, make her strong. She knew she would kill him -- with her bare hands -- she would strangle him. Then her eye caught the glint of a shard of glass from a broken liquor bottle. The shattered glass scrunched and grated beneath her thin black shoes and again, her will fueled by her loathing, she reached for a jagged piece, the pain of bending mollified only by the hatred she felt for this man. Yes, she would stab him.

She imagined her whole being thrusting the point into his flesh, again and again, shredding his heart and lungs.

Clenching the glass in her right hand, she reached the ragged metal edge of the cockpit and she saw him, Jean Levesque. He lay unconscious, face down, his head pressed against the lacey midpoint of the intricately shattered windshield. His blood spread along the spider web of cracked glass, pooling on the instruments below. Pain teased at her consciousness, grew stronger until it made her look away from him, look down at her hand. Her fingers were warm with red liquid, the blood dripping from her palm. Reluctantly, she released the pressure on the broken glass and stared at her lacerated skin. Stunned, the sight broke through her shock long enough to clear her head for a moment. And suddenly she remembered. Levesque knew about Nikolai. Something about Nik, as if he were still alive. She had to find out what this monster knew.

"Jean," she called out angrily. "Jean, can you hear me?" There was no response.

Repulsed by the thought he might move towards her, she felt nausea move in her gut. "Jean, can you hear me?" She couldn't make herself touch him; she felt her knees start to buckle beneath her. Moving away from him, she slowly stepped out into the night air, onto the freshly fallen snow. She must find something to restrain him, some rope to tie him down.

Following the plowed path of destruction left by the plane's descent, Selena shuffled numbly along. She turned awkwardly to look over her shoulder at the hulking aircraft that lay like a slain beast, groaning, exhaling its dying breaths.

In an effort to gain her bearings, Selena gazed at the sky. The night was overcast with a thin cloud cover, but there was a full moon and some light. No stars were visible. She remembered August meant winter in the Southern Hemisphere as she felt the mountainous cold seep into her bones. You've got to stay warm, she reminded herself. Concentrate. You've got to stay warm.

Surveying the crash site, Selena saw twisted and charred pieces of metal that threw dark shadows, menacing and surreal. Multi-colored nylon climbing ropes and clothing hung tangled in high tree limbs. If I could only find some of that rope, she thought. Backing away, she felt something rub against her leg. She stumbled, almost fell, and looked down to find a broken tree branch. The fresh scent of pine boughs filled the air. She tried to take a deep breath, but the stabbing pain in her ribs prevented it. She felt the hairs inside her nose prickle like icy needles.

Moving on, she noticed a dark object on the ground. Its shape seemed familiar. She moved closer and bent down to see, then realized it was her briefcase. Empty and battered, it was still hers, a reminder of who she was, of her existence before this night. Eagerly she stroked the worn leather, and remembered the postcard from Nik. Inside the side pocket, lodged in the corner, she found the card. Even in the dark she could make out the silly Hawaiian shopper. Selena smiled, as if at an old friend, and slid the postcard into her pants pocket. She moved on.

A round orange object in the woods to the right caught her attention, and she walked in that direction. It was a sleeping bag, rolled and tied, coated with a dusting of snow. She made a mental note to pick it up on the way back. A creaking noise came from the plane, and she cringed. Searching for any sign of Jean, she saw only the dark hole of the cockpit. She tried to still her breathing, to listen. Nothing. "Find some rope," she told herself. "Keep looking. Stay focused."

Continuing along the trail of destruction, she reached the edge of a ravine. The cliff dropped at least 300 feet, and at the bottom lay the tail of the plane. On the other side, their trail of damage. It appeared that when the nose of the Metroliner hit the ground, the impact had partially torn the cockpit from the plane, then flipped the aircraft upwards until the tail came down with enough force to rip it off. It had landed in the ravine. Fortunately the midsection jumped enough to make it over the divide, leveled off, and plowed through the brush for another hundred yards. They'd been flying at a fairly low altitude. Jean must have used the treetops to cushion their impact, she realized, cutting their speed with the resistance.

Selena's body began to ache from the cold. She decided to start back towards the wreckage and look in a different direction. Maybe there was something in the cabin she hadn't noticed. She wrapped one arm around her ribs, holding them tight. Deep breathing hurt the most, and she knew she had to be careful not to puncture her lung. As soon as she had tied up Levesque, she would wrap her chest, then make some sort of camp and start a fire.

On the way she kept a lookout for any supplies that might help her survive. There was a small clearing, maybe fifteen by twenty feet, off to her right, and Selena made note of the location; it might be big enough for a fire to signal a rescue plane. She knew instinctively that if she couldn't radio for help, she shouldn't count on being rescued. If she waited and no one came, she'd be too weak to walk out on her own.

Returning, her feet landed quietly on the carpet of snow-covered pine needles. She barely noticed the orange sleeping bag. It was almost white with snow. To free her other arm, she knotted the red blanket around her neck like a cape, then carried the bag back towards the plane, hugging it close to her chest.

Warily, Selena approached the hulking shell of the plane, stopping for a moment at the edge of the thick undergrowth. For a moment, fear overcame her. She was terrified. He's injured, she told herself, maybe dead. He can't hurt you now. Then his deep voice reverberated in the hollow shell of the cabin.

"You fucking bitch!" he hollered, his words loose with mucous and blood. "You've done this! You and that goddamned Russian!" She felt his loathing in hard-edged fear. Now Selena remembered. Levesque had said it just before the crash. Something about Lorillard, about how he had done this, had rigged the plane and tried to get rid of them both at the same time. And the talk about Nikolai, as if he were alive.

There was a sudden crashing noise, as if something had been thrown. Selena heard Jean cry out in pain. Panicked, she backed further into the woods and stood frozen beneath the tall evergreens, unable to move or breathe. Her eyes focused on the half-sheared cockpit.

"You've wrecked everything! You bastard!" Jean cried out. His tone was desperate, his voice broken in pain. More banging and crashing and then he appeared, framed by the ragged edge of metal. Selena gasped in terror. Jean Levesque was leaning against the interior wall of the cabin, holding his stomach. Blood ran from his forehead, his mouth. One arm was broken, the raw white bone exposed, reflecting the moon's light.

Selena dropped the sleeping bag and took off, headed deep into the forest. Holding her rib tight, she ran as fast as she could. She looked back only once to see if he was following. It wasn't until she heard the crack of branches from behind that she knew. He was coming. She could hear his hungry breathing. He was close. She ran faster.

Suddenly Selena tripped and fell forward against her chest. She forced herself not to cry out and managed to crawl quickly to her feet, then braced herself against a tree, breathing in deep gulps of air. Running on, she knew her ankle had been sprained in the fall.

I can't hide, she thought. He'll track me in the snow. I don't know if I can outrun him. He's badly hurt, but he keeps coming, as if nothing could stop him. Selena had to think fast. The mountain climbing equipment -- if she could find the clearing, maybe there'd be something to help her.

"All right, bitch!" Jean hollered. His voice echoed through the still forest. "I'm gonna finish this. Maybe not like we planned, but you're still dead meat."

Selena was struggling for breath. What was he saying? Not like we planned? Finish this? She kept running, limping as fast as she could, looking over her shoulder. Lorillard must have known about this, he must have sent this man to kill her tonight. He must have planned it all, rigged the plane. He planned to kill them both. Then he must have known about the call, about Katya. He planned that, too. He knew I would get on that plane. Then what about Katya? Was she really missing? Or was it all a setup? Maybe Katya was all right. Selena felt a beat of hope push back her fear.

"Why are you doing this?" she called to Jean. "Lorillard tried to kill you."

Levesque's vicious laughter charged the air. He didn't answer. Selena kept on running. Hard as she tried she couldn't get enough oxygen. With every breath the pain seared through her like a hot metal rod. He's still coming, she thought. He's getting closer. How can I stop him?

"Why?" Selena yelled back, her chest heaving in pain with each breath. "What's he trying to do? What's his plan?" Selena could hear Levesque moving in. She took off again; she ran harder.

"Old King Kronos!" Jean hollered. "The King and his damned rocks!" He laughed, the sound bloody and loose in his throat.

"You can't get away with killing me," she yelled back. "The CIA knows I'm here. They'll be looking for me."

The sound of Jean's maniacal laughter sent an alarm shrieking through her body.

"And the Russian thinks you're so smart, Doctor."

What did he mean? Was the CIA involved somehow?

"Where's Dr. Potapov?" she called. Her voice was stronger now, with anger, but she felt the ache in her legs, the drag of her feet in the deepening snow. She was slowing down. Still, Levesque kept coming. He wouldn't stop. She remembered the blanket across her back. I must look like a cardinal in a snowstorm, she thought, an easy target. Limping through the brush, she struggled with the knot at her neck then threw the blanket into the woods.

The pain in her ribs was acute. She knew she couldn't keep going, not for long. I can't hide, she thought. I'll freeze. I've got to attack. It's my only chance.

Jean's cruel laughter again filled the cold night air. She had to rest, to think. Where was the clearing? In the snow everything looked the same. She turned right, took off limping, forced herself to keep up the pace. Then she saw it.

Turning eagerly in that direction, her foot caught on something. Pain ripped across her body as she flew forward onto the ground. She cried out from the agony, then lay there, her face in the cold snow, unable to get up.

Finally she forced herself to her knees, crawled behind the nearest bush, and crouched. Her breath billowed in white clouds before her. Huddled under the canopy of trees, she looked up toward the stars. Over the years, they'd always been her friends, but tonight there were none to be seen.

She heard a branch break and knew he was much closer. The realization frightened her so much that she lost her balance. Her hands reached down into the fresh snow to brace herself, and she felt a round, thin, snake-like coil. Pulling back quickly, it took her a moment to understand.

Selena brushed away the flaky white crystals and saw the mountain climbing line she'd been looking for. But what good would it do now? She tried to pull the cord to her and saw that it lay diagonally across the clearing just ahead. But the line was caught on something in the branches on the other side. It wouldn't budge. As she pulled, the green line rose taut across the open expanse. I can use it to trip him! I'll take him by surprise! But then what? There were only seconds left before he was there.

Her hands groped under the snow until she felt the top of a stone buried in the ground. Frantically she dug with her fingers and nails into the hard, frozen earth, clawing at the rock until it broke free. It was only a little bigger than a baseball, but it was all she had. She placed it at her feet and picked up another smaller stone. This she held tight in her fist.

The green line was visible now, lying across the clearing on the surface of the snow. She wiggled it back and forth, tried to bury it, make it disappear. Carefully, so as not to pull it back up to the surface, she wrapped the line around her palm. What was it stuck on? she wondered. She prayed it would continue to hold.

With one fist buried in the snow she firmly gripped the line. Her hand ached from the cold, but she told herself it was good. It would keep her alert. With the other hand she held the small rock and crouched, waiting, trying to quiet herself. She could hear him clearly now, his passage through the trees and his deep, hard breathing. He was close, but if she leaned around the tree to see him, he might notice her. Instead she judged his position by sound, kept her head and eyes turned sharply to the left for the first sight of him. He was about twelve yards away, she thought, directly behind her and to the right.

She waited a few more seconds then took the stone she clutched in her left hand and threw it as hard as she could, up ahead, beyond the clearing. The pain sliced across her chest with the force of the throw, but the stone landed with enough sound to make him stop in his tracks and search. He turned to the left a bit, towards the noise, and she could hear him pick up his pace. She grabbed the next rock and prayed whatever held the rope on the other end would not break free.

Afraid to move for fear he would spot her, she told herself, Wait. Wait. Be patient. She could feel the vibration of the ground. She heard his voice yell out angrily, directly beside her now, "I'm gonna kill you, you--"

She yanked the cord with every bit of force she had. His legs hit the rope hard, and she felt the line break free at the other end. She careened backwards into the brush. Looking up, she saw the ice axe tied to the other end of the green line. It was hurtling through the air.

In the moonlight everything seemed to happen in slow motion. He flew forward, his feet flipping over his head. His mouth screamed the word, "Biiittcchh!!" His enraged eyes looked immense and white in the darkness.

The green line hurtled gracefully through the night air, pulling the silver ice axe. The razor-sharp edge of the pick glinted with each revolution as it flew, spinning across the clearing, end over end through the dark, finally lodging in the trunk of a tree. Jean Levesque crashed to the ground, then tumbled and rolled. He lay face down in the snow.

Selena waited in the silence, terrified he would get up. Holding the tree trunk for support, she forced herself to her feet. Her eyes never left his body as she walked cautiously toward the clearing. She couldn't hear his breathing. She took another step closer, into the exposed, open space. She could see his face now, his eyes closed, and she waited, wanting to be certain. Suddenly he moaned, opened his eyes and stared at her. For a moment she was frozen in terror, unable to flee as she watched him struggle to his feet, then fall.

She ran limping towards the ice axe. Jean again tried to get up. She grabbed high to reach the silver handle and tugged fiercely. Its ragged edge was deeply embedded in the rough bark of the massive evergreen. She could hear him laughing behind her. He was up now. He was coming closer. With each yank on the axe her ribs shot a fierce pain through her chest. She could hear him breathing. He was almost to her. When the axe suddenly broke free, the momentum whirled her backwards and around. She lost her grip on the handle. The axe fell.

Levesque threw back his head in laughter. Blood trailed from his forehead and from his mouth, but his eyes sparkled with life. She lunged for the axe. He grabbed her just as she took hold of the handle. She spun with all her might, both arms fully extended, sweeping the axe through the air, breaking free of his hold and crying out from the pain as the shining steel flew up, up and around.

She could hear the clean, piercing sound when the sharp point sunk deep into his neck, stopping them both in a deathly quiet. He stood before her for what seemed like many moments, staring with wide eyes that looked at nothing, no longer smiling. She released the handle of the axe and backed away, her legs shaking beneath her. A rattling sound wet with blood surfaced from deep inside him. Finally, the axe still embedded, he fell backwards.

Silence suffused the forest once again. Jean Levesque lay perfectly still, his eyes and mouth open to the falling snow. Selena could hear only her gasping breath. She didn't move. She watched him. She knew he would get up again.

After several minutes, she limped cautiously around his body, keeping a safe distance, and then stood looking down at his face. The talon-like spike of the axe had penetrated beneath his chin and driven its eight-inch, curved blade up through his skull. The steely point surfaced over his right eye. Warm blood seeped down from the silver tip and pooled on the staring eyeball, then streamed down his cheek, a deep, rich, red against the crystalline snow.

Selena stood perfectly still. Her fast, shallow breaths billowed like smoke around her head and faded into the moonlight. When his body jerked abruptly, she shrieked in horror and lurched away. His head fell loosely to the side, spilling the gathered blood from the open eye that stared directly at her. In the angle of moonlight, the engraved "L" on Lorillard's ice axe glinted hypnotically.

It was several minutes before she believed it was really over, that he was really dead. She watched the quiet snow falling over Jean's body, melting on his still-warm skin, and disappearing into the pools of his blood. She left him there, lying on his back in the center of the clearing.

CHAPTER 18

Selena returned to the shell of the plane, trembling with fear and cold. She told herself not to think about Jean anymore. She must concentrate on surviving. She went straight to the mangled cockpit and tried the radio. As she'd suspected, it was crushed and useless. So was the compass. Searching the interior of the plane for supplies, she pulled open every cupboard and chest she could find. It was dark, but she managed to locate two more red blankets. Fortunately, one of the overhead compartments carried camping supplies: tin dishes and waterproof matches, even some dried fruit. Stuffed in the back of a storage closet, she found some clothing in a blue nylon duffle bag.

First she wrapped her chest tightly with a cravat made from the long-sleeved shirts, and then she put on a blue sweatshirt and a yellow rain slicker. The bright color of the rain jacket reminded her of the orange sleeping bag she'd dropped earlier in the woods and, despite her fear, she forced herself to go out and look for it. She found it covered with snow, but inside it was still dry.

Returning to the plane, she painfully lugged sheets of torn metal to the cabin, then leaned them against the gaping hole of the cockpit to block the bitter wind. In the moonlight she was able to find several branches and pine boughs that had been sheared from the trees. These she dragged inside and braced against the seatbacks, using them as insulation against the wind.

Less fearful now, she returned to the forest. Her hands were stiff and cut, but despite her exhaustion and injuries, she forced herself to continue searching for dead branches, leaves and pine needles to build a fire. Stopping for a moment to rest, Selena noticed the snow had stopped. She looked to the sky and saw a clearing between the rapidly moving clouds. The stars were finally visible. Dropping the branches, she smiled. She felt as if she'd been given some encouragement, some sign. Stars could move 100 miles per second, she knew, but because they're so far away they would seem constant, unchanging, for her entire life. She knew the constellations could help her find her way.

This was the Southern Hemisphere, she reminded herself. South of the Equator there would be stars visible that couldn't be seen at home. Selena searched for the Southern Cross. It was the smallest of all the constellations, and for many people a disappointment to behold after hearing its romantic name for so many years. But Selena knew the longer bar of the Southern Cross points almost exactly toward the South Pole of the sky.

The light clouds passing overhead made it difficult to see, but finally she recognized it. There, next to the large, impressive figure of the Centaur, half man, half horse, she could clearly see Alpha Centauri, marking one of the forefeet. It and Beta Centauri, the other forefoot, were both bright, first magnitude stars. And there between the front and back legs of the Centaur was the Southern Cross. It was like suddenly seeing God, and she felt tears burn her eyes with happiness, with the power of life over loss and pain.

She had wondered at times if her daughter were ever taken from her, if such a terrible thing should ever happen, would she still experience this connection to the stars, the rightness of their existence and hers? Probably not for a very long time. But maybe, eventually, her love for the sky would comfort her, remind her of the joy of her love. She could connect with Katya there again, as she did with her mother. For joy wasn't just happiness in extreme, Selena thought. It embraced all life, both pain and pleasure, just as the stars did, unblinking and omniscient.

Selena felt exhaustion set in. She took some bearings to help her the next day. If the Southern Cross points directly south, that meant she should head west, towards that tall group of evergreens. She tried to see further, to give herself a deeper sense of direction, but doubted the shapes she saw at night would prove helpful in the morning. At least it was a start.

Once inside her makeshift den, Selena removed the bottom cushions from two seats and used one to sit on while the other she propped behind her as protection against the cold metal. In the corner she built a small fire and watched as the wind currents lifted the smoke and spun it around in a circle, over her head, then out through the hole of the cockpit. She covered herself with the sleeping bag. From her pockets she took some small rocks and placed them onto the edge of the fire.

It was important to keep her energy up, so she tried to eat some dried fruit and nuts, but couldn't. Instead, she sat transfixed, staring into the flames. Where was Katya? The question was like a ceaseless alarm, a siren, urgent and shrill within her body and her mind. It felt like a relentless, physical call to action. She considered leaving right away, heading down the mountain, but knew that would be foolish. She must survive. She must wait for daylight and warmth. She must find her daughter.

Lorillard had planned to kill both Jean and her. He knew the phone call would come. He knew she would leave to go to her daughter. And Nik? She felt certain he must be alive. Was Lorillard responsible for the hang gliding accident? And what had Jean been yelling about King Kronos? He had said something about the King and his rocks. Selena tried to think, but her mind wasn't clear. If only she could figure out Pierre's plan. SQUIDs, she reminded herself, but she couldn't focus. Her thoughts were a blur, fading in and out.

What would she do tomorrow? She had no compass but she knew the heavens well enough to determine direction. As a girl her father had insisted she take every Red Cross course from life saving to bandage wrapping, just in case. She understood survival was based on finding water, first and foremost, and food, shelter, and signaling for help, if possible. Water wouldn't be a problem with all the snow, she thought. As for food, she remembered how the young Red Cross instructor had taught them bugs were food. A person could eat ants, he'd said. You just had to be sure to pull off their heads; otherwise they'd pinch your tongue. In South America, he'd told them, people ate roasted ants in the movie theaters instead of popcorn. She and her friends had squealed at the thought of it.

Selena smiled at the memory, how she had run home to tell her father. She knew even then his insistence on the Girl Scouts and the Red Cross training was because he was afraid of losing her, the way he had lost his precious Olga. Ironically, all his caution only served to make Selena more rebellious and less afraid.

Selena placed another dried branch on the fire and watched the flames jump and spit. Her father had died five years ago. Their relationship hadn't been an easy one, but remembering him, she longed for the feeling of security he'd always given her.

It was her father who had ensured her love of the stars. He hadn't meant to, of course, and at first she'd hated him for it. She was in junior high school when he insisted she join him on a sailing trip. It had been one of his futile attempts to get to know her, to be closer. Selena hadn't wanted to go, said she would miss her friends at home. Her protests were ignored.

He chartered a 48-foot boat from the Rosey Roads Marina on the military base in Puerto Rico. Together they cruised the Grenadine Islands for three weeks. Expecting to be bored, instead Selena was soon enthralled with the night sky. Every evening after dinner she would lie on deck and watch the stars. The meteor showers were dazzling and combined with the native peace of the outdoors, Selena experienced contentment and a spiritual, primitive wonder she'd never known. It was the best of her memories with her father.

The smell of burning pine and the hiss of flames soothed her. Exhaustion followed close behind and eventually overwhelmed her. She missed Charlie. And Nik. With the rising warmth she realized how blessed she'd been in life. So many people to love.

She dozed for a while. When she woke, she looked at her watch only to find it had been smashed. The fire was fading, and she scattered some damp pine needles over the top, producing smoke before a flame broke free. She placed a good-sized branch over this, but when she leaned back, her body began to shake again, as much from fear and pain, she thought, as from the cold. She wrapped her arms around herself and rocked back and forth, trying to calm her heart. She told herself she was all right, the worst was over, but delayed terror had invaded her body and it responded with a will of its own.

* * * * *

"Damn it, Hambly." Bingham was pacing the room. "This better go as planned."

"I'm sure it will, sir."

Bingham was shaking his head. "Mulroney's really on my back."

"The nuclear inspectors are scheduled to leave in 48 hours, sir."

"I know, I know. Why don't you go tell Mulroney. Maybe he'll cool off and leave me alone. And tell the President, too, while you're at it. That's where this is coming from." Bingham finally sat down with his elbows on his desk and his head between his hands. Hambly knew his boss just needed to let off steam.

"We just received a bulletin from Admiral Kingsley, sir. Operation Blue Whale is proceeding on schedule. The aircraft carrier Reagan will be approaching the Chilean coast in 72 hours."

"Well, thank God for that," Bingham said. He opened a side drawer of his desk and pulled out a small tray. Tying a new fly for his first fishing expedition up at the lake helped relieve the pressure. As soon as this operation is over, he told himself, I'm out of this hellhole. The sooner I get to that cabin, the better. The property was in escrow and due to close in two weeks. And the cash was ready, all $75,000. Thanks to Mr. Pierre Lorillard, Bingham thought.

* * * * *

When Arthur entered Mr. Lorillard's bedroom suite the morning after the dinner party, he found his employer fully dressed and asleep on top of the covers. Pierre's small frame was in the fetal position, curled tight against the night's chill. To Arthur he looked like a sleeping child.

Quietly placing the tray of coffee, juice, and the morning papers on a round table near the patio door, Arthur carefully woke Mr. Lorillard.

"Sir," he said softly, bending over him. Lorillard's eyes darted beneath their closed lids, his hands clenched tightly under his cheek. "Mr. Lorillard, sir."

Pierre woke with a start and sat up quickly. Looking around the room, he appeared confused.

"What is it?" he demanded. "What's the problem?" A person was vulnerable when they were asleep. He didn't like being found that way.

"You have a phone call, sir. Senor Ruiz from the Santiago airport. He said it was important. He's waiting on the line."

Pierre cleared his throat and got quickly to his feet. He brushed his pants and shirt respectably smooth. Rest hadn't come until the early morning hours, sometime after four-thirty. He could not remember his dreams, he never did, but this morning Pierre felt troubled and exhausted. By the time he walked across the room to the telephone, however, he had cleared his head and firmly grasped the situation at hand.

"This is Pierre Lorillard." There was silence in the room as Arthur poured a cup of black coffee and placed it on the desk beside the phone. He went to straighten the bed.

"Are you certain?" Pierre asked, his voice flat. Again silence. "I see. Well, keep me informed. Speak only to me, do you understand?" He hung up the phone and walked with his coffee to the window, then looked at his watch. It was eight o'clock.

Looking out at the storm clouds gathering over the choppy sea, he asked, "Where is Mr. Coons?"

"He's ready to leave for the LIFT, sir, but he said there was no hurry. The helicopter is preparing for departure." Arthur topped off Mr. Lorillard's coffee from the sterling silver pitcher. The morning papers lay untouched, and his employer seemed distracted.

"Is there anything else I can do for you, sir?" he asked with concern.

"I'll be leaving in a few minutes." He looked at his watch. "I'm expecting another call."

Pierre had just received word his plane had crashed in the lower Andes, somewhere east of the LIFT. No signals had as yet been received from the plane's radio direction finding beacons. There must be a malfunction. A search party would be sent to fly over the area, but visibility was poor due to the thick tree growth. No survivors were anticipated.

That took care of two problems, Pierre thought. Jean had been loyal, but he'd become troublesome, was out of control. It was unfortunate, but the man's life had been destroyed many years earlier. He'd never completely recovered.

Dr. Hartmann, however, that was a different matter. A remarkable woman, he thought. She's provocative, both physically and intellectually. But it couldn't be helped. He couldn't risk her testimony before the symposium and before the press that an asteroid was on a collision course with Earth. Lorillard didn't need the competition of a barrage of U.S. nuclear weapons in space. Hartmann's suspicions about Nikolai only exacerbated the situation. Still, Pierre was surprised at the remorse he felt over her death.

Lorillard remained standing as he sipped from his cup of coffee. He forced himself to concentrate on the pressing matter of the moment. Whoever tampered with Dr. Hartmann's research results wanted the faulty information announced before the Star Wars vote. Why? Who? Pierre felt certain he knew.

* * * * *

Over and over again as Hambly patiently waited, Clive Bingham read the memo he held in his hand, then repeated the words in his head. He knows. He knows. Lorillard knows.

Bingham had left CIA headquarters and driven out of the sixty-mile tap zone to make his usual bi-weekly call to Pierre Lorillard. Now his mind sifted the man's words, scrutinized his tone for any hint of exactly what Lorillard understood. He was hard to read, but Bingham was pretty sure he was right.

173

"By the way," Pierre Lorillard had told Bingham casually. "Dr. Hartmann is scheduled to give her report this afternoon. I'm hopeful she won't hurt the Star Wars bill too badly."

"So is the President," Bingham said. Then there had been silence, an empty space that Lorillard left, presumably for Bingham to fill.

"I know you'll keep me informed," Lorillard eventually said, "of any developments."

"Absolutely," Bingham said, then hung up.

It's no good, Clive thought. I smell something foul. Something's stinking up a storm. He read the memo again.

"Dr. Selena Hartmann and Jean Levesque have been in a plane crash in the foothills of the Andes. No survivors expected." Bingham shook his head. Even if Lorillard found out about the altered research results, why would he want to get rid of Hartmann? He stood to benefit more than anybody by passage of the Star Wars bill. Lorillard Labs would benefit in major contracts. It made no sense. If only I had a decent agent in place, Clive thought, shaking his head. The Agency is going to hell and the sooner I get out, the better.

Hambly continued to wait, but Bingham said nothing. This more than anything made Norman anxious. His boss was thinking.

Clive walked to the window. The squirrel hadn't been around for a while and he congratulated himself. I got you, you little bastard. And I'm going to get Lorillard, too. We'll just see.

"Hambly, I want those inspectors to be on the very next plane out of here, do you understand? They need to be down there yesterday. Lorillard's making a move. I just know it. I've got a bad feeling about this. We can't wait any longer."

"Yes sir. I'll take care of it."

"Time to make the plant. Place the call to the *Washington Post*. Immediately. And get me General Rosales. I'd better let him know we're on our way."

Hambly left the room and Bingham continued to stare out the window and puzzle over the situation. Lorillard knows, Bingham thought. He must. But there's no way to be sure. If he's figured out about Hartmann, about the research, what's the bastard going to do? And why?"

* * * * *

"You're making a mistake," Nikolai told Pierre Lorillard. "It's foolish."

"As I told you before, my friend. There are other forces at work here. I hope to explain all of it to you very soon."

When Lorillard had told him Katya was safe and would be moved to the adjoining suite of rooms as soon as the formula was delivered, Nikolai knew he must give Pierre what he wanted. Walking to the computer, he inserted a disc, made some last minute additions to his work, and transferred the file.

"Immediately," Nik said, handing Lorillard the disc.

"She's on her way now," Lorillard assured him.

Confident bastard, Nik thought, his frustration and fury growing at the impossibility of the situation.

"There'll be no more trouble from Jean," Pierre said. "Never again."

It was then Lorillard made the announcement. The LIFT was going Online. ASAP. Appalled, Nik tried desperately to convince Pierre all magnet tests must be completed prior to operation.

"There's an inherent danger," Nik said. "You've got to understand. Superconductors are limited in two distinct ways: Critical Temperature and Critical Current Density, or CCD. If the temperature is too high or the current too strong, superconductivity is lost."

"We've met that challenge," Lorillard said. "Enough tests."

"But what if the magnets quench?" Nik said. "The sudden resistance will produce dangerous amounts of heat. They'll turn red hot and explode."

"In all the tests, quenches reached their plateau well above the operating current," Pierre said, losing his patience. "There's ample margin."

Nikolai could see he was getting nowhere. The man was a maniac. "You're wrong, here, Lorillard. Absolutely wrong."

Pierre chuckled at Nikolai like an indulgent parent.

"You must stop being so afraid, Nik, so negative. Remember on the mountain when you felt you couldn't go on? Determination, my friend. The most powerful engine." Pierre smiled and walked to the door. "I will explain everything. Soon, my friend."

* * * * *

General Enrique Rosales wiped the glob of spilled hot sauce from the shirt of his blue uniform. His feet were propped on his office coffee table and he was watching television. The stress from his belly had finally popped the bottom button of his shirt, but he was too drunk to care. He needed to take a piss, but that would have to wait. On television Pierre Lorillard was giving a news conference, and Rosales wasn't about to miss it.

After Lorillard's dinner party, Enrique had flown back to Santiago in his military jet, then slept at the office. First thing in the morning he called a meeting of his top men. Enough of being bullied, Rosales decided. If there was one thing he'd learned in his 52 years, it was that the toughest bastard always won. Every time. That was a game he knew how to play.

"We're live at Kronos Hall," the news anchorman said. "U.S. Representative Pete Chapman is about to make an announcement."

Enrique Rosales watched Pierre Lorillard enter the hall followed by Chapman and his entourage. Reporters were hustling around them, all barking questions as the men approached the podium.

"Ladies and gentlemen," Pierre said into the microphone. "As the host of this conference, it is with deep regret I make this report. The noted astronomer Dr. Selena Hartmann has been in a plane crash."

Murmurs and sighs rose from the audience of astronomers. A stir of surprise from the gathered press didn't stop their cameras flashing shots of Lorillard's somber face. He continued.

"She and the pilot, Mr. Jean Levesque, are missing and believed dead. Their plane crashed in the foothills of the Andes. As yet the search party has not located the scene of the accident. I will keep you informed of all developments. Representative Chapman?" Lorillard said, moving away from the mike.

"This is a sad time for us all, but I'm hopeful Dr. Hartmann has survived and will be located soon. As many of you know, Dr. Hartmann was due to present her research findings tomorrow on the potential collision of an asteroid with Earth. In her absence and at the request of our host, Pierre Lorillard, I will present an abbreviated version of the scheduled report tomorrow at noon. Let us remember both victims in our prayers and hopes. Thank you."

General Rosales hit the power button on his clicker. Rising with effort from the couch, he brushed the crumbs off his belly and made a sloppy attempt to stand at attention and salute.

"Maòana, señores," he said. "Vaya con Dios."

* * * * *

Lorillard had given him assurances. And limits. Nik paced the floor, distraught over what he had done, reviewing the possibilities. And the dangers. He stopped and stared out the window, waiting.

Any attempt to escape or communicate with others would mean immediate punishment of Katya. If Nik cooperated fully, if the formula tests were successful, they would both be allowed to go free. Katya would be 'found' in the jungles of Costa Rica, the unharmed victim of a failed ransom attempt by guerilla forces. Nikolai would be given a new identity, a position at a prestigious university, and allowed to continue with his work. No one would be harmed. But any attempts to involve the authorities would bring dire consequences. They would not be able to protect themselves.

Nik didn't believe Lorillard, but what did it matter. He could not deny him. He could not risk harm to Katya. He was sick at the thought of what he had done. By giving the formula to Pierre, he felt certain he had changed world history. And not for the better.

Nik was pacing again when he heard the sound of crying. He stopped, stood perfectly still and held his breath. At first he didn't believe his ears. It must be Katya. They had finally brought her.

"Katya!" he yelled, hoping she would hear him through the walls of the room. "Katya! Are you all right?" The crying continued just outside the door.

"Yes," she said through her tears. "I'm all right. But where's my mother? They have Mom!" He heard keys in the lock. The door swung open and there she was, her arms held roughly behind her back by a dull brute of a guard. When she saw Nikolai, she tried to run to him, but the guard jerked her back until she cried out in pain.

"Stop it!" Nik yelled. "You're hurting her, you fool. Stop it!" He ran towards her, stopping only when he saw the barrel of the gun at the back of her head.

As if in justification, the moron said, "Your daughter tried to burn the place down." Nik's body registered shock at the word "daughter."

The guard pulled Katya back into the hallway. "I was supposed to let you see her," he said. "Now she goes in the other room." She began to sob.

"Where's my mother?" she cried.

Running to her Nik called, "Katya!" but the door slammed in his face.

CHAPTER 19

The clarity of a bird's repeated song woke Selena. As soon as she opened her eyes, reality began to seep through her weariness. Only a moment later the image of Jean Levesque's bloody, staring face pierced by the hook of the ice axe rose clearly in her mind. She shuddered.

With her first attempt to move, a sharp pain shot through her chest. After two more attempts, she got to her feet stiffly. Her entire body felt bruised and brutalized. To warm her frozen toes, she curled them inside her thin leather flats. You must move them, she thought. You must increase the circulation, even if it hurts. Her ankle felt swollen and sore, but she knew she would have to walk on it. You've got to find your way down to the foothills, she told herself. You've got to find Katya.

Selena knew Lorillard would not report his plane missing any sooner than he must. If she and Jean survived the crash, he wouldn't want them rescued. She could try to signal by building a fire, but in this dense forest, rescue planes, if there were any, probably wouldn't see it.

Into the chest pocket of the large yellow poncho she put the last two small bags of dried fruit and nuts, then carefully threaded her way out of the plane's shell and stepped into the woods. In the daylight she could see the destruction and chaos of the crash all around her, but it no longer terrified her. She noticed the first light of day was filtering majestically through the tall pines.

Before starting her journey, Selena looked around to see if there was anything else she might need, anything that would help her climb down to the valley. Nothing useful came into view, and she decided the less weight she had to carry, the better.

She thought of the body, lying dead in the clearing just beyond, and for a moment felt an unreasonable fear that it might be gone, that Levesque might have come to life and be looking at her now. Then she had a thought. Maybe there was something on the body, something in his clothes that would help her. Some written clue to Lorillard's plan? A phone number? But would she be able to dig into the pockets of that man, lying dead and frozen? They had Nik at the LIFT. She hadn't seen him, but she felt certain he was there. She had to try.

The snow had covered their footprints and she wandered timidly for a while, fearful she would come upon the body without warning. She constantly searched the woods for movement. It wasn't until she came to the clearing that she knew Levesque was really dead. His fallen body was a muffled shape of white, the violence of its death camouflaged by the softness of the tranquil snow.

Selena approached cautiously, still fearful he might move. Breaking a branch from a shrub, she used it to brush the white powder from his shirt and pants. She left his face covered.

Taking a deep breath, Selena crouched down close. Her hand tried to reach into the pocket of his pants, but the cloth was rigid. She pushed her fingers further. She could feel the stiffness of his dead body against her palm. He was frozen solid. Her fingers searched but found only coins. She moved to the other side.

Again she had to force herself. Her fingers were cold and stinging. She pushed deeper, against the hard folds of the blood-soaked fabric. She felt something cold and metal. Keys. She pulled them out with some effort and decided to keep them. Maybe they would help later.

His wallet must be in his back pocket, she thought. How would she ever lift the heavy body and roll it over? She tried, but the weight was too much for her rib. Sitting down on the ground right beside his waist, she stuck her two feet as far under his body as she could. She pushed hard to raise it a few inches.

There was just enough room for her hand, raw and burning from the wet cold, to find the wallet and pull it out. She let the corpse fall, then climbed to her feet and quickly moved away, still watchful for any sign of movement.

Inside the wallet she found an assortment of credit cards, some Chilean and U.S. money, a California driver's license, all the usual things. There was nothing to give her a clue. Beneath a folded flap she saw the white of paper. Her fingers scratched at the frozen, black leather, pulled the paper loose, and saw a check from "Grand Tour, Inc," for $25,000. It was made out to Clive

Bingham. She couldn't read the signature at the bottom, but it wasn't Pierre Lorillard's.

Clive Bingham? Grand Tour was the name of Lorillard's boat. Did he also have a company by that name? And why Clive Bingham? Was Lorillard paying him off? For what? Selena stuffed the check into her back pocket.

She pulled Jean's license and credit cards from the wallet and threw them on the ground. A folded and torn piece of paper flipped in the breeze along the crust of snow. She ran after it, opened it, and found what looked like the corner of a painting, a watercolor. Vivid colors, purples, reds, dripped to the edge of the paper. Across these colors were the letters 'ya,' written in script.

She recognized it immediately. It was Katya's signature! This belonged to her daughter! This paper, this watercolor, had been made by Katya. Selena felt dizzy. That hideous man had been with her daughter. Selena couldn't breathe and her mind spun. Her knees buckled beneath her and she let herself go, crumpled on the snow. With both hands, she brushed snow across her face, then, blinking, wiped it away. Katya was at the LIFT! Katya must be at the LIFT!

In the next moment, Selena was on her feet. She knew now that nothing could stop her. She was determined to find her daughter.

* * * * *

Pierre Lorillard was used to resistance. He considered it one of the most frustrating weaknesses of human nature, but he understood it. Why not say no, it won't work, it isn't possible? For most people it was easier to tear down something than to make a stand. No one was prepared to risk anything. Nobody had the guts. And what could be safer than saying it won't work? If you were right and it didn't, you'd get to say, 'I told you so,' and look very wise. If perchance something worked, well, everyone would be so pleased they'd forget your resistance. You were just being cautious. So the naysayers far outnumbered people like himself, people who had a vision and weren't afraid to pursue it. It was as true in business and in science as it was in life. Lorillard was convinced that worldwide, people's fear was the most destructive force, the most dangerous aspect of human nature.

When it came time for the KRONOS PROJECT, he knew the resistance would be rampant. He decided to circumvent it, bypass it completely. But today Pierre would make an exception. He was going to give this man one chance. If Nik was as smart as Pierre thought, the Russian would understand the magnitude of the plan and its importance to the future of the world. He would see the virtue in Pierre's foresight.

Lorillard found Nikolai alone in the secured area of the LIFT Control Pod, a single guard on watch at the door. Pierre got right down to business.

"There's something I'd like to show you," he said, a mischievous smile in his pale blue eyes. "Come with me."

"Where is Dr. Hartmann?" Nik demanded before leaving the room. "Has she been hurt? What have you done with her?"

Lorillard hesitated for a moment, but his eyes never lost contact with Nik's. "She is perfectly all right, my friend. I assure you."

"Where is she? If anything's happened to her...."

"I give you my word," Pierre said. "She's safe." He held up both hands.

Nik looked at him with disgust. The man would say anything to get his way. Pierre returned his gaze with steady calm.

"Come with me. You'll see."

With the guard behind him, Nik followed Pierre down the hall, through a security check, towards the central area of the control pod. The doors opened onto a massive, oval-shaped room ringed in glass. A bank of computers and oversized TV screens lined the circumference of the room. Brushed-aluminum walls and counters added to the sterile, but efficient ambiance. In the center, additional monitoring screens rose to the ceiling. Multi-layered control panels occupied the attention of a staff of thirty women and men. This was the nerve center of the LIFT.

The staff worked frantically in a scramble of activity and commotion along the bank of consoles. Nik had never seen the control room in full operation like this before.

"What's going on?" he asked.

"We're preparing to go online," Pierre said. "I've ordered Extreme Status." Lorillard laughed at Nik's look of alarm. "I want the system to be fully operational by Monday."

"That's not possible. What about Core Status? You can't skip that."

Pierre laughed out loud. "I'll explain. Come along." Lorillard approached a high-security elevator in the center of the pod. Reaching for a chain around his neck, he pulled out a black metal card punctuated with a series of indentations, then inserted it into the steel frame of the elevator. The doors opened, and they entered the small, silver compartment. Pierre pressed down. He looked at Nik with a tight-lipped smile that stretched across his face.

The elevator opened onto a narrow corridor. They walked to the right.

Two guards flanked the hallway just outside a double doorway.

"I'll call if I need you," Pierre said, again inserting the black metal card.

It was a stark, yet elegant, circular suite of offices completely decorated in shades of silver and gray, the exterior wall constructed of floor-to-ceiling, one-way glass. The view of the LIFT facility and the desert expanse was so breathtaking as to induce vertigo.

Nik brought his focus back to the room's layout. Ever since Katya's arrival at the control pod, he'd been working on a plan of escape. Any information about the configuration of the LIFT could be useful.

Lorillard walked to an elaborate console of computers standing free form in the center of the room. He made several entries.

"Watch," he said.

On a wall-sized screen Nikolai saw the words KRONOS PROJECT appear with what looked like an artist's rendition of some futuristic space landing. Robotic vehicles were traveling the cratered surface of an irregular body.

"Nik, this is the most exciting project of my life," Pierre Lorillard said. "I want you to be part of it."

* * * * *

Selena looked to the sky. An early morning full moon and the location of the rising sun confirmed the westerly direction she'd charted from last night's Southern Cross. She must focus her energy and attention on moving forward, moving back to life. It was cold, but she felt all right, not frostbitten, and she knew movement would help to raise her body temperature. The sun would soon warm the air. Picking her way through the brush in the fresh, shallow snow, she tried to estimate her distance from the LIFT.

They were headed due east at the time they flew over the control pod. When she moved to the back of the plane they had just passed the other side of the accelerator ring. Before they crashed, the plane had banked. They'd flown south for maybe ten more minutes. Selena estimated they were flying at about 250 miles per hour, and that meant at most they'd be about 40 miles east of the LIFT. They hadn't flown far into the Andes then, and she mustn't be at too great an altitude. This was encouraging. Selena knew one of the most important ingredients for survival was the belief that it was possible. Any negative thoughts would only drain her much-needed energy. Limping badly, she pushed herself to pick up the pace.

Think, she told herself. Concentrate. Why did they take Katya? What is

Lorillard up to? He had planned to kill both her and Jean. He had rigged the plane. Lorillard knew she would get the call, knew she must go to her daughter. And all the time, Katya was there, with him.

Jean had called Lorillard 'King Kronos,' the 'King of Rocks.' It must be relevant. Kronos Hall, King Kronos. But she had looked it up on the computer, she knew the myth of Kronos. There had to be something else to it.

Kronos had something to do with astronomy, she remembered. In one of her early textbooks there had been an illustration, some ancient depiction of the god. The image was vague to her, but she recalled Kronos spitting something out of his mouth. It must have been the babies, she thought. But wait. The stone. He also spit the stone out. That was the illustration. The stone fell to earth and was revered. A temple was built where it landed. It was considered a heavenly stone. That's why astronomers identified with Kronos. They thought the mythology was based on an actual meteorite fall. That's why the illustration had been in her astronomy text. Lorillard was a student of the stars. That's why Lorillard had built the LIFT on the site of the pallasite meteorite. His heavenly stone. His precious stone.

So what did it all mean? Lorillard was King Kronos, the King of Rocks. That's what Jean had called him. Selena knew the answer was there. Why didn't it come to her? She walked on, pushed herself harder.

The rustle of the yellow slicker, her deep breathing, and the crack of branches beneath her cold feet, all disturbed the silent woods. Occasionally she looked up, noticed the cold beauty surrounding her, but it didn't help the pain she felt each time she stepped on her right ankle. Her ribs were incredibly tender and swollen. None of it matters, she told herself. I must get to Katya. And to Nik. I have to reach the LIFT.

As she walked, Selena continued to puzzle over the evidence. The remarkable meteorite Lorillard had on display at his home came to mind. He said he was a collector. Meteorites were stones from heaven, if anything was. And what about the SQUIDs? SQUIDs were the most sensitive measuring devices available to scientists. They were limited only because of the expense and difficulty of maintaining their superconductors at the right temperature and critical density. Nikolai's formula for an advanced superconductor could lessen or do away with those limitations. As hard as she tried, none of it came together.

After two hours Selena rested, sitting atop a large rock. She ate some of the dried fruit and some snow for fluid replacement. Severely fatigued, she knew it was because of the altitude as well as the physical shock to her body.

Her feet were so cold she could barely feel them. She feared frostbite and wondered if she should take the time to build a fire. She had to keep going, she knew. After a few minutes, she took off again.

Selena noticed the sun was moving towards the north. That was right, she told herself. At noon in the northern hemisphere the sun appeared in the southern part of the sky. It was the opposite here. She had been heading due west, and adjusted her course a little to the north.

What else did she know? Think, she told herself. What else have you seen or heard? Review the places you've been, the conversations you've had.

She pictured the four of them gathered around the magnificent meteorite at Zambarano. There was something Lorillard had said. He'd spoken about an article of hers, about the technology involved in precisely charting the course of asteroids. That's right. And she had been surprised. That article had never been published. She wrote it a year ago. How had he read it? He would have needed access to her computer. That was possible, but why?

Checking her location in the woods, Selena noticed the snow wasn't as deep. Despite the cold, she was sweating from the exertion. Eat some snow, she told herself. Don't become dehydrated. She felt utterly exhausted. Keep going, she told herself. You can't stop. Keep thinking.

What about the grounds at Zambarano? Remember the telescopes on Lorillard's balcony? His knowledge of space, his fascination with aliens? That would tie in with his meteorite collecting. And that leads to the Kronos myth. The King of Rocks, hurtling stones down on Earth. "The King of Rocks," Selena repeated out loud. "Rocks?"

She remembered the book in Lorillard's study. The cover had a photograph of a huge chunk of platinum. The book had been about resource depletion of the planet. Resources. Rocks. The King of Rocks.

"Oh my God!" Selena cried out loud. "No! It can't be!" She stopped walking. She hoped she was wrong. But no. That's got to be his plan! It had to be. All of a sudden, everything made sense. The pieces fell together to the tune of trillions of dollars. Why hadn't I seen it before? she thought. Pierre Lorillard was going to attempt to mine asteroids in space!

Selena kept walking, picking up her pace with the excitement of her discovery. Asteroid mining had been talked about for years. There was a devoted contingent of scientists who supported the idea. But no one was seriously considering it now. The basic technology was there, yes. But it wasn't advanced enough. The process would be too dangerous, not only to

184

those attempting the mining, but to the entire planet Earth. No one would dare. No one, she realized, except Pierre Lorillard. He would. Lorillard would believe that he could pull it off. All the recent discussion of defensive nuclear warheads in space would only serve to encourage him, even force his hand.

It was estimated one asteroid could hold as much as $30 trillion worth of precious metals. The value of the platinum group alone, if it could be mined, was incalculable. And asteroids were only the beginning. It was possible the planet Mars was covered with diamonds. And the most valuable of all, Selena thought, was probably the Moon, a resource for helium-3.

Scientists had dreamed of the possibilities, but no one had proposed a serious plan for the immediate future. It would never be approved. The danger was far too great. The margin for error miniscule.

Selena was slowing down. She couldn't help it. The exertion was taking its toll, and she felt she couldn't go on much longer. Just a little more, she told herself, just before she tripped. She grabbed at the branch of a young evergreen, managing to hold herself upright. You've got to keep going, she told herself. Think. Keep thinking.

What about the SQUIDs? They would be used to determine the composition of the asteroid. Lorillard could then pinpoint the exact location of the most precious metals. And Nik's formula would make the SQUIDs work in space, from a robotic probe. It was all there, Selena realized. And it had to be stopped. She could not allow Lorillard to detonate nuclear bombs in space to mine asteroids. The consequences could be catastrophic.

And Nik would never be a party to it either, she thought. That's why Marfa Ivanovna was dead. They had gone after the formula. That's why they needed Katya. If they were capable of accessing her computer, her research, they were capable of discovering Katya was Nik's daughter. Selena felt her balance falter as a roll of fear and nausea spread through her gut. Was Lorillard also responsible for tampering with her research at Keck? Why would he? It made no sense. If he were determined to mine the asteroids, he wouldn't want other nuclear weapons in space. He wouldn't want the Star Wars bill to pass. Her presentation would have almost guaranteed that. Who did it then? Did it have something to do with Clive Bingham?

The pain and exhaustion had completely drained her of energy. Selena felt she could not go on. She kept walking.

CHAPTER 20

"You want me to be part of what?" Nik's voice was anxious. While he worked urgently to decipher the meaning and purpose of what Pierre was showing him, his entire body registered alarm, as if it expected to be surprised by something worse than it could possibly imagine. Nik studied the screen.

"Your formula has allowed me to create a refinement of the SQUID technology. With it, Nik, I intend to mine asteroids." Lorillard watched Nik's shock. "That's right. There's a wealth of precious metals and minerals out there. You know that. All we need to do is harvest them."

Nik could hardly believe his ears. Had Lorillard lost his mind completely? Mining asteroids? That was a dream of the future, not a reasonable expectation of today. Nikolai struggled not to show his thoughts. He needed all the information he could get and that meant encouraging Pierre to go on.

"I don't understand."

"Let me explain," Pierre said. "The strategy of the KRONOS PROJECT would involve locating a near-Earth asteroid, one in close orbit, and precisely plotting its course. When the NEA approached Earth, we'd use explosives to fragment it. Say it's two or three miles across and shaped like a dumbbell, we'd splinter off the back half. The main mass would continue on its orbit."

"On its altered orbit," Nikolai said.

Pierre ignored him. "Additional explosives would counter the forward velocity of the remaining asteroid piece. If the forward momentum was ten miles per hour due north, the explosive would exert a pressure of ten miles per hour due south and effectively stop the piece dead in its tracks. Taking advantage of the Earth's gravitational field, we'd park the asteroid within the Earth/Moon system."

"Too difficult to be precise," Nik said. "What if your explosive is too powerful? It's not that easy."

Pierre only smiled and continued as the diagrams on the screen changed.

"Satellites would land and roving robot vehicles would cut, drill, and load the minerals. A stream of aerodynamically designed transporters of a polycarbonate construction would collect the minerals." Noticing Nikolai's expression of amazement, Pierre said, "The technology is available. It's all possible."

Nikolai nodded. He knew it was true.

"Differentiated asteroids," Pierre said, "the irons and stony-irons, contain concentrations of the noble metals, platinum, gold, osmium and iridium. Fortunately, due to millions of years of collisions, many of these metals will already be exposed making drilling unnecessary.

"Once the cargo is loaded onto the carriers, the shuttles would use a predefined entry corridor, avoiding the gravitational pull of the Moon, and skate down to Earth. Buffeted by atmospheric pressure, their speed would diminish just as a rock skimming over the water is slowed."

"What about reentry?" Nik asked.

"The ablative edges would evaporate, cooling the carriers just as sweat on our bodies does, and protecting them from the destructive forces of reentry." Lorillard looked immensely pleased.

"But what about the danger to Earth?" Nik said. "It could be catastrophic. What if the charges used to affect the course of the asteroids are over-designed? The use of too many explosives in the detonation could cause the main mass of the asteroid to fragment and shower Earth with meteorites. If any of the data are flawed in the working model, the risk could be severe."

"If an asteroid should threaten Earth, we would be in an excellent position to counter its orbital path. We alone would be prepared, through our technology and our experience, to alter its trajectory."

"But what if something goes wrong?" Nik asked, incredulous.

"The rocket technology to do this is already in existence," Pierre said. "Once prepared, the entire mission could be completed within eight months."

He doesn't even hear me, Nik thought. True, it was possible. Everything he was saying could be attempted. But there was very little room for error. And the consequences....

* * * * *

Selena struggled on for three more hours, until she was finally below the snow line, and the worst of the cold was over. Her spirits were flagging severely when she came to a steep drop. Suddenly she could see the valley below and the desert stretched out in the distance. She was going to make it. All right, she told herself. You can rest now. But only for a minute.

As soon as she sat down on the soft ground beneath a tree, she started to black out. Terrified she'd be lost there and never found, she made herself stand up. Katya was at the LIFT. She had to go on. She had to keep going.

She realized Lorillard's goal had nothing to do with the LIFT accelerator. It was only a cover. Lorillard needed a big, complex, multi-billion dollar distraction that would allow him to gather the preeminent physicists of the world. What better way than to build the toy of the century?

It was all clear to her now, why Lorillard had Katya. Nik would never have agreed to give his formula for such a project. He would know the danger of Pierre's plan. One miscalculation and he could send an asteroid spinning through space, headed right for Earth. Only someone as egotistical and arrogant as Lorillard would believe himself capable of such a mission. Only a person convinced of their immense superiority would believe they could win the pool game from hell.

He would have had to force Nik to cooperate. That meant they would have told Nik that Katya was his daughter. How better to control him than to threaten his only living child? The thought of Katya being hurt sent screams of fury through Selena's body. She pushed forward, driving herself on. Lorillard had to be stopped. She must get back.

But her steps were becoming uneven. She was having a hard time keeping her balance. The exhaustion was immense. She felt so heavy. An overwhelming desire to lie down and sleep took hold. Could she have a concussion? It didn't matter. She forced herself to move on, each step more painful than the last. She mustn't stop, she told herself. She had to get down. She had to get back to Katya. And to Nik. Her instincts had been right all along. Another step. She must keep going.

And she did. She kept on until her shoe slipped on a mossy rock and her foot twisted under her. She cried out as she tumbled, over and over again, down the steep hill. Crashing into the shrubbery, she passed out from the pain of her ribs and didn't feel anything when her head hit the boulder.

* * * * *

"Pierre," Nik said. "If it's the platinum group you're after, how will you know which asteroids to mine? Ordinary chondrites won't have them."

"You, my friend, made that possible. Watch the screen."

At Pierre's instructions the computer projected a diagram of a SQUID with detailed specifications. The shape looked angular and primitive, like a Mayan drawing of a stick figure with a wide body.

"I intend to make use of the most advanced SQUIDs to precisely detect the location of the platinum group metals both on and within the asteroid piece. Your superconductor formula enables me to do away with the liquid cryogens altogether and replace them with on-chip electronic coolers, making the SQUIDs smaller, cheaper, and more portable. I'll know exactly where to mine. By reducing the disturbance signals of SQUID noise, I've increased the sensitivity output beyond anything ever achieved before."

Nik realized this was nothing more than some fantastic use of superconductive technology to fulfill Pierre's fantasies, the manifestation of his obsession with outer space. It could also prove more dangerous than all the nuclear bombs on Earth.

"But the value of these minerals and precious metals would plummet once the supply was so great," Nik insisted.

"I intend to control that, my friend. Those channels are already being prepared."

Nikolai had to admit the man was brilliant. He was the boldest, most visionary person Nik had ever known. Everything he created was on a grand scale. Including the potential danger.

"Where are you going to find the facilities to do this?" Nik asked. "The money?"

"I have that all worked out." Pierre was grinning with satisfaction. "It's not as big a problem as you might think. And this is only the beginning. I'm convinced Mars has more diamonds on its surface that we can even imagine. Time and pressure have transformed that planet into a cornucopia of rock-sized gems."

Nikolai knew it to be a fact. Scientists in Tokyo had found that the Martian mantle would be far richer in the necessary carbon. Geological activity would have forced much of this material from the interior to the surface.

"Once we perfect our mining technology, we'll be the first on Mars. But there's something even more important than diamonds, Nik. This is the real goal, the true mission. We must mine the Moon. Japanese investors are already backing a robotic mission there to farm helium-3. A manned mission is to follow. Helium-3, Nik!" Lorillard said. "The future! One space-shuttle cargo could meet the United States' energy needs for a year. Nuclear fusion, Nik. Think of it!"

Nikolai understood nuclear fusion was the mightiest force in the entire universe. Unlike the atom-splitting process of fission that powers nuclear plants, fusion entails heating a gas to more than 100 million degrees centigrade while squeezing it so tightly that the nuclei of its atoms are forced to merge, releasing energy. Fusion powers the Sun, the stars, and thermonuclear weapons. The exploration of deep space would be possible for the first time. But the supply of helium-3 on Earth was extremely limited. The surface gravel of the Moon, however, contained vast amounts of the gas.

"Nik, the profit motive has been responsible for the greatest advances in our civilization's history. Why should the exploration of space be any different? This is the future."

Nik knew this was a future all scientists dreamed of. But the man was far before his time. And dangerous.

"You can't be serious about doing this," Nik said, unable to hide the despair in his voice. "I don't believe you would be that foolish. You could destroy us."

With serious formality, Pierre bowed to Nikolai.

"I would like you to join me in this venture," he said. "As my second in command."

Nik was astounded. What was Lorillard thinking? Now that Nik understood, he realized why Pierre, in his compulsive determination, would complete his project even if it required murder. Nothing would stop him. Nik found himself backing away while trying to camouflage his shock. For now, he must appear to go along with Pierre's distorted and fantastic vision.

"Does Reisman know about this?" Nik asked. "Is he involved?"

"Henry, God bless him, is a man truly devoted to science." Lorillard snickered. "He's made all this possible by his work at the LIFT. I needed a cover and Henry provided it. But the LIFT is nothing but a mind fuck for you scientists. It's mental masturbation, that's all. By building it, I was able to gather the world's most eminent physicists to pursue the correct formula for high-temperature superconductors. As it turned out, you discovered it first." Lorillard looked like a proud father.

"What about Coons?"

"He knows nothing, thinks only of the small, immediate, problems we face on planet Earth. He wouldn't understand that the solution to everything lies out there, through connection with our neighbors in the universe."

Nik looked directly in Pierre Lorillard's eyes. "I need to think about this," he said. "How much time do we have?"

"Three or four days, my friend. That's all. I hope you'll join me, Nik." Pierre placed a hand on Nik's shoulder. "I'm going to change life on planet Earth forever. It will be the most monumental occurrence in history."

* * * * *

Norman Hambly handed his boss the 'Top Secret' memo, then waited. The U.S. aircraft carrier Ronald Reagan was en route to the coast of Chile, arrival time 0800 hours the following day. The news article had been planted in this morning's *Washington Post*. Bingham hadn't heard any complaints from General Rosales in Santiago. All was going as planned.

"Thank you, Norman," Bingham said, feeding the memo through the shredder. "This should be wrapped up soon. Just keep me informed of any activity in the LIFT area."

"Yes, sir," Hambly said and left the room.

Bingham leaned back in his chair. Last night had been his and Eunice's wedding anniversary. He'd told his wife about the cabin on the lake and the little nest egg he'd laid aside. Eunice had been delighted. As Bingham recalled the moment, he realized the expression on her face was one he hadn't seen in many years. She looked proud of him, as if he fulfilled all her expectations. Sometimes you have to take justice into your own hands, he told himself. Eunice deserved to be happy in her old age.

* * * * *

The deep rust and blue pattern of the Indian's woolen poncho was faded from years of wear in the harsh elements. His teeth were stained from chewing coca leaves. Hurrying his llama along the stony path in the foothills of the Andes, Miguel felt anxious to return to his wife and their baby with the basket of small, wild potatoes he'd dug that afternoon. Maria's brother would take some of them to market to sell, the others they would eat.

Occasionally Miguel would have pelts to sell to his brother-in-law, but not often. His people, the Araucanian Indians, had been fierce hunters and warriors in times past, but now they lived in poverty, their homes nothing more than rusty sheets of tin. They had become a tribe known for their basic mistrust of strangers.

Coming around the bend, the large white eyes in Miguel's dark round face stared in alarm at the woman's body. There were no white people here in the foothills, only the tourists who drove their Jeeps near Laguna Verde and the Salar de Maricunga, but never here. Unsure if the woman was alive, Miguel was afraid to touch her. He might be blamed. Instead, he lead his llama around the body and hurried back to Maria. She would know what to do.

The sun was almost setting by the time he returned with his wife. Maria's brimmed hat covered her coarse black hair, and a heavy, fringed shawl was draped across her chest. She carried a sleeping baby in a sling on her back. They laid Selena, still unconscious, on her stomach across the llama's back and walked slowly along the pitted, rocky path to their home.

Hours later, Maria was stoking the fire when Selena regained consciousness. She lay there quietly, her mind fuzzy, in and out of focus, her eyes resting on the woman's rough, strong hands. Flame-tossed shadows danced against the tin walls. Watching them, Selena's eyelids drooped. Her senses rolled back into childhood: The smell of spring rain on dusty asphalt, riding her bike home in the last light of a summer evening, the feel of her mother's hug and her soft breasts against Selena. Images passed in a wash of blue light, as if overexposed in the desert sun.

She was sitting tall in the front seat of the car, feeling very grown up after a day of shopping and lunch in the big city. She crossed her bare legs, pretended not to notice the childish bruises. Her mother's long fingers were wrapped tightly around the steering wheel. The sunlight dropped hard shadows across the dashboard.

Selena was eleven. They had been to see a doctor in Albuquerque, a specialist to treat her recurring ear aches. But her mother didn't like to drive, had only learned because her husband insisted when they moved to the desolate Los Alamos. She maneuvered the Dodge station wagon awkwardly along the curving mountain roads.

Selena was too short to see the desert floor below. Eventually she uncrossed her legs, knelt on the seat to peer out. Already nervous, her mother decided to pull off at a scenic rest stop halfway down the mountain. That's when her upper lip began to swell.

Within moments, she was having difficulty breathing. They hurried back to the car, hoping someone would pass by, hoping someone would help. Her mother managed to start the car and drive further down the mountain, around five curves, Selena counting each one, her hand clutching the arm rest, her eyes wide, darting in terror from her mother to the road.

"Mommy," she said. "Are you all right?"

"My throat is closing up." Her mother could barely speak. The car jerked along as she struggled to stay within the lines. "My face is numb." Her voice was only a raspy whisper. Selena felt helpless, terrified. At that moment she knew something terrible was going to happen unless she prevented it. But what could she do?

They made it around three more curves before her mother began to clutch her throat. She struggled to bring the car to the side of the road, pushed the handle on the steering column into park.

"Mommy," Selena cried. "Tell me what to do. Tell me. Please." Her mother could not answer. One side of her face was swollen beyond recognition. She stared at Selena with red, desperate eyes, then slumped sideways onto the front seat, her head in Selena's lap.

Selena felt her chest go hollow, felt terror immobilize her, struggled for breath. She pushed open the heavy car door, slid out from underneath her mother's head. Running to the walled edge of the scenic rest stop, she peered over the side, saw a white convertible parked far below. Two young couples were standing at the railing, taking turns looking through the silver viewfinder. Selena yelled and waved.

"Help! My mother! Help!" The couples below turned to look, then waved back. Leaning far over the railing, Selena yelled again, then again. She saw them laugh. They didn't understand. She yelled harder, waved with both hands. They ignored her. Selena watched them get into the white car, drive down the mountain, farther and farther away, leaving her alone to save her mother. She ran back to the car.

"Mommy! Mommy!" She shook her mother's shoulder, but she wouldn't answer, she wouldn't open her eyes.

Getting in on the driver's side, Selena pushed her mother's legs out of the way. She tried to remember what her father had said about how to drive the car. She stretched to reach the brake, tried to force the lever behind the steering wheel down. It wouldn't budge. Accidentally, she pulled it forward. It shifted out of park. She felt the car slip forward and in her fright she pulled her leg back from the brake. The car began to roll faster, headed right for the ditch, right into the side of the cliff. Selena slammed the lever back into park. The car jerked to a stop. She started again. She knew she was running out of time.

Inching forward, she slammed the brakes, turned the wheel too far to the right, pulled it back too far to the left. The car spurted forward when she accidentally hit the gas pedal, then jolted to a stop when she threw it into park. Moving only a few feet at a time, she jerked the car slowly around one corner, then the next. She saw her mother's lifeless body roll back and forth on the seat beside her. Selena began to cry.

"Please, God," she begged. "Help me. Please, somebody. Help me......"

The doctors told Selena's father that her mother had been dead for some time before the other car happened by. She had suffered from anaphylactic shock brought on by an allergic reaction, probably to something she'd eaten at lunch. The shock caused her throat to swell until she couldn't breathe. It had been no one's fault. There was nothing Selena could have done, they said. Unless she had known her mother was allergic. Then she could have carried an emergency shot of epinephrine. Only then would her mother have lived.

In the tin hut, Selena slept fitfully, cried out in words the Indian couldn't understand. When Selena woke several hours later, the last thing she could remember was falling down, tumbling over and over on the rough hillside, unable to stop.

Maria fed her and washed the blood from her face and scalp, then put a poultice on her ankle and gently wrapped it. She tied fresh bandages made from strong, woven cotton around her ribs, and gave her a soothing tea to drink. Dressed in a new woolen poncho, Selena slept again, soundly, until she woke the next morning to the sound of a baby crying. She heard people talking outside.

Stiff and sore all over, she limped from the hut, shielding her eyes against the brutal sunlight. The group of people gathered before her became silent and stared.

"Buenos dias," she said and nodded, suddenly aware of the boldly patterned red and black poncho she wore. A half dozen Indians and their children were gathered, many of them carrying baskets of potatoes or bundles of woven fabric and clothing.

"Buenos dias, señora," a young man said, stepping forward.

In her meager Spanish, Selena tried to explain she needed to get to the LIFT accelerator. She said the word over and over again, "LIFT, LIFT," exaggerating its pronunciation. The LIFT was the largest employer in the north of Chile, and even these people knew the word.

The young man listened then translated to the others. Maria watched quietly, then said something Selena could not understand. The young man nodded his head in agreement and turned to Selena, speaking rapidly in Spanish.

"Por favor?" Selena asked. "Es mucho rapido, señor." She could not understand. Again he said the words, slower this time, and she understood enough to know Maria's brother was coming with a truck. It seemed the man delivered fish to the LIFT cafeterias and took the Indians' potatoes and dry goods to sell at the market. His name was Fernando. He would drive her.

From a distance came the rumble and rattle of an approaching vehicle. A trail of dust and dirt curved its way around to the group. It was an old Ford panel truck with a hand-painted, fading swordfish flying through the air under the blue lettering "Pescado de la Mer."

The driver came to a squeaky, dusty stop, and the group of women and children all talked at once as they rounded up their goods and gave them to Fernando to load into the back. After words too fast and furious for her to understand, he handed each one some money.

When the noisy chatter died down, the driver turned to her and beckoned. She brushed her hair off her face and attempted to minimize her limp as the group watched her walk to Maria.

"Muchas gracias, señora," Selena said. She wanted desperately to thanks this woman who saved her life, but could not find the words. "Muchas gracias, señora," she repeated, and lifted the new poncho over her head.

"De nada," Maria said, pulling the poncho back down around Selena. "De nada," she insisted.

Selena looked at the ring on her finger, the one Nik had given to her. She slipped it off and pressed it in Maria's palm. Uncertain whether she would frighten or offend the woman, Selena hugged her warmly. Maria looked shy and embarrassed as Selena limped to the truck and hopped from one leg onto the passenger seat. Someone closed the door behind her, and she was immediately overwhelmed by the odor of raw fish. Whispers and giggles broke out in the waving crowd as Fernando beeped the horn and they took off down the road.

CHAPTER 21

"In Memorium." As Pierre Lorillard's limo pulled up to the steps of the Kronos Conference Center, he reminded himself that his announcement of Dr. Selena Hartmann's research results "In Memorium" would only make them more influential. She would be perceived as a heroine in the fight against nuclear weapons in space. And won't Bingham and the CIA be surprised to learn her message to the world was good news after all. Hartmann 2009 was not on a collision course with Earth.

"One at a time, gentlemen," Lorillard said as he climbed out of the car. "And ladies," he added, nodding to the attractive reporter with a mane of red, wavy hair.

The crowd had been waiting anxiously, and when Pierre charged up the stairs they followed like the tail of a comet, spitting and hissing questions like balls of fire, all yelling at once.

"I'm afraid I have no news on the plane crash," Lorillard said. "Representative Chapman will be presenting Dr. Hartmann's findings in just a few minutes." As he strode through the pillared entrance, the redhead again caught Pierre's eye. Tossing her hair, she waved a piece of paper over the crowd.

"What do you have to say about the *Washington Post* story, sir? Is there a nuclear arsenal here at the LIFT? Do you have a response to those allegations?"

The bustle of followers bunched up behind when Lorillard abruptly stopped. Grabbing the paper, his eyes scanned the printout of an AP article.

"Reliable U.S. sources report Pierre Lorillard's LIFT accelerator could be the site of nuclear weapons plant.... U.S. inspectors being sent to investigate...."

Despite an immense effort to remain in control, Pierre hurled the paper onto the marble floor. The bastards! It was a plant, pure and simple. And obvious. But the consequences could and would be the same. Suspected nuclear weapons would give the U.S. all the excuse they'd need to take control of the LIFT, of the lab, of everything. Pierre didn't stop to answer any of the questions bombarding him, but marched down the center aisle of the conference hall to take the stage.

"Ladies and gentlemen!" Lorillard pounded his fist on the podium bringing to attention the capacity-filled hall of anxious astronomers and news people. "Ladies and gentlemen. Before introducing Representative Pete Chapman, I want to address the allegations made today in a U.S. newspaper." He emphasized each word with a pound of his fist. "There are no nuclear weapons at the LIFT. No nuclear weapons are being produced or stored here. Those allegations are ridiculous and false."

A reporter called out from the front row.

"The *Washington Post* said their sources were reliable. Who are they?"

"Who do you think?" Lorillard asked. "Those allegations are nothing more than sour grapes from the U.S. government. They botched their own SSC in Texas. Now they're trying to interfere with my success. But they're going to fail again, my friends. Because the LIFT accelerator is going online."

A commotion of unrest stirred the audience of astronomers as reporters jumped to their feet and rushed the stage. Photographers flashed shots of Lorillard, his fist raised in the air.

"The world will see the truth before the U.S. can shut down the LIFT and deny all of us the value of this research."

"When, Mr. Lorillard?" the reporters called out. "When will you go online?"

"Very soon. The exact time will be announced later this afternoon. Right now I'm going to put you in the trustworthy hands of Representative Chapman. Ask him if he's seen any nuclear weapons being produced here. He's toured the entire LIFT complex, the labs, the control pod, even my home. Ask him." As Lorillard left the stage, he tried to laugh, but his fury choked him.

"I consider this most unfortunate," Pete Chapman said from the podium, shaking his head. "I've seen no indication whatsoever of any nuclear weapons activity here at the LIFT. Whoever is responsible for this, if it's the U.S.," Chapman said, shocked and fumbling for words, "It's unfortunate. To interrupt or delay the important research going on here would only be detrimental.

Astronomical research stands to benefit immensely from the technological advances at the LIFT. This research may even determine the amount and type of dark matter in the universe. And the LIFT has cost its owners less than the U.S. government spends on two nuclear submarines."

From the sidelines Pierre Lorillard was thoroughly enjoying the show, but he had other matters to tend to. Just before slipping out the stage entrance, however, he congratulated himself. Over the years he'd filled Representative Chapman's campaign chest again and again. Through various puppet corporations and the donation of "soft" money given to the party but destined for a specific candidate, Lorillard had been the representative's primary financial support.

Of course Chapman had never known. But the end result had turned out even better than Pierre anticipated. The press and public believed that Chapman and Lorillard had opposing political views. Chapman was a liberal, an anti-nukes advocate, and a cohort of Hartmann's. His vote and leadership would be instrumental in stopping passage of the Star Wars bill. What better person to have defending the LIFT? With all eyes on the Representative, Lorillard slipped out the stage door unnoticed and waved to his driver.

"To the control pod," he said and climbed into the cool dark limo.

Under the guise of halting the proliferation of nuclear weapons, the United States was about to move in, about to shut him down so that eventually they could confiscate the LIFT accelerator. Why? To build nuclear weapons for space. They wanted the lab and the LIFT technology. First they rigged Hartmann's research for passage of Star Wars, he thought. Now they're trying to take my technology.

"I built it," he said in the privacy of his soundproof compartment. "Nobody else." Lorillard clasped his hands together and squeezed until the blue veins bulged. Clive Bingham has taken my money for the last five years, he thought. The bastard. But I'm not surprised. I've been expecting something like this.

Lorillard congratulated himself on making the decision to go ahead with the Primary Installation and not wait for the final test results. I'll begin the first experiments. Their success will be the best obstacle to the U.S. meddling. There will be a general outcry from the international scientific community. And Chapman's announcement this afternoon will set the groundwork. I'm not going to allow the United States of America to barge in here and take over. No way. I'll call the control pod and begin Extreme Status immediately.

Just as Lorillard went to pick up the phone, it rang. He jerked back momentarily, then laughed at his tense nerves. "Lorillard here," he said.

The voice on the other end seemed to be laughing, too. "Hello, Mr. Lorillard. This is General Enrique Rosales. I'm glad I caught you before it's too late."

* * * * *

Approaching the main gate of the LIFT facility, the white panel truck with the painted swordfish pulled to a stop. The driver quickly jumped out and began speaking in rapid Spanish to the guard while holding his hands around his belly and making an awful face.

"Mi hermosa, Maria, es muy importante, señor, por favor, mi hermosa....."

Selena leaned back in her seat and moaned out the open window of the truck. It was not hard to act as if she were in serious labor and about to deliver a baby at any moment. The sack of small potatoes stuffed beneath her poncho rested on her sore ribs, and the pain was genuine. She had darkened her skin with potato dust and kept the brim of her hat low over her face.

The young guard looked terrified at the prospect of something as messy as delivering a baby. After calling Roos Coons' clinic for permission, he ran quickly to the back of the truck and ordered Fernando to open it for inspection. With his rifle he poked among the baskets of produce and dry goods, the layers of fish on ice, then rushed to open the gate. The stench made him sick.

"Vaya," he ordered. "Vaya usted. Rapido!"

Selena slipped low in the cab as Fernando sped along the newly paved road to the clinic. He parked the truck and she handed him a folded piece of paper. Running up the stairs two at a time, he rushed into the reception area.

"Señor Coons, por favor," Fernando said to the trim nurse at the reception desk. Her hair was white and cut short around perky eyes. Her name tag said, 'Ms. Worthy, RN.'

"Are you the young man with the woman in labor?" Speaking with professional calm and distance, she examined Fernando. He was dressed in a worn suit jacket over an un-ironed white shirt, buttoned to the top with no tie. In his hands he held a black hat. Fernando said nothing.

"They called from the gate," Nurse Worthy said. "Where is she? Why didn't you bring her in?"

"No es posible, señora! Por favor, give to Señor Coons." Following Selena's instructions exactly, Fernando urgently handed the nurse the folded piece of paper. It looked like it was torn from a brown paper bag.

Nurse Worthy looked suspicious. "I'm sorry, señor, but Mr. Coons is a very busy man. I can help you, if you'll just--"

"No es posible, señora. Solamente Senor Coons." Fernando pointed at the piece of paper gripped tightly between the nurse's fingers. "Es muy importante!"

"All right," the woman said. "You wait here, understand? I'll see what I can do." She took off down the hall, her starched uniform swishing as she walked.

The nurse found Mr. Coons in a bright yellow examination room with a mural of oversized frogs and giant water lilies.

"This is my friend, Henrietta," Roos told Nurse Worthy. "My sweetheart here comes to visit me from Peru." The child sat on the examining table, happily kicking her dangling legs. She was dark skinned and wore a turban-like cap sprouting a pink daisy. It flopped over her forehead. The girl's eyes were sunken, but her smile was radiant.

"Hi there." Ms. Worthy said. The girl nodded her head up and down enthusiastically, but didn't say a word. "Excuse me, Mr. Coons, but..."

"Henrietta has a tumor on her larynx," Roos explained. "She can't be talkin' right now, but when we're through with her I bet she'll have a tale to tell, won't ya darlin'?" Roos put his arm around the little girl.

"Excuse me, Mr. Coons," Nurse Worthy said. "But the gate called to say a pregnant Indian woman had begun labor and would we see her. Now her husband is in the lobby, and he says she won't come in. He gave me this." She handed Mr. Coons the folded note. "It looks like nonsense to me, sir, but he says she'll only talk to you."

Roosevelt Coons stared at the words scratched in pencil on the torn brown paper. "Please help! Greek Goddess of the Moon."

"Where is she?" he asked, pulling on his chin. He continued to stare at the paper. "Take me to her."

Roos Coons followed the Indian outside and down the stairs to the parking lot. When they neared the truck, Selena popped her head up. She'd removed the hat and poncho and wiped most of the potato dust from her face, exposing the bruises and cuts from the plane crash and her fall down the hill.

"Oh my God, child," Coons said. "What happened to you?"

"Roos, you've got to listen carefully," Selena told him. "I'm all right, but I need your help."

"But what in tarnation? Where have you been? Come on into the clinic for goodness sake. Let us take care of you."

"I don't want the security cameras to see me, Roos. Pierre tried to have me killed." She could see the disbelief spread across Coons' face. "He did something to the plane, to the oil pressure. We crashed in the Andes. It's true, Roos. Jean's dead."

Selena remembered Jean's face, pierced by the axe, his blood spilling onto the fresh snow. She felt chilled in the midday desert sun. She watched Coons try to comprehend.

"I'm sorry," she said. "But Lorillard's got my daughter. He kidnapped Nikolai Potapov for a secret project. I've got to find them."

"Kidnapped? What secret project are you talking about?"

"He needed Nik's formula for superconductors. Katya is Nik's daughter. Lorillard's using her to threaten Nik."

Roos Coons looked flabbergasted. For a moment he wondered if Dr. Hartmann was in her right mind, but the bruises on her face were real enough to scare him.

"Are you sure you're all right?" he asked. "I don't understand, but we can call the police. If it's true we'll put that ol' weasel right in the hoosegow, lock him up and throw away the keys."

"No, you can't do that. Lorillard controls the security forces here. Roos, he almost killed me. He's dangerous."

"Mr. Coons! Mr. Coons, sir!" Roos turned to see the nurse standing at the top of the stairs waving to him. "Is everything all right? Do you need help, sir?"

"Call the helicopter," Coons hollered. "Tell George to be ready at the air strip." He started to wave her away, then called her back. "Ms. Worthy. Bring me that rifle. The one old Joe gave me. It's in my office."

The nurse hesitated. "The hunting rifle, sir?"

"Yes. Bring it to me. With the ammunition." Roos turned to Selena.

"We've got to find Dr. Reisman," he said. "He can't be involved in this, but maybe he knows where you daughter is. Maybe he can help us get her outta here."

* * * * *

Audience anticipation in Kronos Hall had peaked. Dr. Selena Hartmann's long-awaited results were finally going to be announced. Initial fears that the presentation would not be made due to her disappearance and death, had given way with the announcement of a 24-hour delay. If anyone hadn't been paying attention before, they were now. The audience moaned when

Representative Chapman again asked for their patience.

"It seems we have some technical problems with the video portion," he said. "The staff has assured me it will only be another five minutes." One of the representative's aides approached the podium, and Chapman noticed she was carrying a cigar box tied with a large black bow.

"Excuse me, sir," the young woman said. "You have an emergency phone call." As they walked offstage, she handed him the box of cigars. "These just came for you with instructions they be delivered right away."

"But I don't smoke cigars," Chapman said, taking the portable phone from his aide.

The operator came on the line. "Please hold for the caller."

"Buenos dias, Representative Chapman. This is General Enrique Rosales. You remember me, señor?"

"Certainly," Chapman said stiffly. "I'm about to give a presentation, general. What can I do for you?"

"I understand you are a busy man, senor. I won't keep you. I wanted to make amends for the other night, at dinner. Did you receive my gift?

Pete Chapman looked at the cigar box he was holding. The label said Davidoff #10. "I believe so, general. Does it have a big, black bow?"

"Don't be mislead by the box, señor," Rosales said. "It's not what you think. Please. You must open it and accept my sincere wishes."

"Hold on," Chapman said, and placed the phone on a nearby stool. He pulled the black ribbon off one corner and then the other. When the lid to the cigar box opened a quarter of an inch, the sound of the blast was deafening. The Senator's body was thrown against the wall, his skull shattered and his spine splintered into pieces that fell to the floor.

The overflow crowd in Kronos Hall fled in a panic of screams, shoving and fighting to get out as the stage area crumbled before them. Throughout the LIFT facility, fire alarms and security sirens blared.

* * * * *

In the clinic parking lot Selena and Roosevelt Coons felt the ground shake with the impact of the bomb. Fernando was standing behind Coons and moved closer, covering his head with his arms. Selena could see he was terrified.

"What was that?" she asked.

"Come on," Roos said. "Something's goin' on here, and I gotta talk to Henry. And that devil, Pierre." He turned to Fernando. "Can you drive this thing over to the lab?" he asked, and then realized the fellow was stricken with fear and probably couldn't understand him anyway.

"Go," Selena told Fernando, pointing to the clinic door just as Ms. Worthy headed down the stairs, gun in hand.

Grabbing hold of the rifle like a veteran turkey hunter, Coons told the nurse to take care of Fernando. The Indian's frightened expression beamed with gratitude as she pulled him into the clinic.

"You be careful," Nurse Worthy said before she disappeared behind the tinted glass doors.

Selena quickly pushed herself over to the driver's seat. The pressure on her bruised ribs caused a searing pain across her chest. She started the truck as Ross heaved himself inside. She was backing out before he'd closed the door.

* * * * *

In his glass-enclosed office on the main floor of the control pod, Pierre Lorillard could feel the vibrations from the bomb move up his stocky legs. He knew it was the conference center. Gen. Rosales had been brief and to the point.

"I'm calling to warn you, señor. My sources tell me the Cuernaca guerrillas are planning to attack the LIFT as an anti-U.S. statement. I believe they intend harm to Representative Chapman. My troops are on their way to protect all Chilean citizens and to secure the LIFT. And your safety, señor."

Pierre knew there were no guerillas. Rosales had used his own goons to manufacture trouble as an excuse to move in and confiscate the LIFT before the U.S. arrived and took it. In the process, Enrique Rosales would become a hero to his people instead of a villain being tried for crimes against humanity. The man had a knack for surviving. Again Lorillard shook his head. Not my LIFT, he thought. Nobody's going to take what's mine. Not you, general. Not the United States.

Pierre Lorillard walked to his office intercom system and pressed the 'Full Facility' button.

"PREPARE TO GO ONLINE," he ordered. His voice broadcast deep and full through the control pod and the sound of his words gratified him. He had waited a long time to say them.

"PREPARE TO GO ONLINE! FULL POWER!"

Lorillard had secured what he needed, the essential ingredient, the formula to perfect the SQUIDs. That was all that really mattered. He'd already ordered his jet held ready for take-off at the airstrip. Before the Chilean army hit the gates, he would enjoy himself. Who else should be the one to play with the $5 billion toy he'd created? Who else was entitled to destroy it?

CHAPTER 22

Nik paced the lab floor. From his first days of captivity he had felt desperate for a way to escape. He'd studied the facility diagrams in that basement room, but it wasn't until a few days ago, until Jean Levesque taunted him about Katya, that he'd figured out his plan. That was one of the reasons he'd insisted she be brought to the control pod. He thought his scheme stood a decent chance of working, but he was worried about whether Katya could handle it.

Staring into space, Nik crossed his arms over his chest and pulled on the end of his short beard. Through Selena and Katya he'd been given the chance to make a new life. It was a chance he dearly wanted. But since Katya had been moved to the room down the hall, he'd heard nothing of her, had no idea if she was all right. What if the guards were hurting her? What if she were sick? Surely she must be terrified. That is, he thought, if she's still alive. Nik told himself she must be. Lorillard would not be so foolish as to let anything happen to Katya.

But now he must ask her to do this frightening thing. He prayed it would work. Coming to a standstill in the middle of the lab, Nik placed his hands on the side of his head and squeezed his skull, as if he could release some of the pressure. You've been all through this, he told himself. You don't have any choice. You can't leave your daughter here. Nik's chest tightened. That word, daughter, continued to astonish his heart.

Nik strode to the window. Another problem was the security system at the LIFT. Cameras would monitor their every move, so the only hope would be to work fast. He was deep in these thoughts when the bomb exploded. Feeling the vibration, he reached for the window frame to steady himself.

Horrified, he watched the Kronos Conference Center crumble. Viewed from the control pod, the people running from the exits looked like frantic ants, speechless and desperate. Within minutes he heard Pierre's voice over the intercom give the command.

"ONLINE! FULL POWER! ONLINE! FULL POWER!"

He's started the experiment, Nik thought. I can't believe it. Why now? It must have something to do with the explosion. Nik realized this meant only one thing. It was time to make his move.

He knew they would have to evacuate the accelerator ring. The explosion at the conference center, whatever its cause, was an unexpected bonus. Security would be distracted. With the LIFT going online and the accelerator ring evacuated, they had a chance to make a run for it. But it had to be now.

"Help! Help!" Nik hollered, pounding desperately on the wall. The guard, used to Nik's good behavior, opened the door, and Nik hit him over the head with the back of a chair. Just like in the American movies, he thought. The guard slumped at Nik's feet, his rifle clattered to the floor. Nik quickly stuffed a dirty sock into the man's mouth, then wrapped the guard's wrists with a belt and dragged him behind some boxes where he'd be less visible to security cameras. Using the belt, Nik secured the guard to a pipe, took his pass, hid the rifle, and hurried to the door.

* * * * *

Under the shadow of the pod's web, the white panel truck tore through the curving streets of the LIFT facility. Nearing the central rotary, Selena found the way blocked by rubble from the blast.

"Go that way," Roos said, pointing left. "We can swing around the lab." He held on for dear life as Selena took the corner. He saw her wince and hold her ribs.

"You sure you're all right?"

Selena nodded but couldn't bring herself to smile.

"You don't look so good to me," Roos said.

By the time they pulled into the parking lot, people were running towards the conference center to help victims of the blast. Roos called out to a passing group.

"Have any of you seen Dr. Reisman? Where's Lorillard?"

Without stopping, a woman in a lab coat called back to him. "At the control pod."

Before Selena could put the truck in gear, the ground began to shudder. The crowd of staff and scientists running by came to a frightened halt. Selena and Roos looked at each other in amazement as the truck shook beneath them.

"It's the LIFT!" she said. "Lorillard's started the proton collider!" She looked in the direction of the pod. "We've got to get over there. I've got to find Katya." Selena backed out of the parking lot, threw the truck into first and took off, the tires squealing as she drove away.

If I'm right about his plan, Selena thought, there are two things Lorillard needs to succeed. He knew I had one of them. That's why he wanted me dead. Now I have them both. They're my only bargaining tools, my only real power over him. But if I use that power against him, I'll be destroying everything I've fought for. Am I prepared to do that? If I threaten him, will he believe me? Enough to give me Katya and Nik?

"There's the old weasel's limo," Roos said and pointed to the control pod. "Looks like he's ready to take off."

* * * * *

In the desert three miles from the entrance to the LIFT, a line of green Army tanks and trucks followed the lead jeep of a young Chilean lieutenant dressed in camouflage fatigues and a helmet.

"Contact General Rosales," Lt. Garcia told the private who cradled a radio between his legs. "Report our arrival. Request further orders." The stream of vehicles continued their dusty path through the midday heat of the desert.

Lt. Garcia was more than nervous. He had never before experienced combat. In fact, he'd been chosen to command the only real maneuvers that had taken place on his country's soil in many years. But with the success of this operation, his people would again revere General Rosales, and he, Lt. Garcia, would certainly be promoted to captain.

Perhaps then the general's daughter, Lucia, might consider his affections. Especially since her American fiancé, unlike a real man, a Chilean man, refused to live up to his commitment to her. After all, Lt. Garcia thought, the general himself had suggested the match on the day of his daughter's aborted wedding. "Why in hell can't she marry you?" the general had asked. Indeed, Garcia thought.

"Sir," the radio operator said. "General Rosales' instructions are to continue the maneuvers as planned. Enter the LIFT facility and take control. Use force if necessary. Guerrilla activity has been reported inside the compound."

"Carry on, Corporal." Lt. Garcia raised his head high. He looked determined.

* * * * *

Clive Bingham was furious. Mulroney had just called and given him a tongue-lashing about the activity at the LIFT. All hell was breaking loose down there. Radar screens were picking up what looked like accelerator operations. There were even reported military maneuvers in the area. What in hell was going on? What had gone wrong? How could this happen now, before Hartmann's research results were announced? Damn! How would this impact the Star Wars vote?

"Hambly!" Bingham hollered through the intercom. "Get in here." Norman was through the door in seconds.

"Call the Pentagon. Tell Admiral Kingsley he's got to get aircraft to the LIFT immediately. The entire operation is at stake."

"Sir, the aircraft carrier is still quite a ways off the coast of Chile. Their ETA isn't until tomorrow, sir. At 0800 hours."

"I don't give a shit!" Bingham said, jabbing his finger on the desk. "That could be too late. Something's gone wrong. Lorillard's started the LIFT. Now get going, damn it. We need aircraft!"

"Yes, sir. Right away, sir."

The last thing Bingham needed was to end his career with a fiasco. Operation Blue Whale had been in the planning stages for four years. They couldn't afford to botch it now. Besides, if things didn't go well, there would be an investigation. Not what Bingham wanted. He pushed back his chair and strode to the window. If that General Rosales was involved with this, Clive thought, there'll be a price to pay.

* * * * *

"EIGHT MINUTES TO LOCK-IN! EIGHT MINUTES TO LOCK-IN!"
In dull, lifeless baritone the threatening words reverberated through the chaos and pandemonium of the control pod. Distraught over the explosion at

the conference center and the unexpected orders to go online, much of the staff had already mutinied. Of those left, several technicians laughed nervously as they stared in amazement through the soundproof glass into Pierre Lorillard's office.

Like the embodiment of a mad scientist in a silent movie, Dr. Henry Reisman, the director of the LIFT facility, was gesticulating dramatically, flailing his arms in the air and spitting as he shrieked.

"You promised me!" Reisman yelled at Lorillard. "I was to control the operation of the LIFT!"

Pierre Lorillard pressed the red button on the intercom panel.

"Send some guards down here immediately," he said and continued to gather papers and stuff them into a briefcase. "I'm sorry, sir," the security officer responded. "We're shorthanded because of the explosion."

The blue veins in Lorillard's neck bulged with the effort to control himself. "Then get down here yourself. And don't," he said, "make me repeat that order."

"But you can't go to full power," Reisman pleaded, his face red. "The whole thing could explode if you keep ramping."

"I can't wait," Lorillard insisted. "Don't you understand? They're coming. The CIA is moving in. Chile's army is almost at the gate."

"But don't destroy the LIFT. Let me complete my work."

"I can't allow that."

"Then I'm ruined." Reisman's voice had risen to a screech. "By the time another accelerator is built I'll be dead. You can't do this. It's my life." Reisman lurched towards Lorillard, grabbed him by the neck and tried to shake him, but Pierre's short bull of a body threw the frail old man off with one arm. A guard bolted through the office door and grabbed Dr. Reisman, restrained him with a painful twist of his arm. Henry struggled, mumbling incoherently, spitting and gnarling his words.

"Get him out of here!" Pierre ordered. The guard began to drag Reisman kicking and screaming from the room. "The man's a maniac. I want him out of the control pod."

"He'll destroy everything," Henry cried to the terrified staff. "My work will be ruined! He's going to blow up the LIFT! Don't you understand? You've got to stop him!"

A few of the already anxious staff began to move towards the exit elevators, at first cautiously, one-by-one, then in a bolting, panicked group. Lorillard laughed at their frenzied escape.

"He's right," Pierre hollered. "Go on. Run and hide. You'll miss the Big Bang everybody's been waiting for."

Struggling against the tide of the terrified crowd, an armed guard pushed and shoved until he reached Pierre's office.

"Mr. Lorillard, sir. There's a report at the front gate." The young man was gasping for breath. "The Chilean army is here. They're taking control of the facility, sir. They've got tanks and armored vehicles. The gate has surrendered."

"You see my friends," Pierre called to the desperate crowd fighting for room on the elevator and stairs. "There's no time to lose. You'd better hurry." He turned to the guard. "Let them take it, what's left of it. I have what I want. That's all that matters. They can have their desert back."

The guard looked confused. "Yes sir," he said, and ran to tell his commanding officer. The ominous warning of the intercom only stopped him briefly.

"FIVE MINUTES TO LOCK-IN! FIVE MINUTES TO LOCK-IN!"

* * * * *

With the guard's security pass in hand, Nik rushed down the empty hallway to Katya's room. Inserting the card in the door, he pushed on the latch. It wouldn't budge.

"Who is it?" Katya called, her voice high and strained. "Who is it? What do you want?"

Nik had to hurry. If she cried out, a guard might come. Fumbling with the card, it fell from his hands.

"Who's out there?" Katya yelled louder, terror rising in her throat.

Nik inserted the card once again. This time he heard the click of the lock. The door opened.

Rushing in, he quickly shut the door behind him and turned. There she was, against the far wall, her fear barely masked by a defiant expression. They stood silently staring at one another. Nik could feel the tension that saturated the air. Finally, he could stand it no longer.

"Katya," he said, his voice choking. She was all right. His daughter was safe. He had another chance.

She looked up at this man who was supposed to be her father. Her eyes were full of questions, searching and afraid at the same time. Then she broke free from the restraint of her fear. She ran to him. Like a little girl, she felt the toughness melt and the sobs break through as he hugged her and patted her short, black hair.

"It's going to be all right," he told her. Tears brimmed in his eyes. "It's going to be all right." He wondered why he felt so certain.

When she pulled away, Nikolai stood awkwardly smiling down at her. Katya didn't speak, didn't know what to say. In a moment she withdrew her eyes, embarrassed by what she'd done, unsure what to do next.

"We don't have much time," Nik said. "Listen to me carefully. I've got a plan, but it's dangerous. Are you up to it?"

Katya nodded yes, her wide eyes looking both vulnerable and determined. Nik found himself staring at the lovely young woman before him, amazed and distracted by her youthful beauty. She seemed half-woman, half-child, and he realized he knew nothing about having a daughter. It didn't feel at all like having a son.

"Come on," he said. "We've got some searching to do." Nik used the security card to open the door and checked the hall. Stay close behind me," he said, feeling utterly confused. He put out his hand. She looked away, pretended not to see.

* * * * *

Selena and Roos rode the circular glass elevator up the ten-story shaft of the control pod. When the doors opened onto the circle of glass and technology, no security guards stopped them. No technicians manned the banks of computers.

"Lorillard! Where are you?" With the hunting rifle slung over one arm, Roosevelt Coons barreled through the door of Pierre's office. "What in damnation's goin' on here?" he said, then stepped to the side, revealing his companion.

"Give me my daughter," Selena said. "And Nik. I want them both. Now. Or I'll destroy you and your project."

Pierre stared in silent disbelief. She was back. She had survived. Against his will, Lorillard felt his eyes widen in a smile of respect. Dr. Selena Hartmann had returned.

"I know what you're planning to do," Selena said. She struggled to control the strain of emotion in her voice. She felt no fear, only a furious dense energy in her chest propelling her forward.

"You intend to mine the asteroids," she said. She wanted to attack him, to leap at him and pummel him. Her hatred and anger were so intense, that part of her didn't care what happened. She felt strong enough to destroy him.

Lorillard began to chuckle. He had backed up behind his desk and was leaning against the wall, looking immensely entertained by this woman's ingenuity.

"You needed Nik's formula so you kidnapped him, threatened him with my daughter."

"You rotten guttersnipe," Roos said. "You've been tellin' me a cock 'n bull story all this time!"

"And now I've got the formula," Pierre said. "And I'm going to blow this place to hell."

"What are you talkin' about?" Roos demanded.

"Very simple. I won't have the United States or any other country benefit from my work. I'm going to blow it up."

"My God, man. You can't be serious. What about the clinic? What about all the people here?" Roos took a firm hold on the rifle and stepped back towards the door.

"I want my daughter, Lorillard. And Nik. Where are they?"

"They're going with me," Lorillard said.

The fury inside her pressed for release. "No." Selena said. "They're not."

Lorillard's eyes widened and his lips curled in amusement.

Selena's body jerked with the urge to grab the bronze eagle perched on his desk and smash Lorillard's face in. Instead, she forced herself to speak deliberately.

"I'm the only one who can stop you," she said. "I have the two things you need. And I'll use them." She watched Pierre's eyes narrow to a sharp focus.

Selena nodded her head. "I have the formula, too." From the pocket of her tattered slacks, Selena pulled out the Hawaiian postcard. She held it up for Lorillard to see, then turned it around, showed him the formula. "Nik sent it to me. Unless I get my daughter, I'll be sure the right people find it."

"How do I know that's the formula?" Pierre said, even though he felt certain it was. Why else would it be on the back of a postcard from Hawaii if Nik hadn't sent it? Why else would she be carrying it around with her, even after a plane crash?

"It's the formula," Selena said. She stood before him, her hands on her hips, daring him not to believe her. In the silence that followed, she could hear her heart beat hard and high in her chest.

"That isn't enough to stop me," Pierre said. "Let them have it. They'll get it soon enough anyway."

"You're forgetting something," Selena said. She felt an angry pleasure watching Lorillard squirm. She wanted to strike him down, to hurt him, and the violent urge felt good and right to her. She had never felt such determination. Then the control pod shook with vibration and the loudspeaker blared:

"TWO MINUTES TO LOCK-IN! TWO MINUTES TO LOCK-IN!"

"Stop this damned contraption," Roos hollered. "Are you prepared to die? Just to keep your precious LIFT from the U.S.?" He looked at Pierre and saw only cold intensity. Lorillard's pale eyes looked almost white.

"Not me, my friend. I'll be leaving you shortly. I have important future business to attend to. Isn't that right, Dr. Hartmann?" His voice was laughing.

"There won't be any future business," Selena said. "I'm going to stop it. She mustered all the arrogance she could. "I'll announce the asteroid's going to hit us dead on. I'll say I've changed my mind, my calculations were wrong, and we must have nuclear weapons in space if we're going to survive. I'll say the threat is immediate. Everyone will beat you there, Lorillard. It'll be a traffic jam. You won't stand a chance."

Pierre Lorillard was no longer laughing. He knew she was right. All his work would be lost, his future plans to mine the moon destroyed. He had to get there first, corner the mineral market to make the profit necessary to mine the moon. Dr. Hartmann had to be stopped. Again. He leaned forward, gripped the back of the chair.

"You won't do that," he said. "It's against everything you've worked for. You could destroy our world."

Selena stepped closer and stared him straight in the eye. "I'll do whatever it takes," she said.

Pierre knew then he could never let her go free. He couldn't chance it, even if he gave her Katya and Nik. He had one trump card left. Maybe it would distract her long enough to get the rifle.

"You'd give the U.S. what they want? Even after they tampered with your research? Even after they killed your friend?"

Selena struggled to understand. What was he saying? Charlie? It couldn't be.

"You don't fool me," she told him, but she was shaken. Someone had altered her work. And Charlie had disappeared. Had the U.S. fixed her data to secure passage of Star Wars? Had they done something to Charlie? Selena remembered the check she'd found in Jean's pocket, made out to Clive

Bingham. Lorillard could know about Charlie. Selena felt a sweaty chill creep up her back. Her legs weakened. She tried to hold on, but she felt dread infiltrate her cells, spread across her face. "I want my daughter," she said.

"Then give me the formula," Pierre said.

"Where's that child?" Roos said. "And Nikolai? What in tarnation have you done with them?" Coons stepped closer and stood just behind Selena, the rifle aimed at Lorillard.

Pierre looked at Roosevelt Coons as though he were nothing but a fool. In the next moment, Lorillard leapt forward, pushing Selena against Coons, knocking them both down and grabbing the barrel of the rifle with both hands. Yanking it out of Coons' hands, he scrambled to his feet and aimed the rifle at them both. But Roos was already on his knees. He dove for Pierre, grabbed him by the legs, knocked him off balance, back onto the floor.

"Run," Roos called out. "Get outta here."

Selena saw the rifle skid across the floor and she dove for it, crying out from the pain in her ribs. Pierre grabbed it first. He rolled onto his back with Coons still holding him by the legs. He raised the barrel of the gun, aimed at Selena. Roos threw himself onto Pierre just as he pulled the trigger. The bullet went directly through Coons' heart. He fell to the floor, the full weight of his body on Lorillard.

Selena scrambled, ran limping to the center of the pod, toward the elevator and the emergency stairway. The elevator would get her down faster, but the doors might not close in time. As Pierre struggled to throw off Coons' body, the intercom blared a final warning.

"FINAL COUNTDOWN! PREPARE FOR LOCK-IN! FINAL COUNTDOWN! PREPARE FOR LOCK-IN!"

Selena reached the elevator just as Lorillard broke free. He swung the rifle around to shoot. She ran for the stairs, threw herself against the swinging aluminum doors. Unable to stop her momentum, she rolled down the first flight. As the doors swung closed, she heard the shot and looked up to see the rip in the steel door.

Pierre Lorillard ran to the main control console. Three red lights were flashing as the intercom continued its warning.

"FINAL COUNTDOWN! PREPARE FOR LOCK-IN! FINAL COUNTDOWN!"

Lorillard took a deep breath, and then with both hands, he lowered the lock-in lever. The blinking red lights changed to green and the intercom announced:

214

"LOCK-IN COMPLETE! LOCK-IN COMPLETE! BEGIN FINAL COUNTDOWN!"

Pierre knew his time was running out. He dashed for his office. Stepping on Coons' body, he grabbed his briefcase and charged for the elevator.

* * * * *

Katya cried out. "Mommy!"

Nikolai couldn't believe what he saw. It was Selena. She was on three different monitors.

Working their way along the abandoned halls, Nik and Katya had found the control pod eerily empty of guards. When they reached a door marked Security, Nik listened and waited, then knocked. Nothing. Slipping the security pass into the slot, he heard the lock click. Once inside the empty room, they turned around and there she was -- Selena on the silent monitors, struggling for her life.

"Mommy!" Katya saw her mother dive for the rifle skidding across the floor, saw her mother's face as she cried out in pain, saw a short man struggle against a big one to reach a gun, then aim it at Selena. Katya screamed, ran to the screen and spread her hands across the cold glass, as if she could reach inside and stop it all. It wasn't until Coons blocked the fatal shot with his body that she breathed again. Then she began to shake.

"Stay here," Nik said. "I'm going to get your mother. Don't open this door for anyone but me." Katya never took her eyes off the screen.

She watched the black and white video of her mother running for safety, watched helplessly as that man raised the gun to shoot again, watched as her mother threw herself behind the swinging doors. Was she safe? Had the bullet hit her? Katya didn't know. She couldn't see her mother anymore. Scanning the bank of monitors, she ran from one screen to the next. There were only shots of empty hallways, a parked limousine and a white truck, the airstrip with a plane and a helicopter. And on three screens she saw the man who wanted to kill her mother. Katya was watching the most terrifying movie of her life.

She wanted to run and find her mother, to help her, but Nikolai had told her to stay. She had to do something. That awful voice kept repeating:

"FINAL COUNTDOWN! PREPARE FOR LOCK-IN! FINAL COUNTDOWN!"

Katya began to pound her fists on the screens, moving from one to the next, crying out, "Mommy! Mommy!"

Desperate, she looked toward the door, moved in that direction. Who was he to tell her what to do? Yet something inside her made her listen and obey. She turned and again scanned the monitors, her eyes darting from wall to wall. For the first time she took in the whole room. She realized it was just like the place Jean had taken her that first day.

There were the same levers and switches he had yelled at her for touching. He was responsible for this, that hideous man with his ugly face. Angrily, she grabbed the levers and pushed them up and down, up and down. She saw floor plans light up red, then green, just as they had when Jean yelled at her. Again and again, the screens flashed "OPEN ACCESS," "CLOSED ACCESS."

Katya remembered. Jean had thrown a switch just before they'd gone to see her father. She'd seen it turn from red to green. On the monitors she saw the man with the rifle doing something at a computer. She heard the intercom.

"LOCK-IN COMPLETE! LOCK-IN COMPLETE! BEGIN FINAL COUNTDOWN!"

Katya watched the man smile, then run to another room and grab a briefcase. He dashed for the elevator, near where her mother had gone. Katya had to do something. She began to throw switches, each switch blocking off in bright red another area on the screen. Where was the one she needed? Finally, she saw "CLOSED ACCESS" flash across the elevator and stairway screen. It was outlined in red.

Katya watched Lorillard push the elevator button. The doors didn't open. She watched him push again and again. He was getting angry, beating on the shiny aluminum doors, trying to open them with his hands, kicking, his mouth gnarled, his eyes panicked. His image disappeared when he ran in the direction of the stairway.

"FOURTEEN MINUTES TO COLLISION! FOURTEEN MINUTES TO COLLISION!"

Katya moved to the next screen. She was standing right in front of it, her hands pressed against the glass. She watched, not breathing, as he struggled with the door, struggled to open it, to force it. He threw his body against it. It wasn't until she saw him throw his briefcase on the floor that she began to back away. It was all right. He couldn't get in. He couldn't get to her mother. When the door opened behind her, she jumped in fright and let out a fearful scream.

"Katya! Katya!" Selena ran to her daughter. Katya grabbed hold and clung so tightly, Selena couldn't move. Just as abruptly, her daughter pulled away.

"I've locked him in!" Katya said and ran pointing to the monitor. "Look!" The pod swayed beneath them and Katya again clung to her mother.

"THIRTEEN MINUTES TO COLLISION! THIRTEEN MINUTES TO COLLISION!"

"We have to get out of here," Nik said. "The whole place is about to blow."

"Roos' helicopter is at the airport," Selena said, still holding onto Katya. "Ready to take off. We can take Lorillard's limo." Her eyes searched the monitors. "Where is it? Where's the fish truck?"

"They left," Katya said. The control pod began to shimmy and sway. "Some people ran up, and the limo drove away. Somebody else took the truck."

"There isn't time to make a run for it," Nik said. "The airstrip is too far."

"Lorillard said he's going to destroy the LIFT," Selena said, moving toward the door, pulling Katya with her. "We have to get out of here."

"Wait," Nik said. "There's another way. It's faster. If the ride doesn't kill us."

"TWELVE MINUTES TO COLLISION! TWELVE MINUTES TO COLLISION!"

"How?" Selena said. "We've got to move now."

Nik searched the walls and ceiling, then ran to the corner of the room, climbed onto a chair and reached for the grating of the air vent.

"I need a tool," he said. "Something to pry this open."

Katya pulled open a desk drawer; she found a pencil, then a letter opener.

"ELEVEN MINUTES TO COLLISION! ELEVEN MINUTES TO COLLISION!"

Nik jimmied it between the vent screen and the wall, bending the metal until he forced the vent halfway off. With his hands he pulled and tore until the rest came loose. He looked at Selena and Katya.

"The tubes that lead from the control pod to the accelerator ring provide ventilation. They're two and a half miles long and pressurized to twenty pounds per square inch. It'll be the ride of a lifetime." He looked at his daughter. "Like nothing you've ever seen at Disneyland."

"It can take us to the ring," Selena said. "The airstrip's just outside. Look," she said, pointing to a monitor. "Roos' helicopter is still there."

"If we find the right tube," Nik said. "Some of them carry air samples up to

217

another room for radiation analysis. And there could be blockage." He looked from Selena to Katya and shook his head. "I can't be sure of what's in there."

Selena looked at her daughter, fear and worry lining her face. Like a steel partition rising in her chest, Selena hardened her heart with determination. She turned to Nik. "We have to try."

"Let me take a look," he said. He pulled himself up into the crawlspace of the vent as the intercom blared another warning.

"TEN MINUTES TO COLLISION! TEN MINUTES TO COLLISION!"

Selena and Katya watched Nik disappear into the dark shaft. The control pod shook beneath them. A moment later, Nik stuck his head out of the vent.

"We've got it," he said. "It connects to one of the main tubes. I didn't open the hatch yet, but I can hear the air rushing past." He looked at Katya. "It's fast," he said. "And it's dark as hell. Do you think you can do it?"

With eyes big with fright, Katya looked at her mother, then back at Nik. She didn't speak, just nodded.

Nik wondered if he was doing the right thing. If they got stuck in those tubes no one would ever find them. If they weren't impaled on a piece of metal and dead, it would be a slow, claustrophobic death. They'd be praying for the LIFT to explode and put an end to their misery. He looked to Selena for the answer.

"Let's do it," she said and took Katya's hand.

"I'll go first," Nik said. "Follow me through the shaft and wait. Listen as I fall. If I run into trouble I'll try to cry out, to warn you. You'll have to find another way down. Do you understand?"

Selena and Katya nodded.

"Katya," Selena said. "I want you to follow your father." That word, "father" hung in the air between the three of them, echoing. "I don't want you left here alone. I'll go last."

"Count to thirty before you start," Nik said. We have to space ourselves. I'll see you both at the bottom." He smiled at them, his eyes holding Selena's for a long time, and then he crawled back down the shaft. Katya stepped onto the chair and pulled herself into the vent with a hand-up from her mother. Before Selena followed, she turned for a last look at the monitors. Lorillard was at the control panel, no longer struggling to escape. To her surprise, he looked deliriously happy as he ramped the accelerator higher and higher. You're mad, she thought, insane. For a moment she considered unlocking the pod, letting him go free. Then she heard Nik's voice echo in the vent. She turned away, hoisted herself into the shaft, and never looked back.

"Remember," Nik said in the darkness. "It's going to be a tight, fast ride. The tubes aren't much more than four feet across. Go feet first. And hold your arms close to your body. Keep your hands over your face. There may be bolts or metal seams." Dear God, I hope not, he thought.

He reached the hatch and stopped for a minute before opening it.

"When we get close to the bottom," he said, "when we're almost at the ring, the pressure should let up a bit."

He turned the handle on the tightly sealed hatch and pulled the circular door towards him and up, hooking it to the top of the tube. The roar of air was deafening, and the suction of the pressure pulled on his body like a giant vacuum. It was pitch black in front of him. He maneuvered into a feet-first position.

Katya was edging closer when she felt the warm skin of a large hand on top of her own. Nik gently squeezed, then patted her reassuringly. She thought she heard him say something, but she wasn't sure.

Suddenly Katya felt tears well in her eyes and she choked on a sob rising from deep within her. What was happening to her? She was crying like a little girl. She knew he couldn't hear her, and she was glad. Just before he pushed off, she reached out into the darkness and her hand rested on his thick, wavy hair. The sensation was unexpectedly soft, and Katya thought at that moment she would never forget the feel of it. When she let go, he pushed forward into the deafening rush of air.

Crouching, Katya approached the threatening noise of the tube. In the darkness she counted quietly to herself. "Twenty-five, twenty-six, twenty-seven," all the while listening for a warning call from her father. She knew she'd never hear it above the whistling pitch of the suction. She looked back over her shoulder. She saw the shape of her mother's head, silhouetted in the light from the shaft. She's so beautiful, Katya thought as Selena crawled closer, reaching out to her daughter, embracing her from behind.

"I love you, darling," she whispered. "We'll all be together in just a minute."

Katya didn't want to say goodbye, she didn't want to let go.

"I love you, Mom," she said, then forced herself forward, trying to remember the touch of her mother's hand as the dark air swirled around her, sucked her away.

When Selena drew close and heard the threatening, dark suction, she was amazed her daughter had found the courage. The tube seemed like a terrible black hole that had devoured all Selena cared for. She waited, heard no sound

219

from below, then pushed off into the empty rush of dark space.

Nik crashed through the ventilator screen at the other end of the tunnel with enough force to rip the screws out of the wall and jam both his knees. He was so stunned and out of breath, he couldn't get up off the cement floor. Katya shot through after him and landed right on top. Nik cushioned her fall, but when she rolled off, she cried out as her foot twisted beneath her. Both of them managed to get out of the way before Selena arrived with a thud. They had traveled the distance through the dark tunnel in about four minutes, speeding along in the vacuum of air at almost 38 miles per hour. It had seemed like an eternity.

Selena was standing first, gasping for breath and holding onto the cement wall of the tunnel. A long gash on her arm was bleeding profusely. Nik got to his feet and went to give Katya a hand, but when she tried to get up, her foot buckled beneath her.

"It's broken," she told him.

The intense vibration of the accelerator increased.

"THREE MINUTES TO COLLISION! THREE MINUTES TO COLLISION!"

The noise grew thunderous in the dimly lit tunnel. Cement walls around them began to crumble.

"Come on!" Nik said, his voice echoing through the hollow ring. "He's ramping much too fast! He must have overridden the program. It's going to blow!"

Nik wrapped his arm around Katya's waist. Selena draped her daughter's arm over her shoulder and limping as fast they could, Katya hopping on one foot, they hobbled along the curving tunnel to the exit.

"TWO MINUTES TO COLLISION! TWO MINUTES TO COLLISION!"

There wasn't enough time. Nik bent down and lifted Katya onto his back. They were able to move a little faster. Selena ran ahead and opened the hydraulic, pressurized doors of the elevator, her sleeve soaked with blood. Nik ran through the passageway with Katya hanging from his back, then suddenly lost his grip, letting her slip. Her feet dragged on the cement floor, and she cried out in pain. Selena ran to her. The vibration in the tunnel was intensifying by noticeable increments every ten seconds.

"NINETY SECONDS TO COLLISION! NINETY SECONDS TO COLLISION!"They ran towards the elevator door. Once inside, Nik let Katya slide down the wall and sit on the floor. The high-speed elevator raced to the top. Fifteen seconds later, they came to a sudden halt and all the lights went out.

"We've lost power," Selena said.

"What are we going to do?" Katya asked. In the darkness, she sounded frightened.

"Wait," Nik said. "The emergency generator should kick in. If we're lucky."

"ONE MINUTE TO COLLISION! ONE MINUTE TO COLLISION! FIFTY-NINE! FIFTY-EIGHT! FIFTY-SEVEN! FIFTY-SIX!"

The elevator jarred suddenly and dropped a few inches. They all felt their stomachs rise to their throats. They heard the drone of a generator. The lights came on, and Selena pressed the button for "Ground Level." It worked. The elevator began its ascent.

When the doors opened, the three of them stood bathed in desert sunlight. The helicopter was within sight. Nik waved to the pilot.

"THIRTY! TWENTY-NINE! TWENTY-EIGHT!"

Nik hoisted Katya onto his back, and they ran, ducking under the spinning rotors, their hands covering their eyes from the dust and sand.

"Roos is dead!" Selena hollered. "Let's go! He's dead!"

"NINETEEN! EIGHTEEN! SEVENTEEN! SIXTEEN!"

The copter flew up, clearing the web of the LIFT, then banked to the west just as the blast hit. They watched the massive accelerator ring erupt, creating a mushroom cloud of dirt and smoke. At the center the control pod tilted and jerked in spasms, its support knocked out from underneath.

The air currents from the explosion pulled on the helicopter, tilting it on its side, almost flipping it over, pulling it into the maelstrom of smoke and ash that filled the desert sky. The pilot struggled to regain control.

"Look! Mom!" Katya hollered, but couldn't be heard over the savage noise of destruction from below. She grabbed her mother's arm and pointed. There in the glass expanse of the control pod Selena saw the silhouette of a man spread eagle against the window. Then the entire pod crumbled to the ground and was lost in the surge of black smoke and dust.

The helicopter veered sharply to the right, pulled farther and farther away. They looked back to see the LIFT settle like a dark scar on the white desert sand.

EPILOGUE

Despite the early fall chill, Selena felt overheated as she walked up the steps of the Congressional building in Washington, D.C. Her makeup and dark glasses not only camouflaged what remained of her yellowing bruises, they made her difficult to recognize. It had been three weeks since she returned from Chile, and it seemed to Selena a great deal had happened. She wondered if it would be enough.

Besides all the other challenges, the time had been an emotional roller coaster for everyone concerned. She was still struggling with her grief over Charlie's death. Selena missed her friend terribly. Katya, too, had been hit hard by the loss. Oddly enough, it was Nik who had brought the smiles to their faces, comforted them both.

After the immediate onslaught of pressure from the media to discuss the LIFT debacle, they had tried to just take it easy, to heal, to get to know each other. Like everything else, it wasn't that simple.

Selena crossed the Capitol building rotunda and crowded into the elevator with a group of French tourists. As it rose to the mezzanine, she checked her watch. The vote would have started, and she didn't want to miss the final tally. She wondered if this time she had managed to make the difference. There were so many things beyond her control.

Her daughter's awkwardness and silence around her father flip-flopped with flirtation and a demanding stream of jabber. When she regressed into being a little girl, she wanted Selena all to herself. At those times Nikolai became an intrusive stranger. Through it all, Katya was jealous of the deepening relationship between her mother and Nik. Emotional confusion reigned.

Selena had purchased a new Honda with the insurance money from the Porsche speedster. There was enough left over to buy Katya her own used car when the time was right, and Selena hoped her practicality wouldn't disappoint Charlie too much.

One afternoon Nik had taken his daughter out for driving lessons. As Selena watched through the living room window, Katya pulled into the driveway, the rear wheels of the car bumping over the curb and almost knocking down the mailbox. Nik literally covered his eyes. Selena started to laugh, then, to her surprise, the tears came and wouldn't stop. The gladness she felt was almost too much to bear, and she wished Charlie were with her to share it. Selena's only comfort was in knowing her friend would be so very happy for her, for them all.

The elevator opened and she made her way through the crowds to the mezzanine. Nik had taken Katya to see Russia. He wanted to show his daughter Moscow and St. Petersburg, then Lomonosov, his family's country home. Selena had considered going along, but in the end she decided to let the two of them make the journey alone. There would be another time for her. Besides, she wanted to be here, in Washington, for the vote.

The viewing area was jammed with tourists and Selena, still wearing her sunglasses, jockeyed for position. People stared at her, then made room. The representative from Oklahoma was voting to approve Star Wars, and Selena started biting at the cuticle of her index finger then stopped herself. What if her efforts failed? What if she hadn't done enough? No, she told herself. You did all you could.

With Chapman's death she had lost not only his vote but also his leadership. After renaming her asteroid "NEA Charlie 2009," she announced her research results, but despite her assurances there would be no collision, the Star Wars bill looked like it would pass. That's when Selena decided to take matters into her own hands.

Gazing down at the theater of mahogany desks and royal blue carpet, she took a deep breath as the representative from Oregon voted against Star Wars. What you did, Selena told herself, wasn't wrong. And you'll have to be the only judge of that, because no one else will ever know.

"Dr. Hartmann," Clive Bingham had said on the phone that day. "What a surprise." Judging by his tone, it wasn't an entirely pleasant one.

When she told him about the check for $25,000 she had found in Jean Levesque's pocket, when she told him what she wanted him to do, he hadn't liked it.

"I'd lose my cabin," he said. "That's all the money I have. I gave up my whole life for a few years of peace there."

"You gave up someone else's life, too," Selena said. "Charlie is dead."

"But I was only doing my job," Bingham said.

Selena's voice was cold.

"It's your choice," she said. "That's more than you gave Charlie. Either you do it, or I go to the press. You'll lose your pension. You'll be dishonored as a traitor. You'll probably go to jail. And remember. If anything happens to me, my attorney has a letter with all the relevant information. You'll definitely go to jail then."

At one point, Selena would have enjoyed that even more. She had wanted to turn him in, to make him pay. But she no longer felt that way. If he followed her instructions something good might come of all that had happened. That's what mattered now.

She had told Bingham to get his hands on whatever money he could and use it to buy a vote against Star Wars. She didn't want to know any of the details. He was to figure out how to do it, find out whom to contact, determine who was accessible and receptive. After all, PACS and lobbyists did it all the time. She knew he had the connections. If he could get the money, it was possible. And it might make all the difference.

Selena's breath grew shallow and rapid as she watched the last votes come in. The tally was 217 *for* Star Wars and 215 *against*. As she expected, it was close. Her hands clutched the wood railing. With each of the last votes, she breathed less and less until she thought her chest would break. Then, finally, it was over. Star Wars had been defeated, 217-218.

Selena put her hand on her forehead and dropped her head. Her skin grew flushed and warm. She fought the tears that welled in her eyes behind her glasses, and with each deep breath she realized there had been something far more personal at stake than stopping nuclear weapons in space.

Hurrying for the elevator, Selena walked briskly across the rotunda and down the stairs. The sun was warm on her face, the air no longer chill. Her smile was timid at first, then radiant. Maybe anything *is* possible, she told herself. Maybe it isn't too late.

As her taxi drove off, Selena looked back through the rear window. She felt certain that part of her had been lost in this; part of her had been left behind forever. But she knew she had reclaimed something, too. Something that had been missing for far too many years.

~ ~ ~ ~ ~